MURDER AT THE AIRPORT

Behind them, the madness lasted
for a full hour. Players inched their way
toward the exits, stopping patiently
to autograph loose sheets of paper,
albums, pucks, and even a shirt.

At last, La Guardia was left to its usual
pre-dawn squalor. But it was not until
the first cheerless fingers of light sent the
night shift off duty that an invoice
clerk, hurrying through the parking lot
in a fine drizzle, almost stumbled over an
outflung arm. It was a moment before
he nerved himself to bend down and
look more closely. Then he jerked
upright and pounded back to the terminal.

Someone had to be told—*there was
a corpse in the lot!*

Books by Emma Lathen

EMMA LATHEN

MURDER WITHOUT ICING

PUBLISHED BY POCKET BOOKS NEW YORK

POCKET BOOKS, a Simon & Schuster division of
GULF & WESTERN CORPORATION
1230 Avenue of the Americas, New York, N.Y. 10020

Copyright © 1972 by Emma Lathen

Published by arrangement with Simon and Schuster
Library of Congress Catalog Card Number: 72-83919

ISBN: 0-671-83373-1

First Pocket Books printing August, 1973

10 9 8 7 6

POCKET and colophon are trademarks of Simon & Schuster

Printed in the U.S.A.

CONTENTS

1	OH, SAY CAN YOU SEE	1
2	CENTER ICE	8
3	THIRD MAN IN	15
4	BODY CHECK	25
5	BLUE LINE	32
6	BEHIND THE CAGE	44
7	TWO ON ONE	52
8	HIGH STICKING	63
9	ON THE ROAD	73
10	POWER PLAY	78
11	HAT TRICK	87
12	DIGGING IT OUT	93
13	DELAYED CALL	100
14	LEADING THE RUSH	105
15	FACE-OFF	113
16	A RUDE GESTURE	122
17	SCREEN SHOT	130
18	AN OPEN NET	137
19	PENALTY KILLER	145
20	ON THE FLY	153
21	GOALS AGAINST	160
22	RAGGING THE PUCK	166
23	STICK HANDLING	173
24	AGAINST THE BOARDS	179
25	OFF SIDE	190
26	CUTTING DOWN THE ANGLE	199

MURDER
WITHOUT ICING

1

OH, SAY CAN YOU SEE

WALL STREET, the financial center of the world, exports men as well as capital. Lawyers, bankers and accountants commute regularly to Oslo, Beirut and Lima, while more rarefied specialists wander even farther. The man trudging through cocoa fields in Ghana probably has a desk somewhere along Pearl Street. Wall Street dispatches jute marketers to Lahore, oil-traffic engineers to Kuwait and econometricians to Dar es Salaam. Nepal and Lapland are as much part of its province as Kansas and Nebraska.

To a man, such returning itinerants compare New York unfavorably with these Camelots. This does not in any way distinguish them from the general population. No true Wall Streeter requires a passport in order to complain.

Very frequently such complaint involves the elements.

But this first week in December had been exceptionally mild. As John Putnam Thatcher, senior vice president of the Sloan Guaranty Trust, strolled to work, he decided that attacks on New York's execrable winter would have to wait. It remained to be seen what would take their place.

High-level rent gouging, he soon discovered. At the corner of Broad Street he was hailed by Hugh Waymark, senior partner at Waymark-Sims.

"Siebrack is offering us a new lease, of course," he said, impersonating a hapless tenant. "A thirty-two-percent increase in the rent! They're just trying to see what the market will bear!"

1

Unhappily, Waymark-Sims brokerage fees were fixed by law.

But Waymark's heart was not in the landlord problem. "Oh, well, I guess we'll just have to lump it."

Business, Thatcher suggested, must be good.

"Not bad," Waymark admitted. "By the way, John, I've been wanting to tell you. The Sloan has picked a real winner. It's high time somebody did something to give the city a lift instead of taking what they can get—like Siebrack Brothers."

Thatcher tried, and failed, to think of any recent demonstrations of virtue by the Sloan.

Waymark was continuing: "Shows that Wall Street keeps up with the times. Well, good to see you."

Thatcher watched him bustle off to his centrally located, well-maintained office, then resumed his own leisurely progress, idly pondering Waymark's comments. He understood where Siebrack Brothers stood; the Sloan's posture eluded him.

Billings, the elevator operator at Exchange Place, had another metropolitan problem at the ready.

"I see they're thinking of raising the subway fare again," he said, before the pneumatic doors slid shut.

When Thatcher showed no inclination to discuss the city budget, he, too, moved on to a more optimistic frame of reference.

"That's the way it is. Still, New York's got a good chance, don't you think, Mr. Thatcher?"

Thatcher, who always encouraged positive thinking, agreed.

"It kind of makes you proud of the Sloan," said Billings. "Here we are."

Thatcher strode along the sixth-floor corridor, nodding to subordinates, until he reached his own corner suite.

"Good morning, Miss Corsa," he said.

His admirable secretary was, as always, awaiting him. She did not reply with animadversions on the city of her birth. But neither did she produce any mystifying tribute to the Sloan. Instead, she said, "Mr. Withers just called." Involuntarily, she glanced at the clock. It was unusual for the president of the Sloan to be in his tower suite so early; but then, it was unusual for him to be there at all at this time of year. Bradford Withers customarily sought sunnier climes long before the first snowfall. "He said that he would like to see you as soon as possible."

"Damn," said Thatcher. He thought a moment. "I'll go right up."

Miss Corsa, he was glad to note, approved, although Withers' presence boded ill for a constructive morning. The financial side of banking rarely engaged his volatile attention. Whether it was the staff Christmas party or hospitality for a visiting dignitary, Brad could chew up a good deal of expensive time. Thatcher hoped a prompt visit might be an economy in the long run. So he returned to the elevator and was soon being wafted upward.

This time it was remodeling the Paris branch of the Sloan. But Withers was soon deflected. Like Billings and Hugh Waymark before him, he had some complaints about city life. They were peculiarly his own.

"I've got two dinners this week," he said, making them sound like a real hardship. "Then, there's the Corinthian Club Banquet. And Carrie has us down for a couple of benefits."

This could be interpreted as an indictment of the hectic pace of New York life. Thatcher himself would put it another way.

". . . still, that's what makes New York a great city," Withers said. "And I'm glad the Sloan is making a contribution. I've always said, John, what's good for New York is good for the Sloan."

"Yes indeed," said Thatcher. Whether Withers knew it or not, the Sloan had forty-eight branches scattered over five boroughs operating on this premise. But now, if ever, was a chance to clarify these allusions. And Withers had more time to spare than either Hugh Waymark or Billings.

Exactly how, Thatcher inquired, was the Sloan contributing to metropolitan life? Surely Brad could not mean the Sloan's holdings of Port Authority bonds?

Indignation darkened Withers' pale blue eyes. "I'm talking about the Huskies," he said. "Aren't you following them? Everybody else is." He might have been talking about dereliction from duty.

"The Huskies," said Thatcher as light dawned. He should have guessed. If weather provided the first topic of conversation for New Yorkers, organized sports came a close second. In summer Thatcher expected the Mets or the Yankees. During the football season, he was more remiss. But this was inexcusable.

The New York Huskies were an ice hockey team. And this season the Sloan Guaranty Trust was sponsoring all Husky games, at home and away.

"You know," said Thatcher frankly, "the Huskies slipped my mind." There were extenuating circumstances. He was neither a hockey nor a television fan. He did not share Withers' consuming interest in how the Sloan shaped its public image. "I gather the programs are everything that you—and Public Relations—hoped for."

"More," said Withers. "Sponsoring the Huskies is the best move the Sloan has made in years. It's a wonderful fighting team and they're getting the Sloan message across to a whole new audience. The Huskies appeal to young people."

"And older people, too," said Thatcher, recalling Waymark and Billings.

"What you really should do," said Withers, for once animated by something connected with the Sloan, "is come down to one of the games."

Did Withers himself attend hockey games?

"Damned exciting," said the Sloan's president. "I wouldn't miss one."

If hockey was keeping Bradford Withers in Manhattan at this time of year, it must be damned exciting indeed.

"Now, about these renovations in Paris," said Brad, getting down to serious matters most commendably. During the subsequent half hour, while he weighed the merits of Empire overmantels versus spiral ramps, Thatcher was free to pursue his own thoughts. They were, on the whole, rather chastening.

While he and a large staff were laboring over such abstruse matters as revalued currencies and investment credits, the outside world—which included Bradford Withers —was identifying the Sloan with the destinies of an ice hockey team.

He was not altogether sure that he approved.

Lunch at the Hilton, however, turned his thoughts back to banking. The Municipal Bond Dealers were not even interested in New York. Their attention was focused farther south.

"Down there in Memphis, they're running real bucket shops," said Thatcher's companion. At the dais, the speaker was saying much the same thing in more statesmanlike language.

"How do they get away with it?" Thatcher asked.

Pardee was blunt. "They lie a lot."

But Thatcher knew it takes more than that to peddle fraudulent securities successfully. Gullible buyers are as necessary as unscrupulous sellers. In Memphis, several small firms were developing new wrinkles in an old game.

"They concentrate on small banks," Pardee said. "Would you believe that some banks don't even check up on what they're buying?"

"Deplorable," Thatcher agreed.

It was an exchange he was going to remember in the very near future.

The occasion arose on the journey back to Wall Street. Thatcher found himself sharing a taxi with a distinguished out-of-towner.

"Traffic gets worse all the time, doesn't it?" said Archibald Holland, peering out at the crush. "And the city gets dirtier all the time."

"How are things in Pittsburgh?" asked Thatcher pointedly.

Natives may recite imperfections; visitors, particularly those from Pittsburgh, should show more self-restraint.

"Fine," said Holland, with untroubled assurance.

He should know, Thatcher admitted. The Hollands were Pittsburgh's first family; Holland Steel, one of its industrial giants. And Archibald Holland himself, spare, middle-aged and serious, was one of its foremost citizens.

"I'm glad to have run into you today," he said, after a pause. "I've been wanting to talk to the Sloan."

It was one peer to another, Thatcher saw, even in an immobilized taxicab.

"Yes?" he said cautiously. The Sloan did not handle any Holland business.

"It's about my son, Winthrop," said Holland.

The caution, Thatcher saw, had not been misplaced. A. Winthrop Holland had left Pittsburgh and Holland Steel seven years earlier. Since then he had surfaced in areas within the Sloan's purview. He was the first Holland in generations to try increasing an already immense personal fortune, and he had done so with buccaneer gusto. There had been purchases of newspaper chains in the South; there had been refinancings of toy firms in California. There had been mergers, deals, promotions and plans. "The second Holland empire," one news magazine had put it.

"I may have been wrong in discouraging him from branching out. He seems to be doing quite well now," said his father judiciously. "He's quite pleased with the way things have been going lately. But of course he made some miscalculations when he first started."

As Holland seemed to expect a reply, Thatcher obliged. "Very natural that he should."

Archibald Holland frowned. Possibly he did not regard it as natural. "The time has come for him to reorganize. He will be selling some earlier ventures and increasing his position with the successes. This is a favorable moment for some of these moves. There may be a time lag but I think anyone who participates with him will be satisfied."

This, of course, was a code message. Thatcher had no difficulty unscrambling it. "And how much accommodation would he require while he reorganizes?"

"Not more than a million, I imagine. I thought the Sloan might be interested."

This proposal was not, of itself, strange. Bigger amounts have been handled in even more informal surroundings. The source, however, gave Thatcher pause.

There were Holland banks as well as Holland museums on the Golden Triangle.

"We would be willing to consider it," he said, discovering that he too had adopted a proconsular tone. "But we'd need more detail."

"I'll suggest to Win that he drop by and talk to you," Holland said.

"We'll be glad to see him," Thatcher replied insincerely. But he felt he owed his curiosity something. "Tell me, why the Sloan? You have banks nearer home."

Tactfulness can go only so far. The Hollands not only had banks nearer home, they had them in the family.

But Holland was unembarrassed. "We have decided," he said smoothly, "that unless our participation is kept within certain bounds, people might be justified in saying we benefited unfairly from our relationship with Win."

Thatcher did not believe a word of it. The Hollands had extended all the accommodation they were going to; now they were willing to share Win Holland's pie with others —including the Sloan. It did not sound like disinterested generosity to him.

Holland then surprised him.

"I thought of approaching the Sloan," he said, "because of your current involvement with Win."

Thatcher internally resolved to have an unknown loan officer's head on a plate. "And what involvement is that?" he asked.

"Why, that ice hockey team," Holland said. "The Huskies. Win is an owner. And he was delighted when the Sloan signed them up."

"I'm sure he was," said Thatcher.

But he had not lunched with the bond dealers in vain.

"Miss Corsa," he said, on arrival, "it always pays to check up on what you're buying."

Miss Corsa was accustomed to Mr. Thatcher. She waited.

"The Sloan," he said, "is, in effect, buying the Huskies."

"Six-zero," she replied.

He was taken aback only momentarily. "No, I am not

interested in last night's score. I want someone at the
Sloan who can give me some information about them."

"Mr. Younghusband," she said. "I'll call him for you."

2

CENTER ICE

BUT DEXTER YOUNGHUSBAND, as so often these days, was
not at his desk in the Sloan's public relations department.
He was at rinkside.

On the ice, the New York Huskies were having a workout. Stick smashed against stick, pucks caromed wildly,
players plunged into the boards. Most of the bystanders
were riveted by the action. But two groups had other concerns. Dexter Younghusband was studying a sheaf of photographs. They were proofs for the cover of the next issue
of *This Week in New York*.

"Superb!" he breathed reverently, halting at a picture of
the Husky goaltender making a well-nigh impossible save.

"Look at the one of Siragusa scoring," his companion
urged.

Younghusband bent to his task. If, instead, he had been
listening to the conversation fifteen feet away, he would
have learned that the association between Winthrop Holland and the Sloan Guaranty Trust, presently exercising
John Thatcher, might not be very long-lived.

"I'd have to think about that," Holland was saying
thoughtfully. "I've had a piece of the Huskies for a long
time now."

"Naturally you want to think it over. But it's a good
offer for you." The large man spoke with gentle persistence. "It would give us both what we want. I'm holding

notes of yours that are way past due. You're in a cash bind and it's not convenient to retire them."

"It sure isn't." Holland grinned ruefully. "You know the picture, Frank. I've got the chance of a lifetime, and I'm investing in a big way. Cash is a little tight now, but I could pay you off with a short extension."

"Sure you could," Frank agreed. "But why bother? You're onto something hot and you want to concentrate on that. As for me, I'd like a sports investment. The way the Huskies are going, I figure your interest is worth twice what you paid. Three or four of us would get together and pick it up from you. That way, your notes would be wiped out and you'd end up with a cash surplus."

Holland had jammed his hands into the pockets of his overcoat and rocked back on his heels during this summary. Now he nodded.

"I won't say I don't like the sound of it. But it's still pretty general. Tell you what, Frank. Why don't you get it all down on paper? Your partners, the figures, all that. Then we'll take another look at it."

Frank clapped him on the shoulder. "I'll have it for you in a couple of days. You'll like what you see. And now let's watch this superstar of yours. After all, that's what I came down here for this morning."

Together they strolled toward the far cage where Billy Siragusa, the Huskies' new center, was practicing slap shots. While several rink attendants smoothed a roughened section of ice, Winthrop Holland remembered he was a host.

"Frank, come and meet Dexter Younghusband from the Sloan Guaranty Trust. Dexter, this is Franklin Moore."

Younghusband turned to greet the newcomers. They were both big men, but with a difference. Holland was tall, rangy and boyish. He was wearing a turtleneck shirt and chukka boots. Sideburns and a neck-length crop suited his thick, dark hair. Moore was large, portly and balding. Younghusband's eyes lingered briefly over his handmade shoes and expensive tailoring.

Like many American men, Holland felt impelled to amplify his introductions. "Frank is visiting from Nashville. He's in real estate back home."

Privately Younghusband decided that Moore was in real estate in a big way.

"You know the Sloan is sponsoring the Huskies this season, Frank," Winthrop Holland continued. "And Dexter is the man in charge."

Frank Moore slid into conversation with Southern ease. "It sure looks as if the Sloan is getting its money's worth," he remarked.

There were enthusiastic cries of agreement from all sides.

"Of course, October was nothing to write home about," Younghusband admitted, trying for detachment, "but since then the Huskies have been great. You didn't catch the game last night, by any chance?"

"I sure did. And it was a sweet win." Moore smiled broadly. "That makes it five out of the last seven games, doesn't it?"

Younghusband warmed to this discerning visitor.

"It's Siragusa who's made all the difference."

"That was a smart move, trading for him," Moore agreed. "And he wasn't going anywhere—"

"We thought Mrs. Post was crazy when she insisted on paying so much for him. But it couldn't have worked out better—"

Holland tried to break in on the conversation. "Speaking of Clemmie, is she around anywhere?"

"She went to the office a while back, Mr. Holland," somebody volunteered.

Neither of the principals had paid the slightest attention to the question. They were pelting each other with hockey lore. They finished each other's sentences, supplied missing names, jumped the gun on the punch lines of anecdotes.

Winthrop Holland did not join in. Basically he was not the stuff of which rabid sports fans are made. He was a strong tennis player, an experienced sailor, a veteran skier. But he had invested in the Huskies largely because he had played hockey at Princeton. Although he enjoyed watching a game, he lacked the passion for statistical data. He did not care who had been the League's high scorer in 1966.

He was amused to notice that Moore very quickly took Younghusband out of his depth. The Sloan's PR man was a recent convert. He could cite chapter and verse with great accuracy but he could not sustain a contest about great moments on ice. He was forced back to the present.

"Of course, it's still early in the season, but there's no telling how far the Huskies will go. They're just beginning to play as a team."

Moore nodded sagely. "You upset the balance when you made your trades. It takes time to adjust. But now they're developing a strategy built around Siragusa's style. I'd be surprised if they don't get into the play-offs."

"And they're making New York City hockey-conscious. You should see the letters we get at the Sloan." For a moment the public relations man in Younghusband displaced the team rooter.

"The whole damned country is getting hockey-conscious," Moore corrected him, gesturing with an unlit cigar.

"And why not?" Younghusband challenged. "It's fast, it's exciting, it's beautiful!"

Before Moore could top this, Holland grabbed his elbow for attention. "Look, Frank, I can see you two are going to be at this for a while. And I've got to be running along. The boys here will take care of you if there's anything you want to know."

"That's fine, Win. Thanks for bringing me." Moore turned for a last word. "I'll be sending over those papers in a couple of days. Think about it in the meantime, huh?"

Holland grinned. "Sure. But if the Huskies do as well as you think, the price is going to go up. It might be a lot cheaper for you to wait a couple of months and just take cash."

"No, I'm not hanging around for them to win the Stanley Cup." Moore laughed outright. "But I'd sure like owning them if they do. And what difference does it make to you?"

"There's a lot of sentiment involved, Frank."

Moore was incredulous. "Come off it. You've seen less hockey games than my wife."

"Oh, not for me," Holland hastened to explain. "But Clemmie Post is going to be shook up by this."

"Mrs. Post? What's it got to do with her if you sell your piece of the action?"

"It's only right to talk it over with her."

"Sure you want to tell her about it. But I've seen your agreement. She doesn't have any right of first refusal. She doesn't have any rights at all. This is a simple business deal."

"It may be simple business to you. But the Huskies mean a lot to her."

Mrs. Clementine Post was suspicious from the start.

"Franklin Moore of Nashville?" she echoed accusingly. "I've heard that name before."

Win Holland examined the toe of his boot. "The other day I said I'd be bringing him around." A child could have seen that he was hiding something.

"That's not what I mean!" she snapped.

"You could have heard the name anywhere. He's active in sports. That's why he's interested in the Huskies."

"What sports? He hasn't been active in hockey."

Holland decided he had no further room for maneuver. "He's the one who organized the big heavyweight fight in Nashville. That must be when you heard his name," he said reluctantly.

Mrs. Post's bright blue eyes widened. "A boxing promoter! And you'd sell to that kind of man!"

"I was afraid that would start you off. All he did was get a couple of friends together as a syndicate to back one fight. But it wasn't really their kind of thing. They're much more interested in a going team."

"And who are these famous friends of his?"

"For heaven's sake, Clemmie! You make them sound like the Mafia. Frank Moore is a respectable real estate dealer who happens to be a hockey fan. His friends are just like him. On top of that, they're big home-town boost-

ers." Holland was now speaking persuasively. "You ought
to talk to Frank yourself. Why, he was going to hockey
matches before most people heard of the game. And he
hasn't been wasting his time either. He's a real expert. He
can give you the rundown on every coach and trainer in
the League. And talk about ideas! He's got a barrelful.
There are some trades he's got in mind to strengthen the
defense. And he said he thought the boys weren't getting
enough emphasis on . . ."

The easy flow faltered, then trailed away completely.
Holland looked across the table in open dismay.

"I see." The words were flat. "These new owners take
over."

"No, no! You don't want to look at it that way."
Abruptly Holland changed his tactics. "Dammit, Clemmie, you've always complained that I don't take *enough*
interest."

She glared at him. She was old enough to be his mother
and inevitably she took advantage of this. When Winthrop
Holland's far-flung business activities kept him away for
an entire season, she chided. When her meticulous letters
elicited phone calls from London or the Bahamas saying
Just do whatever you think is best, Clemmie, she tut-tut-
ted. But she had never fooled herself. As far as she was
concerned, she was the owner of the Huskies and she liked
it that way.

What's more, as far as the public of New York City was
concerned, Mrs. Clementine Post was the owner of the
Huskies, and they liked it that way. Her absurd enthusi-
asms and affectations cast an endearing gloss over the
whole team. When the hockey season opened, *The New
York Times* celebrated the event with a front-page picture
of Mrs. Post and her two husky dogs entering the Garden.
When she crammed a knitted cap with the Husky emblem
on her white corkscrew curls and perched her plump little body on skates in Central Park, the tabloids went wild.
If ever the Huskies should win a cup, at least two million
people would expect the presentation to be made to a burbling Mrs. Post.

All this passed through her mind as she maintained her silence.

"Of course, they'd expect to have some say," Holland continued awkwardly. "But what's so wrong about that? They're the kind of people you ought to want for partners. Frank thinks hockey is the coming game. He says that down in Nashville they're all excited about it. The colleges are building rinks and the papers are giving it real coverage. It's what you've said all along. It's going to sweep the country."

Mrs. Post had been concerned before. Now she was militant.

"What is all this about Nashville? Tell me straight out," she demanded. "Does that man have any crazy idea about moving the franchise from New York?"

There was a tense pause.

"He didn't exactly say that," Holland evaded.

"What do you mean by exactly? What the hell did he say?"

"He just said that Nashville was disappointed not to get an expansion team, that it didn't seem fair for New York to have two teams."

Clemmie Post sucked in her breath sharply. Then her jaws clamped into a grim line.

"That settles it. He isn't buying into my team!"

For the first time Winthrop Holland met her eyes squarely. "Clemmie, I've got a right to sell my share, and you know it."

"Yes, I know it," she conceded bitterly. "But it makes a difference who you sell to."

"That's not the way our agreement reads. I'm suggesting a reputable purchaser. That's all you can expect. You may be wrapped up in the Huskies, but I don't have to finance you."

Mrs. Clementine Post had been a wealthy woman from the hour of her birth. She cocked her head alertly.

"Is that an invitation for me to make a counteroffer?"

"No, it's not," he said irritably. "Stop trying to make something complicated out of something simple. Frank Moore has made me an offer in good faith. I'm considering it. Out of courtesy, I've told you about it. That's all there is to it. Hell, I may even decide not to go along."

She smiled wanly. "I didn't really think you'd try to hold me up, Win. I suppose that's one reason I don't want somebody like Franklin Moore sitting in your seat. It's just the sort of thing he'd try to do."

"You don't know anything about him," Holland said, stubbornly loyal.

"All right," she said, shifting to conciliatory tones, "but maybe I won't have to. Just do one thing for me, Win. Don't make any snap decisions. You never can tell."

"Tell what?" he asked blankly.

It was her turn to be evasive.

"Oh, something else might turn up."

3

THIRD MAN IN

AT THE SLOAN, a conference on Great Lakes Steamers was adjourning with a unanimous decision.

"Either we cut our losses," said Walter Bowman, the chief of the Sloan's research department, "or we go down with the ship." He hoisted his considerable bulk and prepared to leave Thatcher's office.

For once, Everett Gabler, who was following suit, agreed with him. "Do these people think that the Sloan simply accepts whatever their accountants say?" he asked indignantly.

Profits, Thatcher pointed out gravely, are the reward for risk taking. Great Lakes Steamers was simply taking its chances on land, as well as on sea.

"Risk taking?" Everett said. "The SEC will call it something else. And if they don't, the Department of Justice will."

Miss Corsa spoke from the doorway. "Mr. Thatcher, will you see Mr. Younghusband now? He has brought some material on the Huskies."

Dexter Younghusband, rising eagerly from a chair, was unacquainted with the mettle of Thatcher's staff. Otherwise, prudence would have deferred his comments until their departure.

"Yes, I thought you might be interested in our revised forecasts for the Husky series. We now have two recent public opinion polls to correct the original survey."

The research department's opinion of Public Relations' polls was no secret. Walter Bowman could not forbear.

"The Huskies are costing us over a million this year, aren't they?" he asked innocently.

PR prided itself on not being penny wise and pound foolish. "We're getting tremendous returns. This summary of our Nielsen ratings proves it."

Everett Gabler took up where Walter had left off. "I, for one," he said sternly, "still regret the decision to drop *Thursday Night at the Symphony*. And not solely on cost grounds."

Younghusband stoutly believed that a good PR man never sees opponents, only potential supporters.

"Perhaps you'd like to see these estimates of audience exposure—" he began.

But he was venturing where the American Institute of Certified Public Accountants often feared to tread.

"And what precisely do you mean," asked Everett with a menacing gleam, "by audience exposure?"

John Thatcher decided it was time to intervene. "In any event, there seems to be agreement that these telecasts have been even more successful than originally anticipated."

Everett, he should have remembered, was a man who could quarrel with anything—including success.

"A weekly symphony was consonant with the dignity of the Sloan," he intoned. "A weekly hockey game is quite different. That fact remains, no matter how many viewers this program has."

On that austere note he departed, taking Bowman with him.

"My message may have misled you, Younghusband," Thatcher said as they retired to the inner office. "I wished to ask you about the ownership of the Huskies."

"Mrs. Clementine Post. A wonderful woman." Younghusband ripped out the answer in one breath. "All by herself, she created a popular image of the Huskies. And that, of course, is half the battle."

Thatcher frowned. "I certainly had the impression that she was the owner. Aren't there sometimes pictures of her in Central Park?"

"That's exactly what I mean. And remember," Younghusband said earnestly, "a picture on the front page is free publicity."

Thatcher ignored the dictum.

"But at lunch today, I heard young Holland referred to as an owner of the Huskies. Where does he fit into this?"

"Young Holland? Oh . . . Win Holland! Well, he owns a share of the Huskies. But Mrs. Post is the executive owner. She's the one who makes the decisions, she's the one who gets into the papers."

Thatcher's hopes as to the usefulness of this interview were hitting a new low. "There are other owners?" he prodded gently.

"Several of them. But they don't count. Mrs. Post is the majority owner, and Win is the next biggest. You'd think with his name that we'd get some free coverage on him, too, but we don't." Younghusband was unable to leave his professional grievances. "After all, think of the headlines about his sister last year."

Thatcher thought about them. It had been a very messy divorce.

"And is that the kind of publicity you want for the Huskies?"

"Good God, no! Hockey is a clean sport. But it shows what a Holland can do when he puts his mind to it." Younghusband sounded wistful. "Of course, Win's never

been around much until this season, he's never really had
the time. You know he has business arrangements all over
the world."

Thatcher was half amused. That last sentence proved to
him, if not to Younghusband, that Win Holland was simply selective in his publicity. He did not wish to be known
as the owner of the Huskies. He wanted to appear before
the world as an emergent tycoon.

"I gather he's more in evidence this year?"

"Yes. We did ask him last month if he'd like to escort
this new singer to one of Clemmie Post's parties, but he
said no. Oh, well," Younghusband sighed, "I suppose it
doesn't make any difference if he's selling out."

Thatcher's amusement came to an abrupt halt. Any one
of his subordinates would have been alerted by his courtesy. "You say that young Holland may be selling his share
in the Huskies? Is that general knowledge?"

If it was, the Holland family should do something about
its communications.

"I don't see how it could be. It just came up a couple of
hours ago when I was at the rink. Win was there with a
guest. I'll bet it was the first time, and what good will it do
us now?" Younghusband noticed Thatcher's face and hurried on, abandoning his petty concerns. "The guest was
somebody in real estate down in Tennessee. He's a hockey
enthusiast from way back and Win owes him some money.
He wants to do a trade. Holland was definitely interested
but it wasn't anything final. I suppose the opposition might
make him think twice."

"What opposition?" Thatcher asked.

Younghusband colored. "There seemed to be some
feeling that Mrs. Post didn't like the idea," he said vague-
ly. "You know how it is. If you're around a place, talking
to people, you can't help overhearing some things."

Thatcher was just as glad that the research department
was not present at these apologies for procurement of information. Walter Bowman could not have been trusted to
control himself. Hard on the heels of this reflection came
the decision to dispense with Public Relations also. There
must be more efficient ways of gathering intelligence than

waiting for it to fall from Younghusband's lips. Within moments he had terminated the conference and was standing by Miss Corsa's desk, debating his next move.

"Everett may be right," he murmured. "A weekly hockey game *is* different." To the best of his knowledge no creditor had ever leaped at the chance of acquiring a full symphony orchestra.

Miss Corsa's voice brought him to his senses. "I asked Mr. Younghusband to leave a Husky schedule. Perhaps you'd like to look at it."

Obediently, he accepted the proffered card. One look told him that Miss Corsa, as usual, had her reasons. She was avoiding the necessity to contradict him in so many words. The Sloan's money was not buying a game a week: at first glance, it seemed to be buying one a day.

"There are seventy-eight games in the regular season," she said. "That does not include the play-offs."

How many times, thought Thatcher, would he have to learn the same lesson? When he wanted general information, his secretary had it. When he wanted specialized information, she could find the appropriate expert. He decided to address himself to the first need.

The fundamentals of ice hockey are brutally simple, and Thatcher did not think they had changed much since his boyhood in New Hampshire. Two teams, each composed of five players plus a goalie, scramble to put the puck into the opposition net—whether the play is on a frozen pond in Ontario or a regulation rink in Chicago.

"But I did not realize," he said aloud, "that the professional schedule is so grueling. They often seem to play four games a week with a good deal of traveling in between. Tell me, Miss Corsa, the National Hockey League is divided into two divisions, isn't it?"

"It is. The New York Huskies are in the Western Division."

"Ah, yes. And the Vancouver Canucks are in the Eastern Division. I remember noticing that. Apparently things look different from the NHL offices in Montreal. But these two divisions play among themselves to determine the final contenders?"

"No, there's a good deal of interdivisional play in the regular season. The divisions were only formed at the time of the expansion." A chilling doubt crossed Miss Corsa's mind. "You do know about the expansion, Mr. Thatcher?"

But here he was on solid ground. Coverage of American athletics is not confined to the sports pages. Plenty of it spills over into *The Wall Street Journal*, where six-figure television budgets, multi-million-dollar sports facilities and deferred-payment contracts are as engrossing as earned-run averages or yards gained on the ground. When in 1967 the National Hockey League launched a new marketing technique, many *Journal* readers recognized the broad outlines. The NHL was simply following a familiar path——by trying to stimulate demand for its product and increasing supply. This meant more teams, more games and more gate receipts. The mechanism for this transformation was the sale of franchises for new hockey teams from Atlanta to Oakland.

"And so," he summarized, "the original six teams were more than doubled in number."

"Yes," agreed Miss Corsa. "The regular season eliminates all but four teams in each division. Then there are three rounds to determine the winner of the Stanley Cup."

"And each round consists of . . . ?"

"Winning four out of seven games. And therefore," she said, returning to her original point, "the Huskies could well play over ninety games."

Thatcher did more than listen; he began to calculate. The Huskies had already swept up such disparate enthusiasts as Hugh Waymark and Billings, Miss Corsa and Brad Withers. Behind these simple partisans lurked the shadowy financial figures of Archibald Holland and Win Holland, Clementine Post and an unknown realtor from Tennessee. Convulsions on one level or another could be expected with the machine-gun rapidity imposed by the NHL schedule. The Sloan Guaranty Trust, Thatcher began to think, might well have a tiger by the tail.

"It is time that I learned more about the ownership of the Huskies," he announced.

"Mr. Trinkam," said Miss Corsa intelligently.

Thatcher was impressed. Charlie Trinkam, his second in command in the trust department, led a notable extra-curricular life. It had never taken him anywhere near an ice hockey rink. If it now developed that Charlie had abandoned his lifelong study of women in favor of the Huskies, then New York was truly witnessing an unprece-dented spectacle.

Fortunately, Miss Corsa was not privy to these thoughts. But she noted that her employer was mystified and acted to dispel confusion.

"The Edwin Post estate," she amplified. "Mr. Trinkam handles it."

Thatcher had barely absorbed this fact when the subject of their conversation appeared from the corridor. Charlie Trinkam, looking harassed, wasted no time on prelimi-naries.

"John," he demanded, "do you know anything about this Winthrop Holland?"

"I was just on my way to ask you about Mrs. Clemen-tine Post," Thatcher retorted.

Charlie lifted his eyes to the ceiling as if seeking higher guidance. "What the hell is going on with that team?" he growled.

"As a large portion of New York is under the impres-sion that it's a branch of the Sloan, don't you think we'd better find out?" Thatcher was already heading back to-ward his desk.

By the time Trinkam was settled, his naturally ebullient spirits were beginning to assert themselves.

"It's a shame you weren't ten minutes earlier, John," he said. "Then you could have had a shot at handling Clem-mie yourself."

"Oh, she's been here at the Sloan, has she? Probably another little fact that Younghusband forgot to mention," Thatcher remarked.

"I'm surprised you didn't hear her shouting yourself." Charlie grinned. "A forceful woman, Clemmie, when her dander's up."

The indulgence in his voice explained why more than one trust officer on the sixth floor routinely surrendered

the account to Charlie when death substituted a widow for
the original client.

"I gather she's annoyed about Holland's plans. We'll get
to that in a moment. Right now, I would like some background. Did Mrs. Post inherit the Huskies from her husband?"

"God, no! Ed Post was as conservative as they come.
For that matter, I don't think Clemmie would have been
interested then. What happened was that both her daughters married and moved away. Then Ed died and she was
at loose ends. You know what women are like when that
happens." Charlie shook his head darkly.

Thatcher, himself a widower with three married children, only knew the reverse of the coin.

"Yes?" he said encouragingly.

"It can take them in a lot of ways—good works, spiritu-
alism, gigolos. But with Clemmie, it happened to be the
time when the NHL was expanding, so she went in for ice
hockey. For a long while there I was afraid it was going to
cost her more than any of the others would have." Charlie
reserved idiosyncrasy for after hours. In financial matters
he was unassailably orthodox.

"Did she pay too much for the team?"

"There wasn't any team, that was the trouble. She had
to beat down a bunch of people. The NHL wanted to ex-
pand into new cities and New York already had the
Rangers. So they had two objections. First, they said New
York could never support two hockey teams. Second,
she'd have to pay an indemnity to the Rangers for invad-
ing their territory. But Clemmie was all fired up and raring
to go. She dickered with the Rangers for almost a year.
And, of course, she kept waving the cash in front of
them."

Thatcher was beginning to be interested in Mrs. Post.
"And she convinced them?" he asked skeptically.

"No, I wouldn't say that. They never believed there was
enough support for two teams. They simply decided that
the one who'd be hurt wouldn't be the Rangers. And for
years it looked as if they were right. The Huskies stayed in
last place and they couldn't fill the Garden. This year

everything's different. It's standing room only, they've got a big television contract and the promotional sales are booming for the Christmas season. Clemmie's getting a damn good income from her million and a half and some day there'll be healthy capital gains. She enjoys rubbing my nose in that." Charlie grinned unrepentantly. "That's because I told her she was crazy when she first got the bug."

It was, of course, always gratifying to learn that a Sloan client had made a profitable investment. It would have been even more so if the bank's advice had been correct.

"Mrs. Post is not the only one doing well out of the Huskies," Thatcher observed. "Presumably the other owners are, too, including young Holland."

"From what I hear of that wonder boy's investments, he can use some luck. Or he could if he wasn't a Holland. It must be nice to have half of Pennsylvania behind you."

"Now, Younghusband tells me that Mrs. Post is the majority owner. So I assume—"

But Charlie sat bolt upright, bringing the front legs of his chair down with a crash. "Not on your life! That's what the ruckus is about. Clemmie owns about forty percent and Holland holds about twenty-five. The rest was taken up by five or six people Clemmie talked into buying."

"Ah!" Thatcher was practically purring. "The classic situation. Mrs. Post has substantial control only as long as nobody organizes the other interests."

"Sure, but it's been that way for years. What I can't understand is Clemmie's story that Win Holland has decided to sell and is looking around for buyers. If he didn't unload during the bad years, why do it now in the middle of the season? The team may be worth a lot more in a couple of months."

"It's not a simple sale. At least not if Younghusband has managed to get something right for once," Thatcher modified cautiously. "It's a partial swap. The buyer seems to be the initiator. The bait for Holland is clearing some debts."

"Well, that makes a lot more sense. Particularly if Holland is getting active on some other front."

Thatcher repeated the gist of his conversation with Archibald Holland.

"Sure." Charlie hailed this confirmation. "I knew Clemmie must be wrong somewhere. From Holland's point of view, it's not a bad offer. He wants to get moving on some other deal, and this gives him a chance to clear the decks and wind up with cash. Poor Clemmie!"

"Why is this buyer so objectionable to her?"

"To hear her tell it, he's a refugee from Leavenworth. He once backed a boxing match or a horse race or something. But that's not it. His real crime is that he's interested in hockey. He's got some ideas about running the team himself. On top of that, he might like to move the franchise south."

"Could he do that?"

Charlie shrugged. "All these teams seem to move around like jumping beans these days. I suppose if Nashville put up a big enough premium, he could. Clemmie hasn't spoken to Moore herself. And I discouraged her from trying. In fact, I told her to shut up all along the front."

"Do you think you had any effect?" Thatcher could not believe a woman who had battered the NHL and the Rangers into submission was easily silenced.

"I've got two things going for me. First, I told her it was too early to start a fuss. When a team's playing four games a week, its value can change damn fast."

"How fast?" Thatcher asked dubiously.

"God, I don't know. It was just something to say. My real inspiration was point number two." Charlie paused in self-congratulation.

Thatcher was very suspicious. "And that was . . . ?"

"I told her she should talk to Younghusband about a Sloan welcome home for the team. They're going out to the Coast for a bunch of games. If they win them, I said she ought to work on a big show of local support. That might change Moore's ideas."

Charlie was waiting for applause. He did not get it.

"I only hope that Brad doesn't hear about this," said Thatcher with deep misgivings.

4

BODY CHECK

IF JOHN THATCHER had spent more time at Shea Stadium, he would have realized that Bradford Withers was only one of the problems posed by a welcome home for the Huskies. Dexter Younghusband was a publicity man who knew the public only as a set of statistics. He carefully organized a ceremony restricted to interested parties. In attendance would be owners, players' wives, select pressmen and, of course, the sponsor—the Sloan Guaranty Trust. Each speech and gesture would be rehearsed down to the last rose petal. Not until the next day would Greater New York play its part by reading the papers, watching television and listening to talk programs.

Events conspired against him. In crisp succession the Huskies defeated San Francisco, Vancouver and Los Angeles. Simultaneously two teams leading the division slipped badly, moving the Huskies that much closer to a sure berth in the play-offs. Furthermore, La Guardia Airport is not private property.

Under these circumstances, Younghusband's decorous plans were doomed from the start. His formal cast of characters arrived at La Guardia at four o'clock in the morning to find a mob of several thousand before them. New York City was taking matters into its own hands. The Huskies would get a real tribute. They might also be torn to pieces by their admirers.

"I hope you're satisfied." It was not Thatcher's best time of day.

Charlie Trinkam looked around the terminal in pained surprise. "I just wanted to get Clemmie out of my hair," he said sadly.

Several paces ahead of them, even Brad Withers had noticed something unusual. "Younghusband, what are all these people doing here?" he was asking.

But one person had no doubts about the success of the occasion.

"Charlie!" shrieked Clementine Post, materializing from the throng. She was wrapped in a mink coat and a six-foot scarf in the Husky colors of red and gold. "Isn't it wonderful the way everyone has turned out? What a marvelous idea of yours."

Charlie was sardonic. "I'm glad you like it."

But Clemmie would not have noticed if he had been downing hemlock. She was busy blowing kisses to the crowd. They responded with cries of recognition and vast roars of enthusiasm.

"That's Clemmie Post!"

"Sock 'em, Clemmie!"

It was some moments before Mrs. Post remembered her companions. Then she clasped Charlie's arm impulsively, her eyes alight with excitement, and breathed, "Everything is just grand."

Trinkam snatched at a legitimate bone of contention. "A week ago you were in my office claiming everything had gone up in flames. Make up your mind, Clemmie."

"That was a week ago. Frank Moore won't be able to buy the Huskies now."

"You mean the price will have risen too much?"

Clemmie Post was affronted. "I wasn't talking about money," she said reproachfully.

Charlie and Thatcher exchanged looks over her head. Two lifetimes in banking had taught them that the rich surpass everyone else in sensitivity to the sordidness of cold cash.

"Then, what were you talking about?"

"Why, after three games like this, Win won't dream of

selling. He'll be too enthusiastic. It's barely a third of the way through the season. Anything can happen. Good heavens, the Huskies might bring home the Stanley Cup. And then Win would have dozens of people wanting to buy him out. I suppose," she conceded, "you could call that money."

"You have your own names for things," Charlie said amiably, "but all the same, I think you're right about Holland."

Thatcher was inclined to agree. After three dramatic victories and a season in which anything could happen ahead, it would now be difficult to set a price agreeable to both buyer and seller.

"I really should get hold of Milt the minute he's off the plane," Clemmie was musing to herself. "Otherwise he's likely to tackle Win right away."

Charlie's suspicions were roused. "Clemmie, I thought we agreed you were going to keep this under your hat for the time being."

She blushed. "Oh, I'm sure he already knew." She continued with deep satisfaction. "And he was livid. Particularly about Moore wanting to improve things. After all, Milt is the coach and general manager."

"I suppose you've been trying to organize a revolt."

"The team has a right to know what's going on. Besides, you can't keep things like this a secret. Half of them had already heard about it."

"It's your team," Charlie conceded. "But is this the time to stir them up?"

Clementine Post had the last word. "It hasn't done their playing any harm, has it?"

Without giving him a chance to reply, she beckoned imperiously over his shoulder. "Win! Win! We're all over here," she called, then lowered her voice to hiss, "You see. This is the first time Win Holland has had enough team spirit to come to a welcome home."

Charlie hissed right back. "And who is that he's toting around with him? If it's Moore, the deal may still be on."

"Nonsense! Win probably thinks he has to be polite to the man as long as he's in town."

Nothing could have exceeded her own graciousness when Franklin Moore was presented to her. "Win's told me about your interest in the Huskies, Mr. Moore. I'm glad you were able to be with us this morning. We're all very proud of them."

"You sure have a right to be proud, Mrs. Post. I couldn't get out to the Coast, the way I would have liked to, but I watched it all on television. They played outstanding hockey, all three nights."

Like her team, Clemmie seized the opportunity to score a point. "And I thought the coaching was good, too. Using Kerr to check Oddi really paid off."

"I don't see how you can ask for better coaching than the kind that wins three out of three," he replied blandly.

Now her probing began. "We all have high hopes for the rest of the season. Even Win is going to think a lot more of the Huskies."

The response came not from Moore, but from Holland. "Come on, Clemmie. Frank and I have already been into all that."

"And if you want to know, Mrs. Post, Win is thinking a little too highly of the Huskies right now. At least for my pocketbook." Moore was philosophic. "Your chances on this kind of deal come and go, they don't stand still. But there comes a time to decide whether you're going to fish or cut bait. I suppose I'll have to clean up my business and go home without a hockey team."

Clementine Post beamed. Moore twinkled down at her. Only Win Holland was embarrassed.

"That's enough business for now," he protested. "We're supposed to be here to celebrate."

Good-naturedly Moore took the hint. "The Sloan deserves some thanks, too," he said to Thatcher. "You're certainly not pinching pennies on the television coverage. There must be cameras all over the place, the way they shift from long-range shots to close-ups. Actually, you see more than when you're at rinkside."

Thatcher recognized a heaven-sent opening. "I know there were endless conferences about the coverage of the

games. But you want to talk to our real experts. Brad!"
He waved to a nearby twosome. "Brad, this is Franklin
Moore, who's interested in the camera work for the Huskies. Bradford Withers is our president, and what he
doesn't know about the subject Dexter Younghusband
does."

He stepped back to watch Withers and Moore plunge
into technicalities, ably seconded by Younghusband and
Mrs. Post. Relief, however, was premature.

He had hoped to immobilize the hockey element so that
he could escape with Charlie. But someone fell into stride
between them.

"Of course Clemmie is a great gal, just great," Win
Holland said.

"Yes?" said Charlie discouragingly.

"But she does get excited sometimes. Hell, she was
plain unreasonable when I first told her about Frank
Moore's offer. I knew she was planning to see you about
it, and I was glad. I hoped someone could talk sense to
her."

"She seems pretty calm today."

"I probably have you to thank for that."

Charlie did not have to signal for assistance. He and
Thatcher had fended off fishing expeditions before.

"That's right, Charlie, you did say something about
Mrs. Post coming to the bank." Thatcher turned to Holland. "I remember because it was on the same day that
your father spoke to me about you."

There was a pause. Then Win Holland grinned. "I suppose that means you're sick of hearing about the Huskies.
But there's no pleasing both of them. Now that Clemmie's
glad because I'm not selling out, my father will be fuming.
He doesn't think an ice hockey team is the right occupa-
tion for a Holland. But then, he doesn't think anything is
except Holland Steel."

Thatcher said that was not an uncommon attitude in
families traditionally tied to one firm.

"Too damned traditionally," Holland grumbled. "It
isn't as if I didn't give Holland Steel a fair trial. Why

should the family mind so much because I decided to leave?"

Reviewing what he had read of young Holland's recent history, Thatcher thought the family should have applauded. It was better by far to have him waste a million or two of his private fortune than to have him mismanage Holland Steel.

Aloud he said, "Every man has to decide for himself how he wants to spend his life."

"That's just what I told my father," Win said eagerly. "But he still doesn't understand. I'll bet he was after you to pick up my interest in the Huskies and maybe one or two other investments, so I could return to the fold."

Thatcher replied that Archibald Holland had spoken of accommodation in only the broadest terms.

Nevertheless Win persisted in trying to extract more detail. Thatcher was not annoyed. After all, he had no obligations to Holland senior.

Before they exhausted their exchange, a disembodied voice overhead announced that the special flight from Los Angeles had landed and passengers would be debarking through Gate 28.

Immediately the air vibrated with excitement. Uniformed guards deployed themselves for battle, the crowd surged forward, press photographers began taking background pictures. The welcoming committee sorted itself out, ragged cheering sections went into action, and, from nowhere, hundreds of homemade signs and banners suddenly unfurled.

Thatcher detached Brad Withers from Moore and moved into the front lines where Dexter Younghusband was haranguing a reporter. Clementine Post and Win Holland looked exalted behind her massive bouquet of roses. Finally the doors opened.

Promptly on cue, Withers stepped forward, wrung the hand of the first man out and began his laudation. The man, one of the team masseurs, looked frightened. But the faux pas was barely noticed in the furor created by the emergence of the second passenger.

"Way to go, Billy!"

"Rah! Rah! Billy Siragusa!"

"You should've killed him, Billy!"

Withers braced himself for another attempt, a suitable number of flash bulbs exploded, the team milled forward to be clutched by imploring hands. In the seething confusion Thatcher was conscious of only a few interrupted vignettes.

A newly injured player looked first at the wall of yelling humanity, then down at his crutches.

Clemmie Post buttonholed a wiry, gray-haired man and talked earnestly as she led him away.

A long-haired man in a silk sports jacket was listening to Billy Siragusa as Thatcher passed.

"Go ahead and wait for me in the lot, Neil. I'll be out to the car when I'm through in here. . . ."

Then the rope barrier gave way, and Thatcher and Charlie Trinkam had their work cut out for them shepherding Withers to the Sloan limousine.

Behind them, the madness lasted for a full hour. Players inched their way toward the exits, stopping patiently to autograph loose sheets of paper, albums, pucks, and even a shirt. They laughed at quips, responded to sallies, grinned into Polaroids.

At last, La Guardia was left to its usual pre-dawn squalor. Here and there a broom was pushed through the litter, incoming freight was checked, post-office trucks moved. But it was not until the first cheerless fingers of light sent the night shift off duty that an invoice clerk, hurrying through the parking lot in the fine drizzle, almost stumbled over an outflung arm.

Clutching at a slippery fender, he stared stupidly from the dark figure lying in a crumpled heap to the darker stain patching the damp asphalt. It was a moment before he nerved himself to bend down and look more closely. Then he jerked upright and pounded back to the terminal.

"There's a dead man out there! Somebody's been shot!"

The new excitement that gripped the airport was a mirror image of the old. Again there were rope barriers, uniformed men, cameras flashing.

And even a familiar name.

"Franklin T. Moore," the policeman holding the victim's wallet read aloud. "He was from Nashville, Tennessee."

5

BLUE LINE

FRANKLIN MOORE'S BODY was discovered at daybreak. Within hours, the New York City Police Department had activated procedures designed to produce information about the dead man. Teletype inquiries were dispatched to Nashville; the medical examiner was exploring the gunshot wound behind Moore's ear; airline desks and downtown hotels were being queried.

But by nine o'clock, very few facts had surfaced.

"We've got a body," said Captain Kallen. "And a name."

Consulting a list, his subordinate amplified. "He had two hundred dollars in his wallet," he said. "Plus every credit card going."

"And he was shot at close range," said Kallen. "A lot that tells us. I'm getting a feeling about this one, Joe. We're going to have to do a lot of waiting."

But, even as he spoke, a patrolman entered the office.

"Courtesy of the *Daily News*," he announced, handing Kallen a ten-by-twelve glossy. "They said they weren't planning to use it—until Moore's name and La Guardia rang a bell with someone. They thought we'd like to have a copy of our own. Saves ten cents."

"What's this?" Kallen grumbled, reaching for his glasses.

His assistant already had a stubby finger on one of the men smiling into the camera.

"The name he gave the photographer," said the patrolman, "was Franklin Moore."

Kallen studied the picture. Then he looked up. "Okay, what's the story?"

"The welcome home for the Huskies," said the patrolman. "The *Daily News* had a man covering it. The team flew into La Guardia at four-fifteen this morning—that's straight from United Airlines. And there was a big turnout to meet them. That's from everybody in the terminal, and Traffic Division as well."

"A hockey fan, huh?" said Kallen. "Well, that's something. He could have been jetting to Iceland."

Joe, still intent on the photograph, nodded. "You can say that again. He was a hockey fan with capital letters. You know who this is standing next to him? It's Clemmie Post. I've seen a million pictures of her."

They all had.

"But what about the other two?"

Joe did not recognize them, but the patrolman was proud of having done the spadework. "A. Winthrop Holland," he said. "The *News* says he's Clemmie's partner."

Kallen whistled soundlessly.

Joe too was impressed. "So Moore was at La Guardia with the Husky owners? I'm almost afraid to ask—but who's this other guy? The one with his mouth open?"

"That," said the patrolman, "is Bradford Withers. He's president of the Sloan Guaranty Trust."

"Great," said Joe. "Three of a kind."

Captain Kallen had tilted his chair back to stare at the ceiling for a moment. Righting himself with a thud, he said, "Three of a kind isn't bad for openers, Joe. Don't you forget it. At least, we're starting at the top. Okay, here's how we handle it."

Joe took note of Kallen's instructions. He did not have to be told to pay special attention to the final admonition:

"Tell the boys to play it carefully. I still have a feeling about this one. Only it's changed in the last few minutes."

Detective Cary O'Brien drew A. Winthrop Holland.

"An apartment in the sixties," said Central Records. "Also a business address—Holwin Enterprises. That's on Forty-seventh Street."

"What time do millionaires go to work?" O'Brien asked.

One millionaire, he found, was hard at it by ten-thirty in the morning.

"Frank Moore!" Win Holland exclaimed when the receptionist finally capitulated. "My God! Of course . . . anything I can do to help. Come in . . . it's just that we are all tied up . . . but come in. . . ."

As he followed Holland, O'Brien saw that, despite her freezing British accent, the receptionist had been telling no more than the truth.

To judge by appearances, it was a busy morning at Holwin Enterprises. A large desk overflowed with legal documents, scrawled notes, lists of figures. Cylindrical ashes in the large ashtrays told of cigarettes burning themselves out unnoticed; the wastebaskets had not been emptied.

Beside the desk, writing on a pad, sat a sallow man with smoothly combed hair. His rumpled jacket suggested he had spent the night in his clothes, possibly at this desk. Intent upon his notes, he did not look up.

"My God, Anton," Holland said abruptly. "Frank Moore's had some sort of accident." He indicated a chair for O'Brien with a casual wave. "This is my associate, Dr. Dietrich. O'Brien here is from the police. He's got some questions."

Dietrich spoke with almost no accent. "An automobile accident?" he asked, his pencil arrested in midair.

Holland shrugged.

O'Brien had already broken the news once. "As I told Mr. Holland," he repeated, "Moore was shot to death."

Dietrich said somberly, "That is a tragedy."

"Yes." Holland had no patience for empty formalities. "And O'Brien wants to talk to me."

"Now?" Dietrich frowned. "But Mayne will be telephoning from London any instant."

Holland was not really listening. "Let me know when he does," he said absently.

"Very well." Dietrich rose and began selecting items from the desk. "I shall review the data in my own office. Then, if he should call, we shall be ready."

"Fine, Anton. Why don't you do that?"

Dr. Dietrich marched to the door with slightly pigeon-toed gait. There he paused for a final remark. "What about getting in touch with Armbruster?"

"I'll think about it." Holland waited until the door closed before saying apologetically: "Sorry about that. Now, Frank Moore—you said he was shot?" For the first time he seemed to assimilate the word. *"Shot?"*

Detective O'Brien briefly outlined what the police had found at La Guardia.

"But what was he doing in the parking lot?" Holland asked.

"That's what we're trying to find out."

"Unbelievable," said Holland, almost to himself.

"You were at La Guardia yourself this morning, we understand," O'Brien said.

"Sure. You'd better let me explain." Holland made a visible effort to order his thoughts. "I own a piece of the Huskies. When I mentioned the welcome home to Frank he said he'd like to come. I warned him that I'd have to hang around for the whole thing and ride back in the team bus. He said that was okay. If it dragged out too long, he'd leave by himself. So I picked him up at his hotel, and we went out to the airport together. We must have gotten there about four o'clock. We talked to some people until the team arrived. . . ."

O'Brien had produced a notebook. "Can you give me their names?"

"Some of them, anyway. There was the guy covering for *Ice and Blade,* and Clemmie Post and some people from the Sloan."

Impatiently he rose to his feet and rubbed the nape of his neck. "Hell, I don't know how much I can help you.

Once the team arrived, I know I lost sight of Moore. We were making speeches and posing for the cameras— No, wait a minute. I do remember seeing Frank once after that. He was talking to Billy Siragusa. But that was right at the beginning. There was a tremendous crowd out there, you know, and it just went on and on. That's why I wasn't surprised when Frank wasn't around at the end. I wouldn't have stayed myself if I didn't have to. I thought he'd grabbed a cab or gotten a lift."

"Are you sure he wasn't around? You said there was a big crowd. Could he have missed the bus?"

Holland shook his head. "The team didn't leave until everybody else was clearing out. You could see who was there, the last ten or fifteen minutes. And we all knew we'd be able to go pretty soon."

O'Brien consulted his notes. "You suggested a cab or a lift. Now who would have given him a lift?"

"Almost anybody. A lot of people had cars out there. And in the last two weeks I introduced Frank to everybody who hangs around the Huskies." Holland was restive. "What difference does that make? He didn't get a lift. He was there at La Guardia all the time."

"In the parking lot," O'Brien reminded him. "Now, Mr. Holland, I suppose Moore was visiting from Nashville. Is that why he's only been meeting people in the last two weeks?"

"That's right. He was staying at the Roosevelt, incidentally. We had dinner a couple of times and took in all the hockey games at the Garden. Oh, and he came out to a practice session once."

Detective O'Brien was beginning to be puzzled. "Mr. Moore was a friend of yours?"

"Sure," said Holland. "That is, we did business together. But I've known him a couple of years. You could call us friends."

"Do you know why he was in New York? Was it just a holiday?"

"No. This was a business trip for Frank."

"And on a business trip he went out to La Guardia at four o'clock in the morning for this welcome home?"

O'Brien knew that expense-account trips often involve extracurricular activities, but this was a new one.

Win Holland hastened to enlighten him. "The business Frank had with me was trying to buy the Huskies, anyway my share of them."

"I see." O'Brien revised his thinking. "You'd better tell me more about that, Mr. Holland."

Holland ran a hand through his hair. "I don't know that there's much to tell. Frank and I had done a few deals with each other before."

"Concerning hockey?"

"No, no. Standard real estate deals—that was Frank's line. I sold him an office building when I closed down one of the Holland newspapers. Let's see, that must have been two or three years ago. I held his notes on that for a year and, by the time they were paid off, he'd subdivided some land outside of Vicksburg. Holwin Enterprises took about seven acres for a shopping center. That's what I thought he was seeing me about on this trip. But it turned out that he'd gotten the hockey bug in a big way. He and some friends of his wanted to pick up my interest. He thought the Huskies had a great future."

"And that's why he was spending so much time at the games and finally at the welcome home?" said the detective.

"That's right. Of course, it was partly pleasure. I'd never seen him so excited about anything. He really knew a lot more about hockey than I do." Holland sighed. "Poor Frank, what a terrible thing to happen."

Just then Dr. Dietrich entered the room. "Excuse me," he said. "Mayne is on the line. I think you must talk to him, Win."

He looked toward O'Brien, but Holland was already on his feet, striding out.

"I'll take it in your office."

Dr. Dietrich stepped out of his way. "Be sure to tell him that under no circumstances will you refinance," he said.

"Right," said Holland.

Dietrich did not follow him. He advanced a pace and

said heavily, "It is a shocking event, that Mr. Moore
should have died in such a way."

O'Brien preferred getting information to giving it. "Did
you know him, too?"

"I was introduced to him. I have seen him briefly on
several occasions, here in this office." Dietrich paused.
"One thing I noticed. You say that Mr. Moore's body was
found only this morning. But you come to Mr. Holland
immediately. Surely there are others closer. . . ."

No question of this sort had occurred to Holland,
O'Brien noted.

"The Huskies," he replied unhelpfully.

"Ah, yes," said Dietrich with comprehension. "I am not
a sports follower. I had forgotten that."

O'Brien was curious. "Doesn't Holwin Enterprises have
anything to do with the Huskies?"

"No, the team is one of Mr. Holland's personal interests. Here, we handle financial affairs."

Even during police interrogations, Detective O'Brien
thought sourly as Holland reappeared.

"He says he's made his last offer."

Dietrich turned. "Did you suggest another option? Possibly that would solve the problem."

"He's still on the phone, Anton. Why don't you talk to
him?"

"Yes, of course."

Dietrich was already hurrying out. Holland hesitated,
then returned to his desk.

"This is some day," he said wearily. "First Frank. Then
Mayne. Where were we?"

In fact, they were no longer in the same place. O'Brien
had reviewed some of Holland's earlier replies.

"Moore's plans to get himself a piece of the Huskies—
was that all right with everyone? Nobody minded the idea
of him moving in?"

Win Holland's answers had been coming readily. Now
they suddenly dried up. "Why should anybody mind?" he
asked sharply. "It happens every day. You just have to
read the sports pages. It's like any other commercial trans-
action."

O'Brien remembered that Captain Kallen had said to play it carefully. He had not ordered his subordinate to leave the field at the first sign of resistance.

"And it didn't make any difference to you?" he pressed. "You weren't annoyed at his trying to get your share?"

To the detective's surprise, Holland's face cleared.

"Oh, me!" he said unguardedly. "Christ, I didn't mind. At first I was all for it. You've got the wrong idea. Frank wasn't trying to twist anybody's arm. He was simply making an offer. And as I said, I was inclined to take him up. It was only at the airport this morning that we decided not to go through with it."

"Why was that?"

Win Holland was transparently pleased to turn the talk to the proposed trade.

"The Huskies were beginning to look damn good after that round on the Coast, even to me. I raised the price, and Frank wouldn't go that high. But he understood the realities, he knew he should have moved faster. The time to pick up a team is before they look good to the whole world."

"You only told him this at La Guardia? Would you say that until then he thought he was going to get the Huskies? Would he have been talking about it to other people?"

"I really don't know. Of course, some people he had to talk to—the ones who were coming in with him. You'd have to ask them how he felt."

"I suppose so," said O'Brien, closing his notebook. He wanted to end the interview on an unstrained note. He was quite pleased with the results of this first round. In spite of those attempts at camouflage, he had garnered one important fact.

If Win Holland had not objected strenuously to Moore's ambitions about the Huskies, somebody else certainly had.

"Franklin Moore," said Clemmie Post when the maid ushered Detective Vernon Marling into her living room. "Yes, I know Moore. What on earth are the police asking questions for? Oh, why don't you sit down here?"

She gestured him toward an enormous scarlet sofa that

exactly matched the silk pants suit she was wearing. Two Siberian huskies uncurled themselves from a rug before the fireplace and padded over to inspect the newcomer.

Mrs. Post reassured him. "Don't worry. Rocket and Pocket love everybody," she said dotingly.

Marling was a cat lover. Furthermore, the icy-blue eyes set in sooty masks intimidated him.

"See?" she chirped as the dogs, losing interest, returned to their rug. "I'm having a second cup of coffee. Can I get you one?"

When Marling refused, she went on gaily, "Now, then. Tell me how Frank Moore has been getting into trouble with the police."

The spacious room was brilliant with sunshine. There were yellow primroses on the table, which still held the remains of Clemmie's breakfast. She herself was everything that the newspapers had led Vernon Marling, a hockey fan, to expect. He was sorry to intrude murder into this cloudless atmosphere.

"I'm afraid he's been killed, Mrs. Post," he said quietly.

Mrs. Post had been lifting her cup and saucer as the announcement was made. She froze and stared wildly about as if uncertain what to do with them.

Marling had received the same information for dissemination as Detective O'Brien.

". . . in the parking lot at La Guardia. His body was found several hours after the welcome home for the Huskies. We'd like to find out everything we can about his last movements."

"I see," she said, putting down her coffee and straightening her shoulders. "Well, ask me all the questions you want. I'll tell you anything I can. But I'm afraid that's very little. I barely saw him at all last night."

She was no longer the same woman.

"You did see him, though."

"Yes." Mrs. Post reconsidered her answer. "For a very short while."

"Do you know what time that was?"

Mr. Post thought for a moment. "It must have been before the team arrived. Yes, of course. After that I was

busy with the welcoming ceremonies, right until we all
went home in the bus."

Marling's reading had already told him that Mrs. Post
always rode on the bus with her players.

"Did you notice Mr. Moore at all after you had spoken
with him?"

She was exaggeratedly patient. "No, I've just told you. I
was in the middle of things. I couldn't have noticed Mr.
Moore, even if I had wanted to."

There was no ignoring the hostility in that last phrase.

"Er—he was a friend of yours?"

"Certainly not!"

Marling persevered. "But you knew him?"

"I knew of him," she corrected. "He was an associate of
A. Winthrop Holland, who is part owner of the Huskies. I
had seen them together at rinkside." Her tone was chill. "I
did not wish to know Mr. Moore."

This sounded promising.

"Why not?"

"He was not a desirable type of man." Mrs. Post
paused dramatically. "He was a boxing promoter."

Detective Marling waited for too long before he realized
that was the end.

"I see," he said at last.

"And I was right!" Clemmie's bitterness suddenly burst
the dam. "Getting himself killed in some kind of Mafia
shoot-out! You can see the kind of people he was involved
with."

"Is that why you thought he might be in trouble with
the police? Because he was a boxing promoter?"

"I didn't think anything of the sort until you walked in.
You just said you wanted to talk to me about Franklin
Moore." She was outraged. "If only it had happened
someplace else. Why did he have to go and get himself
killed in the middle of our welcome home? I'll never for-
give Win Holland."

With the best will in the world, Marling was finding it
hard to see the endearing zany he had been prepared for.
Mrs. Post sounded discouragingly cold-hearted.

"Now, about your conversation with Mr. Moore. What did you talk about?"

This earned him a quick, unfriendly look. "It was merely an exchange of courtesies. Mr. Moore congratulated me on the recent Husky wins."

"He was interested in hockey?"

"I assumed so from his presence." She was growing more *grande dame* by the moment. "But I have explained to you that I had just met the man. I am afraid I cannot tell you anything else about him."

"Thank you very much," said Detective Marling, rising. He had his instructions and he was going to hew to them.

One thing, however, was certain. He would never think of her as Clemmie again.

There was, of course, yet another figure in the *Daily News* photograph. But the police descent on the Sloan Guaranty Trust caused virtually no discomfort. They learned that the Sloan contingent had left, en bloc, almost immediately after the team had arrived at the airport. They received unadorned factual statements from John Thatcher and Charlie Trinkam about Frank Moore's earlier movements. They listened stoically to a rambling discourse from Bradford Withers in which the future chances of the Huskies and the art of television sports coverage jostled uneasily for prominence. Then they departed.

"It's Public Relations that's causing all the trouble," complained Charlie Trinkam, collapsing into a chair in Withers' office.

John Thatcher sat down beside him and tried, unsuccessfully, to reserve judgment. Perhaps there was justification, he suggested, for Younghusband's first burst of activity.

"Fat chance of the *News* going along," Charlie muttered.

Dexter Younghusband had barely waited for the police to clear the building before launching a misguided attempt to pressure the *News* into cropping Withers out of its picture.

"True," Thatcher agreed. "Nor does the picture matter. Still, what I object to is his subsequent conduct."

For Dexter Younghusband, having failed to protect the Sloan, had enlarged his mandate to include the Huskies and gone haring up to their office.

"Even that wouldn't be so bad. It's these hourly bulletins to Brad that have put the fat in the fire."

Doleful tidings from Younghusband had caused Withers to summon his lieutenants to this council of war. Both had been snatched from important conferences. Before Thatcher could reply, Withers entered and was in full flight.

"You're here. Good, good. The police are getting entirely out of hand. Younghusband tells me they've been questioning Mrs. Post and Holland."

"But, Brad," Thatcher observed, "after all, they questioned you."

Parallels were always a mistake with Withers.

"I feel we should all cooperate with the authorities wherever we can," he replied with one of his rapid swings from indignation to virtue. "I hope I made that clear from my own example."

Charlie Trinkam's instincts were kindly. "You sure did."

"But, Brad," Thatcher continued, "if the police can talk to you, why not to Mrs. Post and young Holland?"

Withers had already forgotten his original plaint. Lowering his voice impressively, he almost whispered, "I haven't told you how bad things are. The police are threatening to go to the Huskies."

"Well, that's too bad," Thatcher said diplomatically, "but the players were there at the airport."

Withers was having one of his forceful days. "I told Younghusband that I'd consider getting an opinion of counsel."

It was a pity, Thatcher reflected, that the general confusion regarding the Sloan's role vis-à-vis the Huskies should extend to the bank's president.

Withers went on. "Younghusband tells me that Mrs. Post is very worried about the team being bothered."

Thatcher exchanged a look with Charlie. Trinkam had levered himself upright. "I told Clemmie she'd regret giving everybody an earful," he said more in sorrow than in anger.

Withers thought Charlie had misunderstood. "They're playing Toronto, you know," he added gravely.

"I doubt if it will affect their skating," said Thatcher, who also had kindly instincts.

Withers was a grasper of straws. "You think the Huskies will just brush it all off?" he inquired hopefully.

That far Thatcher was not prepared to go.

"On the contrary. I expect they'll be very interested."

6

BEHIND THE CAGE

NEW YORK CITY is the proud home of basketball and ice hockey teams, the favorite site of certain track events, the first port of call of Lippizaner stallions, Russian bears and Scottish bagpipers.

The demands on Madison Square Garden are correspondingly great, and professional teams practice elsewhere. Therefore the police were not surprised to learn that they would have to travel out to Long Island to interview the Huskies. The team was at an ice rink in Mineola. And within minutes of arrival, Captain Kallen discovered that this geographical fact could have a bearing on his case.

"No," Coach Milt Forsburg explained. "We didn't all go back together after the welcome home. You see, it depends on where the players live."

"I thought the team traveled to and from airports in a

bus," Kallen objected. He had hoped to eliminate the Huskies in one stroke.

Forsburg enlightened him. "Look, we've got players from the age of twenty to forty, most of them from Canada. During the season, their life centers around the Garden and the rink here in Mineola. The unmarried ones take apartments in the city. But the married men bring their families down, and they mostly live in houses on Long Island. That way, they're close to Mineola and to the airports."

The captain could see what was coming. The airports lay between Mineola and Manhattan. "So the married ones don't go into the city at all. It would be the wrong direction for them," he concluded.

"Right. Either they've left a car in the parking lot or they take a cab, or they get picked up by their wives. A guy like Pete Levoisier, for instance, his wife picks him up. It doesn't make any difference what time we get in—three, four, or even five o'clock in the morning—she's always there." He was pleased to cite this instance of wholesome family life. Nonetheless, it appeared to bewilder him. Either Levoisier was an unlikely object for wifely devotion or the manager's own home life had not prepared him for paragons.

"All right," summarized Captain Kallen. "So, the ones who've got houses on the Island stay on the Island. The others all take the bus into the city."

The coach shook his head regretfully. It was not that simple. "Some of the others get met, too. When a player makes a name for himself, he starts attracting his own fans —guys who like to be seen around town with a personality. Now Billy Siragusa, he got picked up by one of his friends." There was a meaningful pause. "By Neil Gruen, no less!"

He expected Kallen to be impressed. Neil Gruen needed no explanation. He owned the city's most fashionable discotheque, believed in the swinging approach to life and was his own best publicity.

The police could take Neil Gruen in stride. "Well, things may be better than I thought," said the captain. "I expected you to tell me the whole team bundled out the front door and into the bus. We could have crossed them off that way, but we wouldn't have had any witnesses. Instead, a bunch of them were fanning out through the parking lot."

"With their wives and friends," the coach said firmly.

"That doesn't make them blind, does it? You never can tell what one of them may have noticed."

"It's easy to see that hockey isn't your game, Captain," Forsburg rejoined. "These boys had just come back from a grueling week. First, we flew out to California the day after a big game in the Garden. Then we kept chugging up and down the Coast—the first game in Frisco, then north to Vancouver, then south to L.A. When the boys weren't in a game and they weren't on a plane, they were practicing. By the time we got to La Guardia, everybody was dead beat. We weren't noticing anything. All we cared about was getting into a real bed."

He had made a bad guess. Captain Kallen was a hockey fan of many years' standing. He had watched too many games to be misled about the physical stamina of the players. They were young and resilient, and they had been able to doze for several hours on the flight home.

"Even if they were asleep on their feet when they landed, there was that welcome home to wake them up," said Kallen. "And I'm not asking them to remember something about a stranger. After all, Moore was thinking of buying the team. They must have been curious about him—what he was like, what his plans were. Enough to notice him if they passed him."

But Milt Forsburg disagreed. "You've got the wrong end of the stick. Win Holland was playing this one close to his chest. Nothing had been decided yet, and no one realized how important Moore might become. Oh, I don't say the boys didn't see him around the rink, but that was all. We didn't really know what was in the wind."

"No one knew anything about the deal?" The captain was openly skeptical. "That isn't the way things work."

"There may have been a few rumors going around. But

that's all. Frank Moore didn't have anything to do with us."

An hour and a half later Forsburg was enunciating the same theory, this time to his team.

"It was only a formality," he said in the locker room. "The police found out Moore was at La Guardia for the welcome home. But it doesn't have anything to do with us."

Pete Levoisier was a big dark man with a placid face. He had already bundled his equipment into a bag and handed it to a trainer. Now he was dressed to go home. "Sure, Milt," he said readily. "Don't worry. We understand. The police were just checking."

"And a hell of a lot of good it did them," commented a burly young man knotting his tie. "Who was going to notice anything in that parking lot yesterday morning? It was dark, it was raining. I had trouble enough finding Neil Gruen's car until he had the sense to flash his headlights."

Trust Billy Siragusa not to miss a chance to mention Gruen, the coach thought sourly. Forsburg always told the press that Siragusa was a natural team leader, both on the ice and off. It was not the truth as far as the locker room was concerned—not since he had started ramming his new fame down his teammates' throats.

Paul Imrie, whose hair-trigger temper made him a terror in action, rose to the bait immediately. "If you came into the city on the bus like the rest of us, you wouldn't have these little troubles."

But it was Levoisier who answered him. "They grilled everyone who went into the parking lot. But we were just like Billy, too busy trying to find our car to see anything else. Eileen forgot where she parked it."

His wife was famous for this habit. The Levoisier family had once been carless for three days while Pete spent his spare hours searching through a giant shopping center, where Eileen had misplaced their station wagon.

Milt Forsburg was grateful for the tactful intervention. He realized that the best thing he could do was withdraw.

He paused only long enough to say, "Don't let this upset you, fellas. It doesn't have anything to do with us."

"That's right, Milt," Siragusa replied promptly. "Not with any of us."

No sooner had the door closed than the analysis began.

"What the hell did you mean by that crack, Billy?" asked a goalie.

Billy laughed sarcastically. "You don't think that Milt is wetting his pants because he's worried about us, do you?"

While the goalie frowned, the team innocent said, "Well, who else can he be worried about?"

Paul Imrie had no trouble with that one. "We didn't have anything to lose by Moore. What difference does it make to us if he buys a share of the team? We never saw Holland until we were climbing out of the cellar. He'd be no loss."

There were no supporters of the Holland interest. What Imrie said was true. Winthrop Holland was a virtual stranger. Nonetheless the present ownership did not lack defenders.

"Mrs. Post isn't like that," the innocent said stoutly.

Imrie looked at him in exasperation. "No, she isn't. So maybe the less said the better," he snapped.

But the goalie had come to his own conclusions. "Mrs. Post is the one that Milt is in a sweat about. You know how she felt about Moore. Christ, she was hollering a blue streak. Everyone heard her. She was hollering for her lawyers, hollering for her bankers, hollering at Holland."

"Well, there's one thing we can be thankful for." Pete Levoisier automatically produced the word of comfort. "No one can say she hollered at Moore. She wouldn't even talk to him."

"Of course, the thing that really got her going was the idea of Moore moving the team to Tennessee," said a right wing chattily. "Personally she's not so wild about Holland that she wouldn't like to trade him in."

"But not for a boxing promoter. I don't know where she got the idea that Moore spent his life setting up bouts." A defense man shook his head knowledgeably. "He just did it that once as far as I know."

"And you're the one who would know," rejoined the wing.

A trainer silently scooped up the last bag. The management should hear this! How long, he wondered, could Milt Forsburg claim that the team had not been following the whole ownership wrangle? For that matter, how far was he deceiving himself?

"No matter how you slice it, you can't blame Milt for being worried," said the goalie. "You saw how he punched home to the cops that bit about Mrs. Post coming back on the bus with us—the way she always does. It was true enough as far as it went. He said that she rode in on the front seat with him as usual. What he didn't mention was that they weren't around while we were signing autographs. There must have been an hour when she could have been anywhere."

Billy Siragusa's laugh jarred the quiet in the room.

"Use your head, man!" His crooked features were alight with malice. "Forsburg isn't worried about anyone but himself. What was so wrong with Moore's deal as far as Clemmie Post was concerned? Sure, she didn't like it. But she wasn't going to be left out in the cold. She'd still have her share of the Huskies. She'd still have a big say in things. Forsburg was the one whose neck was on the line if Moore had big ideas about changes. You heard that garbage about not being satisfied with the coaching. Well, how do you cure that little problem? You get yourself a new coach!"

This was too much for them. Most of the protests were not flattering to Milt Forsburg. The general opinion was that he was too chicken, too lazy, too willing to let someone else do the dirty work, to go to such lengths to defend his job.

Billy Siragusa was undismayed by the wave of objections.

"Oh, I didn't say he shot anybody. I know damn well he didn't. All I said was that he's worried about the cops getting suspicious. That's why he's giving us all this jazz about Moore not having anything to do with us, *any* of us.

That's the official Husky line and he wants us to stick with it."

Pete Levoisier remained unconvinced. "It doesn't matter one hoot in hell what Moore thought about Milt. Not even if he owned the team one hundred percent. So long as a team is winning games, then no owner is going to fire the coach. It just doesn't happen. And Milt knows that as well as I do."

"He was steaming when he heard about it," Siragusa insisted. "So, all right, he wouldn't be fired when he was winning. What about the first time we lost? Next year, the year after, then it'd be the ax."

"Ah, dry up." Paul Imrie had had enough. "Every coach in the League lives with the threat of being fired some year. And if we're talking about people steaming over Moore's plans, what about you? When you heard he wanted to move the franchise away from New York, you went through the roof."

"I can make my bonus any place they put down ice," Siragusa declared swiftly.

"But how are you going to spend it?" Imrie shot back. "Where are you going to find the beautiful people in the sticks? Neil Gruen isn't going to jet down to Nashville. What happens to your bachelor pad and your models and discotheques? You've just gotten your first whiff of the sweet life and you don't want to lose it."

Paul Imrie had the great advantage of genuinely delighting in combat, physical or verbal. His companions all had their fair share of aggressiveness in one form or another. But the spark that ignited them was usually connected with the game by which they earned their living. They threw themselves into body checks to protect their end of the ice. Or they joined frays as an exercise in team solidarity. But Paul Imrie fought for the sheer joy of it. He was a constant occupant of the penalty box, he was always being thrown out of games. And if he had not started the fight in the first place—which was all too likely—he was the one who led the team off the bench to turn a slugging match into a donnybrook. He was also the most loquacious man in professional hockey. Referees had penalized him for sheer pertinacity. Owners had yielded to his salary demands out of exhaustion.

Billy Siragusa did not relish being out-argued. For him it was winning that mattered. He promptly looked for another target.

"Sure, I like living near the big time," he said with such reasonableness that Imrie was disappointed. "But, what the hell, Nashville wouldn't be forever. I'd be traded sooner or later. And as long as I shoot those goals in, I can get what I want. But what about the poor guys who can't? They're not big names. The only thing they've got going for them is that they're with a local club. Take that away, and everything goes down the drain."

Pete Levoisier was methodically checking the contents of his pockets, clearly a man with a place for everything. Now he looked up.

"I suppose you mean me."

"Well, Pete, you told us yourself that those skating clubs of yours are finally beginning to pay off. You've been waiting around a long time for them to click. If we moved to Nashville, what would happen? It's a little late in the day for you to start all over again down in Tennessee."

In his own way, Levoisier could be almost as unsatisfactory an opponent as Paul Imrie.

"No, I wouldn't like to leave New York," he said stolidly. "I guess none of us would, at least not the ones who've been here a long time. But I don't think any of us murdered a total stranger for a reason like that."

There was a collective sigh of relief. Pete Levoisier was a notorious peacemaker. But he had done more than still dissension this time. He had defused a situation that was rapidly becoming awkward for the entire team. They all recognized the discomfort; each had his own diagnosis.

"That kid Siragusa, he's getting a swelled head," thought one.

"It's the first time the team has had a real chance for the play-offs. The closer it comes, the more nervous we'll get."

"Once the coach starts running scared, it's bound to affect the team."

These explanations were not fanciful. The problems of superstar, coach and play-offs were real enough—but so was another, which Billy Siragusa's perversity was highlighting.

Captain Kallen had restricted himself to asking: Where were you? What did you see? What did you do?

Billy Siragusa was asking different questions. What was Franklin Moore going to do? How was he planning to do it? Whom would it affect?

And Franklin Moore had been murdered.

Older and wiser members of the team were content to bury their private thoughts. But the innocent never knew what his thoughts were until he heard them spoken aloud.

"You know something?" he said, painfully following the path of discovery. "Moore was a menace to all of us. Now that he's dead we're a lot better off."

7

TWO ON ONE

LOOKING BACK, John Putnam Thatcher was forced to admit that he had underestimated the extent of the Sloan's involvement with the New York Huskies until almost too late. The point of no return was left behind at precisely ten-sixteen, Eastern Standard Time, on the night of December twenty-fifth.

Millions of Americans and Canadians had stayed up late Christmas Eve to struggle with knockdown toys. They had then been routed from bed by their children; they had opened packages, gone to church, cooked turkeys, entertained guests—welcome or not. This they had done with a display of Pickwickian cheer very alien to their workaday demeanor. Naturally, the strain was too much. By eight o'clock they were ready to slump into armchairs and return to the adult world. It would take two hours of hard body checking to redress the balance.

The Forum in Montreal was the arena that night. The Canadiens were currently in possession of the Stanley Cup, as they had been too often. For a scrappy expansion team hoping to make the play-offs, they were murderous competition. The best New York could hope for was a game worth watching, instead of a debacle.

At the end of the first period, the score was unexpectedly 2-2. Pete Levoisier had surpassed himself, hammering in two goals only a minute apart. The second period saw brilliant skating, furious drives the length of the rink, and acrobatic saves by both goalies—but no change in score. With pressure mounting, the third period was a duplication of the second until twelve seconds before the end of the game. Then Paul Imrie stole the puck and passed to Billy Siragusa. Siragusa outskated a forward, advanced into Canadien territory, slid the puck between the skates of a defenseman, and picked it up on the other side. A feint to the right drew Montreal's goalie off center. Then Siragusa backhanded the puck toward the net.

The announcer's voice had been rising with excitement. Now it broke through all known human registers.

"It's in!" he squawked. "It's a goal. Oh, my God, we've won!"

He flung his arms wide in triumph, then promptly disappeared from view as his chair crashed backward.

At that moment the New York Huskies became sports page darlings, the announcer became a household name, and John Thatcher should have seen what was coming.

Throughout the previous summer, the existence of Jeremiah V. Drake had imperiled the Sloan's sponsorship of the Huskies. For twenty-three years he had been the Voice of the Sloan on the Thursday night symphony broadcasts. In mellifluous accents he had introduced the program of the evening, embellishing it with gems of musical arcana. Omniscience yielded to grave camaraderie during intermissions when Drake chatted with various luminaries from

Bayreuth, Spoleto and Salzburg. At dignified intervals he
reminded his audience of the many facilities available at
the Sloan's forty-eight branches.

With the heroic decision to supplant the symphony by
the Huskies, the problem of Jeremiah V. Drake came to
the fore. Many possibilities were canvassed. The suggestion
of retirement received a blow when it developed that Drake
was a youthful fifty years old.

"God, I thought he was at least a hundred," marveled
Charlie Trinkam when this was reported.

Then surely he could be used in some other form of
publicity, urged one of those men who never see what the
trouble is.

"But it's his voice that everyone associates with the
Sloan," objected George Lancer, chairman of the board.
Lancer's circle of acquaintants encouraged an unrealistic
estimate of the number of people who associated *Thursday Night at the Symphony* with anything.

The solution was a long time coming. To fire Drake was
unthinkable, to retire him was inappropriate, to use him in
any other medium was impossible. Lights burned late in
PR until a compromise was advanced. If Mr. Drake continued to deliver a word for the Sloan, perhaps he could
also support the play-by-play announcer by bringing late
viewers up to date on the score. Did he think he could do
that?

"I suppose so," Drake responded unenthusiastically.
However, he was as anxious as anyone to resolve the im-
passe. Squaring his shoulders manfully, he said, "Anyway,
I can try."

But Fate is a notorious prankster. During the very first
game of the season, with a face-off called, camera and mi-
crophone shifted to Jeremiah V. Drake "for a few words
from our sponsor." Normally there would have been a
dead period of at least a minute. This time, however, the
puck came out of the face-off onto the stick of a charging
wing. Now it is axiomatic in all sports coverage that the
sponsor's time should never intrude on the action. An alert
switch immediately cut in the camera focused on the ice.
And Drake, to his own eternal astonishment, ceased his

prattle about home financing and produced an accurate, compelling description of the play. A sportscaster had been born.

"Fine!" said everybody down in PR. "That may take care of one problem. We'll give it a try for a couple of weeks."

For a brief period there were hopes that a metamorphosis was being accomplished. Gone was the mellifluence, gone was the gravity and, most startling of all, gone was the measured baritone. In moments of stress the Drake voice had a range that many instrumentalists with the symphony might envy. He deplored a loss of the puck in a basso growl, he followed the fast action with a series of barking yelps, and he signaled climactic moments by soaring into falsetto.

Nevertheless, heads were soon shaking. A fifty-year-old man can change in just so many ways, and twenty-three years is a long time. Jeremiah Drake's voice adapted itself, his emotional spectrum exploded, but his vocabulary remained unaltered. Stunned sports fans heard about great choral rushes, about slap shots *con brio,* about passing *agitato* and penalty-killing *molto expressivo.*

Drake had achieved the impossible. The Sloan had doubted his ability to stoop to the acultural depths of sportscasting. He had not even tried. He had elevated ice hockey to an art form.

When the first ratings came in, there was stupefaction in PR.

"They like it!" they gasped incredulously. "In fact, they're wild about it. Drake's becoming a personality."

Jerry Drake—the Jeremiah disappeared early—might simply have become the man who inaugurated a new mode in sports coverage, were it not for the final feature which endeared him to his listeners. Like so many opera buffs, he was unashamedly partisan. There was no nonsense about wanting to see a good, clean game and may the best man win. When the puck went in, announcers in Boston and Chicago trumpeted "Score!" With Jerry, it was either an ecstatic "We scored!" or a despairing "They scored!"

By the time the Huskies were in fifth place, Jerry Drake was taking them into every living room in New York and, willy-nilly, taking the Sloan along.

John Thatcher's appreciation of this iron yoking was hastened by a series of random blows. First there was the *affaire* of the calendars.

Every Christmas the Sloan Guaranty Trust presented its more deserving clients with a chaste but elegant desk diary. Bound in fatly padded morocco leather, stamped with the owner's initials in gold, it contained not only an appointments section but also many interesting tables and maps. Some fortunate recipients considered it indispensable. Others had always accepted it with civility.

This year was different. Barely had the holidays ended when the ingrates began to telephone. Someone had told them, they said, that there was a hockey calendar available at the Sloan. With pictures of the Huskies in action. *That* was the one they wanted.

The leather diaries had gone into production in October. The hockey calendars were last-minute efforts, piled on the counters. They were cheap, they were cardboard, and they were much cherished. John Thatcher had just approved a fourth printing.

Then came a rush of calls from his Wall Street acquaintances. Cordially they invited him to lunch, sincerely they hoped he had enjoyed the holidays, earnestly they inquired about his family. Thatcher, of course, was no stranger to a sudden concern for his well-being. This is characteristic of corporate presidents seeking expanded credit lines, of underwriters selling new issues, of investment counselors wanting inside information. But luncheon with Thomas Robichaux, of Robichaux & Devane, investment bankers, showed that times had changed.

"Wonderful thing the Sloan's doing, sponsoring the Huskies," Robichaux began cheerfully.

Thatcher was automatically on guard. For thirty years Tom had never stopped complaining. Why this sudden geniality?

"I suppose so," he answered warily. "It's working out well for the bank."

"It's certainly made New York hockey-conscious." Robichaux was practically caroling by now. "Hell, even Henrietta wants to see the Huskies. Can you believe it?"

Thatcher had never met the current Mrs. Robichaux, but he had met her predecessors. That was enough.

"She says it's the thing to do," Robichaux explained. "So I promised to take her to that big Black Hawk game at the Garden next week."

"Splendid," said Thatcher perfunctorily.

"No, it's not splendid. I wish you'd listen, John. I said I promised to take her to the Garden next week. You can see where that leaves me."

John Thatcher had never been one to reject shortcuts. "Where?"

Robichaux was becoming testier by the moment. "Now, John, if you don't want to help, just say so. But don't play games with me."

"What do you—oh, you mean the Garden is sold out?"

"The Garden was sold out weeks ago." Tom's impatience was subsiding into his natural mournfulness. "But it's my scalper who's let me down. I've been using the same man for years and now he says he can't help me. At any price. That's the kind of loyalty you get these days."

Sad to say, Thatcher's reaction was one of parochial pride.

"We're certainly getting our money's worth out of that team."

"What's more, with this Jerry Drake, you seem to be tied in more than most sponsors. So—" Tom Robichaux had been heading somewhere all the time—"the Sloan must have some tickets up its sleeve."

"What's that?" Thatcher had been lost in his calculations. "Oh, all right, Tom, I'll do what I can."

As day succeeded day and supplicant followed supplicant, what Thatcher could do became less and less. Shortly before the Black Hawk game, an important customer could not be provided with tickets.

"But for Mr. and Mrs. Ainstruther," Public Relations said seriously, "we could find places in the Sloan box."

"We have a box?"

"Mr. Withers uses it all the time," PR reported proudly. In their opinion, the dignitaries of the bank too often limited their support of publicity to a pitiful budget. "We've had a big distribution for pictures of him there."

Thatcher frowned. He had not forgotten that the last time Bradford Withers had been photographed at a Husky event he had shared the spotlight with a murder victim. Still, if the Sloan had finally found a use for its president's meager talents, was it his place to carp? "Then I can tell Fred Ainstruther you'll take care of him?"

"Absolutely. That will make fourteen in the box."

Thatcher blinked. But worse was to come.

The promptness of Miss Corsa's entry indicated that she had been waiting for the little green light on her telephone to expire.

"Mr. Lancer has had to go home with the flu," she announced without preamble.

"I am sorry to hear that," said Thatcher, as he always did. George Lancer was regularly felled by influenza every January for three days. Both he and his wife were skilled veterans of the drink-plenty-of-fluids-take-aspirin-and-go-to-bed regimen.

"He called before he left and asked if you could keep his two o'clock appointment at Central Park. I told him you did not have any afternoon commitments."

Pinch-hitting for George was also a regular January feature. Rarely, however, did it involve traveling north of City Hall.

"Central Park?"

"Yes, you will be presenting the Sloan awards to the three most valuable players of the Parks Department Pee-Wee League."

George, Thatcher thought uncharitably, sometimes let his sense of duty get out of hand. It was too late now to fob off this chore on some underling. You cannot send a file clerk to represent the chairman of the board.

"I suppose it's unavoidable," he said resignedly. "Exactly where do I go?"

"You won't have any trouble finding it, Mr. Thatcher. The stand has been erected next to the boathouse."

A grim suspicion stirred.

"Miss Corsa, do you mean this ceremony is outdoors? It's twenty degrees and it's going to start snowing any minute!"

"Yes," she replied with a rare show of enthusiasm, "aren't they lucky to have such good weather?"

With George in bed and Miss Corsa losing her senses, Thatcher wondered what condition the Sloan would be in by the time he returned. But as he plodded through the slush to hail a cab, it was brought home to him that Miss Corsa, as usual, was accurately reflecting the sentiments of the financial district. All around him staid Wall Streeters who had been anathematizing the weather for decades were giving tongue to some uncharacteristic cries.

Muffled to the ears, they called in passing: "Grand weather for skating, isn't it?"

Or, with a merry chuckle: "Hope it keeps up now that we've got a good hard freeze."

Wall Street was awash in bromides. At Central Park everything was workmanlike bustle. As soon as Thatcher introduced himself, he was taken under the wing of a Parks Department official.

"That's too bad about Mr. Lancer. I know he was looking forward to this afternoon," said the young man without sarcasm. "Now, have they told you about our schedule?"

"Only that I am to present these savings bonds to the three winning boys."

"Not winning. It's a team that will win."

The future tense was warning enough. For the first time Thatcher examined his surroundings. His eye fell on two diminutive goalies, roughing the ice before their nets with painstaking care.

"I see," he said. "There's going to be a game."

"Oh, yes. First we have the game. Then, while the judges are conferring over their score sheets, there will be a demonstration of some hockey fundamentals by a member of the Huskies. After that, the three most valuable players will be announced and the prizes awarded. Is that clear?"

It was too clear. The ring of spectators was growing rapidly. Parents and schoolmates were loyally turning out to support their own. They stamped their feet, slapped their arms and shouted encouragement to each other. Two hawkers were doing a brisk trade with coffee and hot dogs. It all made for a colorful, animated scene.

With a disgruntled eye Thatcher observed that no such informality prevailed on the dais to which he had been directed. Officials of Pee-Wee Leagues and judges of athletic merit are men of weight and substance. They do not frivol about with paper cups and dabs of mustard. The front row was abuzz with preparations. Stopwatches, sheets of lined paper, and pencils were at the ready. Instinctively Thatcher headed farther back. The last two rows were deserted, with the single exception of a bulky, morose-looking man who did not seem to know what to do with himself. He had slouched down in his rickety folding chair, his hands deep in the pockets of his overcoat and his eyes fixed on an empty sky.

Deciding that he was not going to add solitary confinement to his other discomforts, Thatcher selected an adjacent seat. As the sloucher made no move to acknowledge his presence, he began to fear that he had intruded on one of nature's anchorites. But after several moments of immobility, his companion lowered his gaze and said, in a slow, lugubrious voice, "It's going to snow."

Clearly a man of few words, and those very much to the point.

Thatcher agreed that the outlook was not pleasant. In fairness he added that most of the participants seemed to be enjoying themselves.

This was received thoughtfully. Then came a long, dispassionate examination of the crowd, the players now skating onto the ice, the tensing backs directly ahead. Finally: "It's all right for them."

Much as Thatcher wanted to pursue this promising conversation, the opening face-off made him hesitate in deference to any possible interest in the match. He need not have worried. At the first scramble before a net the voice said, "I guess everybody's watching the game now," and an arm groped downward to emerge with a thermos bottle. A practiced twist produced cups and a thread of rising steam. Several seconds later Thatcher was sipping coffee laced with whisky. He congratulated his newfound friend on his foresight.

"I come to a lot of these things," he said simply.

Thatcher introduced himself and explained his role in the festivities. If there ever were a next time, he said, he would come supplied.

"My name is Pete Levoisier. I play center for the Huskies."

"Then you're giving a lesson in technique later on. And you have to do this sort of thing often?"

"Today's not so bad." Levoisier sighed. "Sometimes I have to make a speech."

Thatcher could see that would be hard on a man of his habits. "And I suppose the demands are increasing all the time."

"We take turns at it. They're always after us to autograph things, and lately they even want us on talk shows." He sounded bleak.

"Still, a good year must be gratifying." Thatcher chose his words with care. He wished to allude to current success without tactless reminder of past failure.

But Pete Levoisier was not the man to see offense where none was intended. Brightening, he informed Thatcher that his real luck was in getting a break at the right time. "Not too soon and not too late," he explained.

"I can understand why you wouldn't want it too late." Thatcher was beginning to take Levoisier's measure. He was not the gabby kind, but he used words with rare efficiency. His short sentences were like railroad engines hauling long freight trains. Occasionally they were overloaded. "You need time to capitalize on the situation. But why not too soon?"

"I'd have wasted it. Now I know what to do with it."

Levoisier was not in the habit of talking about himself. But light prodding elicited the facts. He had grown up poor and married young. Until expansion he had made a very modest salary. Then things changed. For the past five years he had been learning about investing.

"I suppose you've always known about that sort of thing," he said without envy, "but it was news to me. I thought all you had to do was make money. I didn't realize that's only the first step. Then you've got to find out how to put the money to work. Even that isn't the end of it."

This was meat and drink to Thatcher. "Yes. As soon as your investment begins yielding a return, you have to do something with the return."

"That's just it." Levoisier was almost lively. "Take our skating club. Eileen—she's my wife—she thought that one up. I was scared of the idea, and at first we did everything wrong. But we lived through it. Then last year, it really started to pay off. So, by God if we didn't open a second one."

Thatcher had followed every word with unfeigned attention. In effect, Pete Levoisier was outlining a principle that all junior trust officers had to be taught. It took full-time instruction by a skilled staff to drum it into their heads. Even so, few of them achieved the bone-deep feeling for the subject evinced by a professional hockey player who had done it alone in his spare hours. Thatcher found himself wishing that a little raw material like this would occasionally find its way into the Sloan's recruitment office. But he was a realist. If the Sloan wanted a Pete Levoisier, they were going to have to develop their own farm system. A natural consequence of these thoughts turned his eyes to the ice. None of the ten-year-olds slapping the puck looked to him like exceptionally promising bankers.

"Do they look like NHL material?" he asked.

Levoisier scrutinized the field critically. "Mostly their skating isn't good enough," he decided. "Number Twenty-seven isn't bad."

Number Twenty-seven looked exactly like all the others to Thatcher. He said as much.

"Watch him," advised the expert. "He moves in all directions—right, left, forward, backward. He doesn't favor any side. There—look at Sixteen. See how he always wants to turn clockwise. That's all wrong."

Once you knew what to look for, it was quite simple.

Levoisier was warming to his theme. "And that goalie. The one in green. He's got a lot of snap, but he's doing more work than he has to. Waiting for the forward to fire and then jumping for the puck isn't the way to do it. He should come out of the cage and cut down the angle; then the guy with the puck is likely to miss."

"Yes," said Thatcher, bending his mind to elementary geometry.

Their roles had neatly reversed. Now Thatcher was making the fundamental discoveries before an approving specialist.

By the time the game ended, the thermos bottle was empty. Thatcher had learned a good deal about ice hockey and about Pete Levoisier. He was not surprised when the short lesson in stick handling that followed was given with conscientious thoroughness.

He was also not surprised when the first boy up the steps for his savings bond was Number Twenty-seven.

8

HIGH STICKING

CENTRAL PARK had been more enjoyable than anticipated. Nonetheless it had been a mistake, John Thatcher concluded. For weeks every economist in the country had been predicting an end to the slump. Industrial production, housing starts and retail sales were all going up. The market had embraced devaluation like a long-sought bride. During his absence, the Dow-Jones averages had been bouncing frenetically. This was no time for a prudent man to take his eyes off the beta factors.

Even Brad Withers seemed to agree. He was on the line within ten minutes of Thatcher's return. "I don't like the sound of things, John," he began apocalyptically.

Thatcher, still deep in the gross national product, was puzzled. Had rumors of the market's unusual activity penetrated to Withers' aerie in the tower? And if so, how? It would be a brave man who intruded the stock exchange into the Sloan's presidential suite. Yet there was no gainsaying the genuine concern now emanating from thirty floors overhead. A firm but soothing response was indicated.

"I doubt if there's cause for real alarm, Brad," he said calmly. "Things always become a little difficult after the holidays."

"But this year is different. There's too much at stake right now."

It was perfectly true. The Sloan's recent move out of the bond market had been more massive than usual. But Brad could not be referring to that. Things were bad enough at the Sloan with a chief executive resolutely excluding finance from his calculus. They would be a lot worse if he developed an interest in the subject.

"We take precautions against certain contingencies, you know." Thatcher broke this news gently before venturing onto a note of finality. "However, I'm very glad that you've brought the problem to my attention and I'll get onto it right away."

Immense relief poured along the wire. "That's just what I was going to suggest, John. These young men are all very well in their place and I've discussed this thoroughly with Younghusband. I know you'll take care not to hurt his feelings, but when you consider how much is involved—"

"You've been discussing the bond market with Younghusband?" Thatcher was bemused.

"The bond market?" Withers was outraged. "Good God, John, I'm talking about the Huskies. We can't take the chance of any bad feeling. But I'm sure you'll be able

to straighten the whole affair out. I have every confidence . . ."

Withers' confidence in his subordinates was well found-
ed. But the strange reluctance with which they so often
greeted his demands had persuaded him that their diffi-
dence required encouragement.

As on previous occasions, Thatcher rejected the temptation to reason with Brad. The years had shown that
leaving Withers in his quagmires consumed more time and
effort, in the long run, than getting in at the beginning.

Unknown to Thatcher, the beginning had taken place
several days ago when Billy Siragusa received an introduc-
tory lesson in economics from Neil Gruen.

"Billy," Gruen said, passing the bread basket, "when
are you going to get it into your head that playing beautiful hockey isn't enough?"

Billy stiffened. He had become accustomed to a steady
flow of adulation. These days criticism was rare—and un-
welcome.

"What do you mean? I'm going to win the Calder Trophy this season. And that's just the beginning. Next year
I'll do even better."

"Sure." Gruen was contemptuous. "And what are you
getting out of all this?"

"You should hang around your own club, Neil. I guess
you didn't hear about what happened last night."

With a flick of his hand Gruen dismissed last night. "I
heard. People are lining up to meet you, and some of them
are pretty important."

"You're damned right they are." Billy reached for the
magazine by his side in the booth. "Did you catch this lead
story in *Sports Illustrated*? Says I'm going to end up the
most valuable player in the League. And do you have any
idea the kind of contract I'll get when this one expires?"

"And do you have any idea what you're passing up?"

"I'm not passing anything up. I'm getting it all. And I'll
get more." Unconsciously Siragusa stroked his picture on

the cover of the magazine. "What makes you think you know more about hockey than I do?"

"Not hockey," Gruen corrected him. "Money."

Billy cocked his head. Neil Gruen had started with nothing. Now he had everything—riches, publicity, the beautiful life. He did not cast his achievement in terms of the simpler virtues. Instead he talked about being clever, recognizing opportunities, doing your own thing. Billy responded to his maxims as twelve-year-olds had once responded to Horatio Alger.

"But I am making money," he said defensively. "And my contract isn't up until—"

"Forget the contract. That goes without saying. But what about the rest of the gravy? You're talking about magazines, about people wanting to meet you. That means you're a name. The Husky management knows it, all right. They've got applications for licenses and endorsements by the barrel. Mostly because of you. Isn't it time you cut yourself a piece of the pie?"

"I get a share of the take."

"Chicken feed! Get smart and cash in while the going's good. You won't be a hockey player forever. In twenty-five years the name Siragusa won't be worth a cent."

Billy shifted uncomfortably. He enjoyed looking into the golden future, but there was such a thing as looking too far ahead.

"I'll make a mint by then," he muttered.

"You will if you play your cards right. You've got to start selling yourself. You've got to stop other people from doing it and giving you a measly percentage. It's time you became a businessman."

It was against Siragusa's principles to say that he knew nothing about business. He achieved the same goal by saying "You mean sitting around an office? That's not my bag."

Gruen was exasperated. "You hire somebody for that part. Do it now and you can double your take. In ten years you can retire."

"It sounds good," Billy admitted dubiously, "but how do I start?"

"By telling that management of yours the free ride is over. Then you get yourself a lawyer to do the haggling. And if you're smart, you begin thinking of the people you meet here at the club. Some of them are guys who'd like the chance to buy into a business with the Siragusa name."

Billy, lukewarm to talk of percentages and licenses, was obviously dazzled by the vision of a business with the Siragusa name.

Gruen eyed him appraisingly. The inspection was not unkindly—but it was the way a potential purchaser might look at a racehorse. Gruen was planning to make money right along with Billy; now was the time to make sure his wind was good.

"Why can't I get the lawyer first," Billy suggested tentatively, "and let him talk to the management for me?"

"That's not the way to do it. You're serving notice that you're a big boy now." Gruen leaned forward compellingly. "Listen, this is what you do. . . ."

"So far, you have told me of no extraordinary difficulty," Thatcher said irritably. "This star of the Huskies wants more money. That is understandable, foreseeable and none of our business."

Dexter Younghusband was not his usual ingratiating self. "It's all the fault of this crazy system they've got. The management sells Husky endorsements, the players' share goes into a kitty, and at the end of the year every member of the team gets an equal cut."

"That is asking for trouble," Thatcher conceded. "I suppose the popular players are the ones in demand."

"Until this year there wasn't anything worth talking about. But now a manufacturer wants to bring out a big line of hockey jerseys in the Husky colors with the number seventeen on the back—that's Siragusa's number—and tie it in with some promotion by Billy. He says he'll be damned if his share is going to any kitty for the rest of the team."

"They can look forward to a good many situations of that sort if they don't change their system. But what does this have to do with the Sloan?"

Charlie Trinkam was the third participant in this conference. And his temper had not been improved by having it take place after five o'clock. "First, they suck us into their murders. Now they try to saddle us with their problem players. Next, I suppose they'll want us to get together a scratch team and take to the ice."

John Thatcher's memory for grievance was fully as long as Trinkam's. "You've left out an accommodation of credit for Winthrop Holland," he said acidly.

"If you'll just let me explain," Younghusband pleaded. "The Husky management has suggested that, in view of the successful collaboration between the Sloan and the team, the bank might have promotion work for some of the other players. That would help even things up."

Charlie stared at him. "What?" he asked weakly.

Thatcher was made of sterner stuff. "You mean they are asking us to employ unknown players in order to underwrite their troubles with Siragusa?"

"Well, that's what it boils down to," Younghusband said unhappily.

"And they had the effrontery to make this appalling proposal to you?"

"No, I just heard about it." Younghusband experienced some difficulty in continuing. He looked for inspiration first at the floor, then at the ceiling. Finally, in a voice of doom, he said, "Mr. Withers has become friendly with Mrs. Post."

There was a long silence.

"I see," said Thatcher at last.

"That's our Clemmie for you," Charlie Trinkam remarked to no one in particular.

Dexter Younghusband wanted them to know how bad things were. "They have adjoining boxes at the Garden. They see each other two nights a week."

"Of course, we would like to be helpful," Thatcher said untruthfully. "But we are already paying a substantial sum for television rights. Nor is the team in any difficulty with its gate receipts. This is basically an internal problem. They have enough income. They simply don't know how to share it."

Younghusband mistook this musing as a lecture. Resentfully he blurted, "Try explaining that to Mr. Withers."

His seniors satisfied themselves with silent rebuke.

"On the whole," Thatcher continued smoothly, "I think we would do better to make our explanations to Mrs. Post. Tell me, do you think she has any idea how much the Sloan should pay for such endorsements?"

"No, I'm sure she doesn't."

"Then it has just become an insignificant amount. Please remember that, if she should raise the subject in your presence."

Younghusband was hopeful. "You're going to tell her yourself?"

Clementine Post might not be able to extract money from the Sloan, Thatcher reflected, but she was racking up an impressive score on time. She had started with Charlie Trinkam, gone on to Brad Withers, and now . . .

"I'm afraid it is unavoidable," he decided.

Charlie stirred in his corner. "She'll invite you to dinner," he warned.

"I don't know what makes you think that. I'm not planning to make this a social occasion."

"I think she's decided the Sloan can be a big help to her."

"I had John Thatcher to dinner last night. From the Sloan," Clemmie Post announced. "He really wanted to be helpful, but it turns out that endorsements for the bank wouldn't do any good anyway. I had no idea that banks were so stingy. Their fees wouldn't come anywhere near evening things up."

She was sitting at the only desk in the dingy office maintained by the Huskies on Thirty-fifth Street. Her dress was from Paris and her diamond clip from Cartier's, but she did not look out of place beneath the framed pictures of bygone Husky lines. In recent years she had spent a great deal of time here.

Milt Forsburg sat opposite her in a straight-backed chair. He could see clouds ahead. "We'd just be making things worse, even if the Sloan was willing to go along.

The whole point of the kitty was to make the favored players share with the rookies."

Mrs. Post bit her lip. The kitty had been her idea originally, forced upon a reluctant Milt Forsburg. She did not enjoy having her words thrown back at her after the arrangement had proved unworkable. But she was saving her fire for the main issue.

"I still feel the principle is a good one. It gives an incentive to everyone. But it was never designed for conditions like this."

"What's so special about them? We're winning. It's only natural that our promotions do better."

Clemmie kept herself in check. "That's not what I meant, Milt. I was talking about an offer like this, where the manufacturer wants to put Billy's number on the Husky jersey and really make it a Siragusa item. It's only natural Billy should feel he's entitled to more than the other players."

"He's the high scorer on the team. He's the one all the manufacturers will want to feature. I can see a lot of cases like this coming up."

"Well, we're not talking about a lot of cases. We're talking about this one. And I really do feel we're going to have to do things Billy's way. If you think about it from his point of view, you have to admit it's only reasonable."

"What about trying it from someone else's point of view?" Milt Forsburg was very sour. "Say Paul Imrie's or Pete Levoisier's? For five years they practically supported the kitty single-handed. They shared with those rookies you were so worried about. Now that they're not at the top of the pole any more, they get frozen out."

Clemmie was prompt to point out the difference. "But, Milt, in those days there was practically no money involved."

"Which means they were a lot hungrier and it was harder to give something up. But they did it, and they've got a right to their fair share now."

"As a matter of fact, they don't have any rights." Clemmie had the grace to be embarrassed. "I just happened to look at our contract form this morning."

Forsburg knew that by the time Clemmie was examining her legal position, it was hopeless to argue. But still he tried. "It's the way we've always done things in this club. It's what all the boys expect."

"It's not what Billy expects. He told me so himself."

Now that the cat was out of the bag, she stared at him, daring him to object. Milt Forsburg frowned. It was no shock to him that Billy Siragusa had gone over his head. Players had done it before and players would do it again. Far more galling was his suspicion that Mrs. Post was courting these communications, then being secretive about them. But he refused to be diverted.

"You can't play hockey with one man."

"We're relying on Billy. You know it as well as I do. For heaven's sake, Milt, he's made twenty-six goals so far this year."

"Not unassisted," growled Forsburg.

Clemmie's bewilderment was overdone. "What on earth do you mean by that?"

"I'm just asking you to look at the point totals. Imrie's only made nine goals this season, but he has almost as many points as Billy. That's because he's set Billy up for over half his goals."

"Somebody has to get an assist on goals. Paul's lucky enough to be playing in the same line." Clemmie then proved she was no stranger to the ratings. "How many points did he get last year?"

"Paul played pretty good hockey last season," said Forsburg, refusing to budge an inch. "But he was setting up a lousy center."

"Well, we're not going to disagree about that. But the fact is, Paul and all the rest are playing better this year because Billy has inspired them with the desire to win. Until he came along they all thought they were born losers."

Forsburg closed his eyes briefly. The idealization of Billy Siragusa as a prophet leading his team to the promised land was a little too rich for his stomach. Normally his complaint against owners was that they wouldn't leave the team alone. For the first time he found himself wishing that Clemmie could be closer to her players. It might cure her of this habit of believing the romantic hokum produced by the team's publicity staff.

"They're going to be convinced they're losers if we start raiding their kitty."

"Nobody is raiding anything," Clemmie said sharply. "We're just making sure that Billy gets what he's earned. On that my mind is made up."

"All right, all right." Forsburg shrugged his capitulation. "I'll tell him he's won."

"No, Milt, I'll talk to him after practice."

Forsburg's mouth tightened. "I'm the one he came to."

"Yes, I know, but this will give me a chance to explain to him that I'm making an exception just this once, that this isn't going to be a general practice."

"The kid's already got the idea that any time he doesn't like my decisions he can come running to you. What about the time you didn't want him fined for being late to practice?"

"Fine Billy for a little thing like that?" she scoffed. "No, that settles it. I'm the one who'll tell him. Even though you're doing him a favor, you'll make it sound like a criminal sentence. I don't know what you have against Billy, Milt."

"I don't have anything against him," the coach said. "Not if he's handled right."

"You concentrate on the rest of the team and let me handle Billy. You just don't have the touch." Her voice was lightly mischievous.

But Milt Forsburg was not feeling playful. "Does that mean I'm supposed to tell the others about this decision?"

It figured, he thought to himself. Clemmie would want things arranged so that she told her star about the extra money he would get while her coach told the others about what they would not get.

Her eyes widened. "I don't see any need for the others to know about this understanding. At least not until the final accounting."

"These things get around." He did not add that Billy would be chortling his triumph abroad within ten minutes of getting the good news. Milt Forsburg had other matters on his mind. "You don't really think this has solved anything, do you?"

"What on earth are you worrying about now?"

Forsburg was already on his feet. "Billy was just trying this one on for size. Before you know it, he'll be back for all the market will bear." He was underlining every word, sounding a warning in every syllable.

But Clemmie Post blithely ignored all the signals. "No, he won't," she said confidently. "Not after I've talked with him."

9

ON THE ROAD

FRANKLIN MOORE was dead, buried and, in some quarters forgotten.

Clementine Post, for example, was clumsily juggling the claims of Billy Siragusa and seventeen other Huskies with mystifying purpose. She might know how the act would end, but Milt Forsburg did not. A. Winthrop Holland remained closeted in his office, still studying Dr. Anton Dietrich's notes, still waiting for a breakthrough from London. His father, as befitted his station in life, heeded the latest storm warnings and emplaned for the Holland compound in Antigua. And John Thatcher was keeping an eagle eye on the American Exchange.

Others were not so single-minded when it came to murder—among them, the New York City Police Department. Quietly, persistently, they cast a net wide, then proceeded to draw it in.

As might be expected, they began with requests for cooperation addressed to the authorities in Nashville, Ten-

nessee. What manner of man was Franklin Moore, they
asked. Who were his associates? What were his activities?
And, on an earthier level, what was all this about his being
a boxing promoter? Was he mixed up with gambling
money? Had he stepped on any toes?

The answers arrived with commendable promptitude.
Moore was a native of Nashville; his life was an open
book. A full dossier on his business interests had been assembled. They were dauntingly respectable, as were his
friends. Win Holland had been scrupulously accurate in
his account of the boxing match. It represented an isolated
venture on the part of several local worthies. They had not
been pleased with the experiment.

"That was three or four years ago," explained one of
them. "The tourist season had been a flop and we thought
it would give a shot in the arm to the hotels and restaurants. Next time we'll know better. We should have gotten
the American Dental Association to hold its meeting
here."

The speaker was Judge Andrew Cheek, lecturer at the
local law school, successful lawyer and ex-judge.

"They were wondering if it could have anything to do
with his murder," the policeman explained.

"That's New York for you," Cheek said irately. "First
they let Frank get gunned down, then they try to blacken
his name. Frank was an ordinary businessman. He followed sports—but it was just a hobby for him. The way it
is with me."

Here was an opening.

"They wanted to know if we could tell them anything
about Moore's plans for the Huskies."

Cheek looked at him with shrewd eyes. "Oh, so they've
gotten onto that, have they? Doubt if it'll do them much
good."

"You knew about it, sir?"

"To a certain extent. A week or so before he was killed,
Frank called me from New York. I wasn't expecting to
hear from him. And he was all excited. He said he'd run
into a golden opportunity to buy into a hockey team, and
was I interested." The judge shook his head at the memory.

"I told him I'd have to think it over. It's one thing to invest in a Nashville event. But I wasn't sure I wanted to put money into a New York team. Frank told me not to take too much time. He said he'd have to move fast."

"Did Mr. Moore go to New York because of this team?"

"No, no. I knew all about his trip. It was standard business, the same as it always was. He'd go up about every six months or so."

"Then how did he happen to get involved with the Huskies?"

Judge Cheek pondered. "Let me think—yes, I remember. He had dealings with this Win Holland. Holland was thinking of unloading his share of the Huskies and he liked the idea of clearing his books with Frank as part of the bargain. You know he's one of *the* Hollands." The judge chuckled triumphantly. "That should prove to New York that Frank's associates in sports were respectable."

"Yes, sir." The policeman tactfully did not mention that it was the Nashville associates New York suspected. Instead he asked for, and received, a complete membership list of Moore's boxing syndicate. Before he departed he had a final question.

"You wouldn't know how Moore's affairs are left now, would you, sir?"

"I can't give you the details. You'll have to go to Ed Pollet for that. But I can tell you roughly. Moore Realty will probably be wound up as part of the probate. It was really a one-man show. There won't be any trouble over that. Frank was smart, and he always saw to it that he got what he paid for and a little over. Plenty of people around town will be bidding for his holdings. By the time it's all settled, say in seven or eight months, the heirs will be well fixed for life."

"And they are—?"

"His children, of course. Let's see, his ex-wife and the boys are living in Tulsa. They must be twelve or thirteen by now."

The Hotel Roosevelt in New York was not as informative. But even they produced corroboration for Judge Cheek's story. Telephone records showed that Franklin

Moore had made no long-distance calls, other than to his office, until a week before his murder. Then the lines to Nashville had hummed. Everyone on Judge Cheek's list had been called at least once, many of them several times.

"And they all tell the same story as Judge Cheek," reported one of Captain Kallen's subordinates. "Moore wanted to know if they were willing to join in the Husky deal. Those were his only out-of-town calls."

Even the cab rank in front of the hotel had its mite to contribute. Until a week before his murder, Moore had emerged from the hotel each day with the usual destinations—brokerage houses, downtown offices, fashionable restaurants. Then, suddenly, his travels had become more circumscribed. He went to Madison Square Garden, he went to Win Holland's office, and, on one red-letter day for the cabby, he went twenty-five miles out to the rink in Mineola.

"We talked to all those brokers and real estate men he saw at the beginning of his visit," the same subordinate noted. "According to them, it was routine buying and selling. And they've got documents to prove it. One of them had Moore out to his house in Westchester for dinner. Says he was the same as usual—relaxed and easygoing."

Mention of the welcome home for the Huskies did revive one elusive memory at the night desk of the Roosevelt.

"I think we have a complaint slip on Mr. Moore," a clerk volunteered.

"What's that?" The detective was immediately alert. Orgies in the room upstairs or brawls in the bar downstairs could go a long way toward explaining death at La Guardia.

"It was when the Huskies were on the Coast. What a time we had." The clerk shuddered delicately. "Half of our guests had their television sets blaring until one-thirty, and the other half kept calling the desk about the noise. I could look it up for you if you like."

"Never mind," snarled the detective.

But he was a thorough man, and before he was done, he had elicited the same tale from the maid, the elevator boy and the waiters. Franklin Moore had been uniformly genial and undemanding.

"Nobody noticed anything out of the ordinary. He didn't strike anyone as the kind to get into trouble. Hell," said the subordinate despairingly, "even his ex only has good words for him."

The former Mrs. Franklin Moore, now Mrs. James Wright, had been tracked down in Oklahoma. She had immediately scouted the suggestion that Moore could have been involved in a rancorous dispute culminating in violence.

"Oh, no, not Frank," she told the police over the phone. "I'm sure it wasn't anything personal. He was so good-natured. Of course, he liked you to pull your weight, but he was really very easy to get along with. I just didn't know enough to appreciate him in those days."

She had contributed nothing except, of course, a passing curiosity as to what Mr. James Wright was like.

Officially the Husky story about Franklin Moore remained what it had been. But the army of questioners had bypassed the principals to reach informants who were not keeping tight rein on their tongues. They talked with the rink attendants who brought coffee to the players, they talked with assistant trainers who sharpened skates and taped sticks, they talked with the crews who manned the ice-making equipment.

And a new picture began to take shape. For the first time Frank Moore stopped sounding like a candidate for the Chamber of Commerce's Man of the Year and started to sound like a potential murder victim. He had been a disturbing influence rupturing many expectations. Somebody might have decided to do something about it.

The signed statements piling up at Police Headquarters were now worth studying, particularly between the lines. The whole history of Moore's take-over bid was laid bare. Win Holland's financial tangles were plain to see. Other facts emerged as well.

Clementine Post had been furious.

Milt Forsburg had been scared.

Billy Siragusa had been resentful.

Pete Levoisier had been worried.

Kallen and his subordinate looked at the pile in thoughtful silence. The slowly closing net had finally hit an obstruction. Now it was drawn tight around a small knot of people.

"I guess we can scratch everything about Moore except his last week," said Captain Kallen at last. "It all comes down to the Huskies."

10

POWER PLAY

NEW YORK CITY as a whole agreed with Captain Kallen. It all came down to the Huskies, now firmly ensconced in fourth place of the Western Division. While the team took one day off, their fans ransacked drawers and wallets for the small celluloid rectangles headed "The Sloan Brings You the Husky Schedule."

What they found there made them shake their heads. Within the week, the Huskies were playing the Bruins, in Boston Garden. Then there was a return match in New York. After that, the St. Louis Blues were coming to town.

"They're games we want to win," declared Coach Forsburg.

"Want!" Pat Ricco, in Flatbush, exploded when he read this. "What does he mean, *want*? That's no way to talk. We've *got* to win."

"You're going to be late, Pat," his wife said, consulting the kitchen clock. But this morning Ace Refrigeration would have to wait. Ricco had some arithmetic to do.

"Two out of three puts us within three points of third.

That's not good enough. We need a clean sweep. Three out of three."

"They're sure to be in the play-offs" his wife said mildly.

"They've got to make first place," he replied magnificently.

Mrs. Ricco accepted this edict. "Still, you'd better get going," she said from the sink.

Her husband did not budge.

"Absolutely," he said. "First place—or nothing."

Ricco was, as he said himself, a real Husky fan. Like all his ilk, he had been transfigured.

For six long years, while the Huskies had occupied the cellar of the Western Division, Ricco and his fellows had trudged up to the highest tier of Madison Square Garden to watch the team being outskated and outpointed by all rivals. He had learned stoicism. The Huskies had given him an occasional win; they had also produced twelve-game losing streaks. Nor had this season begun auspiciously; twenty-four out of twenty-five editors polled by Associated Press predicted that the Huskies had an outside chance of bettering their place in the standings. They might, said the experts, finish next to last.

Suddenly the year for which he had been waiting was upon Pat Ricco. And he wanted blood.

"First, they've got to beat the Bruins—twice," he said. "Then they've got to take the Blues. We've had enough excuses. Now they've got to win!"

His ferocity was shared by millions of his fellow New Yorkers. Tributes to the coach, the team and the season to date were confined to the sports pages. Elsewhere the martial tone was sounded. "Hit 'Em Huskies," said bumper stickers on every cab. "All the Way! This Is Husky Country!" Thanks to some quick work by the Sloan's public relations department, cars in Chinatown struck a more transcendental note: "This Is the Year of the Husky!"

"No ifs or buts about it," said Ricco, speaking for multitudes. "It's the least they can do for us. The Huskies have got to make first place!"

"Two to one at the end of the first period," the cabby

reported before John Thatcher opened the door. "The crowd went wild when Siragusa scored. Booed and threw things for two minutes. They're animals up in Boston!"

Thatcher settled himself.

"But the Huskies are making the Bruins look like a bunch of bums," said the cabby. "Where to, mister?"

Thatcher barely had time to give the address.

"Thank God, they'll be on home ice the next time they meet Boston," said the cabby, accelerating briskly. "And St. Louis, too. The home-town crowd helps. Billy said so in the morning paper. Read it?"

When Thatcher replied in the negative, the driver shot a covert glance into the rearview mirror, as if to see what specimen of man this was.

Thanks to the Sloan's continuing involvement with the Huskies, Thatcher was able to reply. "You don't think that the Huskies lack depth?" he said.

Depth figured heavily in all the closely reasoned assessments of the Huskies' chances that he had been subjected to.

Reassured about his passenger, the cabby grew wise. "That's what worries me. Depth. Nobody's skating better than the Huskies—not even Boston. But they haven't got much of a bench. Still . . ."

Despite the lack of depth, he confided, he thought the Huskies would beat Boston—twice. Then they would beat St. Louis. Then, first place. After that . . .

The Seagram Building arrived before they got to the Stanley Cup.

Pocketing his tip without thanks, the driver contributed a final observation: "The kind of team the Huskies are, they've got to win!"

"Three to two, Huskies, at the end of the second period," said Lucy Lancer to her dinner table four days later. "And they beat them in Boston. I'm sure they can do it tonight—at home. Perhaps we can take our coffee inside and watch the third period."

Her husband and guests all rose with eloquent alacrity. Only the Peruvian Consul-General was taken aback.

Thatcher sympathized with him. Lucy, the wife of George C. Lancer, entertained on a grand scale. Candles and silver gleamed on the table; a faultless meal had been faultlessly served. The gentlemen were in black tie, and Lucy herself was regal in taffeta and diamonds. One's thoughts did not automatically turn to ice hockey.

Señor Ibañez, however, made a diplomatic recovery. "You are a sports fan?" he inquired, following the ladies into the living room.

"A Husky fan," Lucy corrected him. "Everybody in New York is."

"I have observed much interest in the team," Ibañez agreed suavely.

From the set where he was dialing, George Lancer remarked that it was rare to see such enthusiasm uniting New Yorkers.

Ibañez spoke with authority. "It is true that there is widespread excitement about this hockey team. But, of course, it does not compare to the fervor of soccer fans. Soccer fans, after all, have been known to start wars."

Before anybody could respond, the picture came into focus. If they were not starting a war at Madison Square Garden, they were conducting a battle royal. Both the Boston Bruins and the Huskies were at the sidelines. They were watching the stands, where the whole house was on its feet—screaming. The aisles were thronged with a maelstrom of humanity, through which—as the camera showed—a wedge of policemen was struggling to make headway. The target was a free-for-all behind the Husky net. A confusing melee was in progress, with fists swinging.

The *casus belli* was, it developed, a banner introduced by a contingent from Boston.

"Husky fans," throbbed Jerry Drake, "just aren't going to take that sitting down!"

"Good for them," applauded the bearded architect sitting opposite Lucy.

"You approve?" asked Señor Ibañez. The screen now showed a close-up of police ringing three men and slowly moving them out of their seats to the accompaniment of boos from the crowd.

The architect, who had spent dinner analyzing the shameful spores of violence in American society, became severe.

"The Huskies are in a tremendous fight," he said. "And we're all in the fight with them."

By the time the St. Louis Blues came to town, the Huskies were getting national and international coverage. Even in the Canadian press, game accounts ran second to vivid background features.

"When they took two from the Bruins," wrote one veteran columnist in the Toronto *Star*, "the Huskies captured the heart of New York. This fighting young team, now battling for third place, has stirred a blasé metropolis. Wherever you go in Gotham, there's just one topic of conversation. Waiters, bartenders, shop girls, society women —all of them are Husky mad. . . ."

American journalists are more forthright than their Canadian colleagues.

"The Huskies' fans," wrote a stringer for the Boston *Record American*, "have turned into animals."

Real savagery did not erupt, however, until two days later. The Huskies routed St. Louis and moved into undisputed possession of third place. Unfortunately this was the day when the Husky organization chose to announce its preliminary plans for the distribution of play-off tickets.

"Season ticket holders," said the press release, "will be given the option of buying five additional tickets for each game."

This staid announcement triggered a storm of vilification. Season ticket holders? What about the loyal few who filled the galleries for the Huskies? What about the humble folk who had come in, night after night, from New Jersey, from Brooklyn, from Flatbush?

"The Huskies," thundered an editorial in *Newsday,* "owe New York a lot, and they're paying—by delivering some of the finest hockey this city has ever seen. But that's not enough. Reserving play-off tickets for season ticket holders is a slap in the face to thousands of loyal fans. . . ."

Hastily, the Husky management backtracked. Play-off tickets, it announced, would be distributed on a first come, first served basis, starting in three days.

Now it was the season ticket holders' turn. Who had really supported the team, they wanted to know. But while they protested to every paper and radio station in town, the line was forming. The first young couple appeared at Madison Square Garden. They were carrying sleeping bags, a portable stove and a small infant.

"The Huskies will make it all the way," they told an inquiring TV interviewer. "Venus is in conjunction with Mars. The Huskies will finish the season in first place. And win the play-offs."

The season ticket holders were out of luck. Their moment in the sun had passed. Now it was the turn of a motley crew of astrologers, palmists and similar mystics.

"We Gypsies know," said one Joseph Barbusso. "The Huskies must finish the season in first place."

"Four points out of second place!" Dexter Younghusband was pale as he stared into some private Nirvana. "It's almost unbelievable."

"I understand," said Thatcher kindly, "that we now refer to it as the impossible dream."

Like depth, this was a phrase that figured heavily in the reading material Younghusband had been forwarding to him.

Younghusband came back to earth. "Now, the Sloan has made arrangements for several blocks of play-off tickets," he began.

"You're asking for trouble," Thatcher interrupted.

Younghusband nodded. "Yes, we want to give the matter serious thought. The demand is going to be terrific. It certainly would not be right for the Sloan simply to make them available to our biggest customers."

It would be very wrong. More to the point, it would also undo the impact of the Sloan's sponsorship of the Huskies, as well as constitute an open invitation to smashed windows. Thatcher reflected on ways and means for a moment.

"Why not run a contest?" he suggested. "You should get a big response—and, incidentally, underscore the Sloan's role in all this."

"A contest," said Younghusband, savoring it. "By George . . ."

Accordingly, before the Huskies' game with Minnesota, the Sloan had an important announcement to make.

"Good evening, Husky fans," said Jerry Drake. "The Sloan Guaranty Trust is pleased to bring you tonight's game between the New York Huskies and the Minnesota North Stars. But first here is a challenge for all of you. Would you like to win tickets to the play-offs—here and on the road? Well, the Sloan is going to give you an opportunity to do just that. Here's what you have to do. . . ."

What Husky fans had to do was write a letter explaining why the Huskies had vaulted from last place to their present eminence.

". . . judged by a panel of sports experts, who will look for real hockey know-how. Send each letter to the Sloan Guaranty Trust—Box One, Two, Three—New York 10001. The winners will be awarded four tickets to each play-off game, and an expense-paid tour to . . ."

The Huskies beat Minnesota five to one.

And seventy-three thousand, six hundred and fifty-two of their fans promptly sat down and composed. Preliminary reading, so Younghusband reported some days later, showed a striking consensus.

The Huskies were a winning team, their fans felt, because they had the desire to win.

"Not very original," Thatcher commented.

"Perhaps you'd like to look over some of them," Younghusband invited, gesturing to the mountain of correspondence he had brought with him.

"I'm afraid I won't have time," Thatcher said swiftly. "I am attending a dinner this evening."

Even as he spoke, he contemplated the strange delights being offered him these days. Public Relations, he decided, had lost sight of the fact that the Sloan Guaranty Trust was engaged primarily in the banking business.

"There was one rather unusual way of phrasing it." Dexter Younghusband was happily blind to the impression he was making. "I was taken with it."

According to Master Benjamin Morton, aged eight, Far Rockaway, the Huskies were winners because "they had to be."

"Striking," Thatcher agreed politely, his thoughts veering to a new desideratum.

If there were any place in the greater metropolitan area where people were not assessing the Huskies' chances, he would like to be there.

Curiously enough, John Putnam Thatcher could have found such a haven in the Husky dressing room. Most of the team had departed immediately after practice.

Paul Imrie had no time to think about standings. He was consumed with his wrongs.

"Pete, for God's sake, are you telling me you're going to take this lying down?"

Even in repose Pete Levoisier's face was melancholy. Now it was a tragic mask. "Eileen won't like it," he said heavily.

"You're damn right she won't."

From the day of the marriage it had been clear who would contribute the spark of pugnacity to the Levoisier ménage. Pete, off the ice, was large and graceless and slow. Eileen was small, quick and fiery. Some of the team disliked her and talked of henpecking. But Paul Imrie, himself five foot seven of concentrated belligerence, thought she was good for Pete. Right now she might be an ally.

"She'll be burning," he said, hammering the idea home. "Christ, Pete, have you ever figured out how much you've lost on this kitty system in the last five years?"

Levoisier shook his head in silent misery.

"Well, I have! I did it just before I cornered Clemmie Post, and it comes to damn near ten thousand dollars."

A flicker of animation crossed Pete's face. "Oh, you've already seen her. Why didn't you tell me?"

"I *am* telling you." Imrie was shifting his weight from foot to foot like a boxer weaving in for the punch. "That's why I was late down here. I knew she'd try and sneak out before we were dressed."

Over the years Clementine Post had learned to be unavailable when she had behaved badly to her players.

"What did she say?" Levoisier asked dully.

"What the hell do you think she said? You know what she's like. She gave me a lot of hot air about team spirit and not rocking the boat. She also had the nerve to tell me we've all got to remember that Billy is very special."

"She's hooked on him." Levoisier was fatalistic. "Maybe it's her age or something. She thinks he's a choirboy."

Imrie laughed harshly. "Not any more, she doesn't. She started complaining about Forsburg leaking the new arrangement to us. It did me a lot of good to tell her that darling Billy was the one who blew it. He must have told us two minutes after the deal was fixed up."

"What difference does it make who told us? I suppose she said the same as Billy, that there's nothing about the kitty in our contract."

Levoisier had risen, but he was standing aimlessly in the center of the room. Imrie, meanwhile, had been dressing with his usual catlike speed.

"Yeah, she said if we'd just be patient this year, everything would be regularized next year." Imrie growled menacingly. "I told her she didn't know how right she was. But I still haven't given up on this year. When she talks about team spirit, she wants a setup where it's every man for Billy and Billy for himself."

"Yeah," Levoisier said.

For the first time Imrie noticed his teammate's inertness. "Pete, I want to talk to you, but I don't want to hang around here," he said, leading the way to the door. "Let's get ourselves a beer."

"Sure." Still Pete Levoisier hesitated. "But let's go to Barney's."

Imrie's stride faltered. Like most teams, the Huskies tended to fragment into small companionable groups. Eileen Levoisier was hospitable by nature, and she kept open house for Pete's friends, particularly the bachelors like Paul Imrie. Most beer-drinking was done in the Levoisier home. There was only one conclusion for Imrie to draw. If Pete didn't want to take him home, it was because of reluctance to face Eileen. And Eileen was Pete's confidante, his counselor, his ever-present comfort in time of trouble. This must be bigger than Billy's raid on the kitty.

Paul Imrie's cockiness was gone as he said, "Sure, let's go to Barney's."

Not until they had carried their steins to a corner booth did Pete unburden himself.

"It's like this, Paul. While you were talking to Mrs. Post, Billy was talking to me. . . ."

11

HAT TRICK

EXPERTS usually deepen their knowledge by narrowing their vision. Thatcher was reminded of his truth later that evening at a fund-raising dinner. He was sitting opposite Stanton Carruthers, a distinguished trust and estate lawyer. The roast beef had just been served, and although it was not as succulent as it might have been, it was still preferable to that which lay ahead.

Once again, Harvard had a new dean. The latest incumbent was on his rounds across the country meeting influential alumni. To the potential donors of Wall Street he would automatically be presented as a prudent innovator, embracing the future yet safeguarding the past. He would be introduced by a perennial fixture of the university. Professor Gimble had never left Cambridge, Massachusetts, which remained for him the cockpit of the universe. He would refer to famous now-defunct scholars of years past as Diggory, Wild Bill and JB. To the embarrassment of his listeners he would wallow through anecdotes about what the Digger said and did on occasions which should have passed into oblivion. Gimble never doubted that every member of his blue-ribbon audience considered four years of adolescence as life's pinnacle.

Under the circumstances it was only human for the diners, who had already determined their annual contribution down to the last cent, to remain in the present as long as possible before being swamped by relentless nostalgia. The subject that sprang to mind was the New York Huskies.

"If they win the next three they could move into second place."

"What good does that do? Under the new rules, to make any difference, the Huskies have to go to first place."

Several voices immediately chimed in with additional esoterica: East Division against West Division, the Lady Byng Trophy, the rumors about Coach Milt Forsburg. . . .

"Who are the Huskies?"

It was Stanton Carruthers, his glasses firmly settled on his nose, his voice as precise as if he were raising the possibility of a grandchild conceived by artificial insemination.

At this point, when a flow of information could have been of real help, it abruptly halted. A bond dealer several seats away finally recovered enough to explain about hockey in general and the Huskies in particular.

"Thank you," said Carruthers. "That was very interesting."

This statement was so patiently at variance with his real feelings that it cast a chill the length of the table. Nevertheless, several zealots proffered detailed critiques of the team, the coaching, the management. At first it seemed as if these efforts had met with improbable success. A slight softening became visible in Carruthers' glacial features; a latent gleam appeared behind the glasses.

"Just a moment." Carruthers searched a faultless memory. "There is something I should remember about the Huskies."

Most of his hearers were staggered by the temperance of his assertion. But John Thatcher knew exactly what was likely to be deemed worthy of the memory of a trust and estates lawyer. "Holland," he said gently. "Winthrop Holland."

"Ah, of course." The gleam surfaced. "I recall now that he's the owner."

Several people insisted on telling him about Clementine Post. But although Mrs. Post had a fortune respectable enough for any Wall Street firm of lawyers, she did not stop them in their tracks like a Rockefeller, a Du Pont— or a Holland.

Carruthers was impatient of this niggling and, to a certain extent, saddened that the Hollands should not be preeminent in everything they touched. "Amazing family," he murmured respectfully. "They've been going strong for generations now."

The bond dealer reserved his esteem for the wealthy who were numbered among his clients. "What's so wonderful about them? They're just rich."

But more detached minds could not accept this.

The bond dealer was reminded of the scions of wealth now taking their versatile talents into politics, into good works, into ecology—while someone else minded the store.

"But not the Hollands!"

"Of course, they've been shrewd about marriage," commented one man, narrowing his eyes keenly. "The Holland girls always bring in promising executives."

"Daughters are not the only problem," blurted old Grimstead of Grimstead & Shaw, currency specialists.

There was a respectful silence. Grimstead's only son, now middle-aged, was still finding himself in a Parisian atelier. It boded ill for the financial success of the evening that his father harbored a grudge against Harvard as the source of this prolonged identity crisis.

Thatcher ignored the detour. "Well, this Holland isn't minding the store."

"You mean hockey is more than a hobby to him?" Carruthers was genuinely shocked.

"No, no." Justice to Win Holland required the negative. "He's not very interested in the Huskies."

"I don't know what makes you think hockey is some kind of a hobby. I admit it hasn't hit the big time yet, but sports in general aren't the peanuts they used to be." The speaker, a VP at Consolidated Edison, had his own definition of peanuts. "In the old days a baseball team relied on gate receipts to keep going. And a retired player got a job selling insurance. But now!"

He paused for effect, and in that instant he lost the floor. Baseball, it developed, had spread its tentacles to touch almost every occupant of the table.

"Gate receipts!" snorted the president of a major network. "They can fill the stadium at every game and still their big income is their television contract. Do you realize that nothing, absolutely nothing, can compete with a big game? The situation comedies, the soaps, why even—" he took a deep breath—"even movies might just as well go off the screen when the Mets are playing the Phillies."

As it was his network that carried several games of the week, there was no regret in his voice.

Not so with the chairman of a company specializing in razors, razor blades and shaving cream. "The players are more sophisticated, too. In the old days you could get an endorsement from them for five hundred dollars. Now, for one shot of a faceful of lather, they want an arm and a leg. And," he said, shaking his head sadly, "what's more, they get it."

"Of course they do." Now it was the turn of an entrepreneur whose discount houses dominated shopping centers from New York to Chicago. "You boys are wrong if you think hockey isn't moving right up there. The tip-off came when the National Hockey League formed a subsidiary solely to handle promotional licenses. I don't say the craze has hit the whole country yet—but it will. Every one of my New York stores had a special section for Christmas just to sell Husky items. And they all paid off."

Years of publishing a financial weekly had trained one alumnus in the art of drawing logical conclusions. "Hockey sounds like big business," he said.

"It's becoming big business," the retailer corrected. "If they'd been dealing with real money for years, everything would be cut and dried. But they're still feeling their way. That's why you can get a snarl like the one they're having about the use of Billy Siragusa's name."

"I didn't realize, Elman, that you were concerned with Siragusa's difficulties," said Thatcher.

"Me and every store east of the Mississippi," Elman replied jovially. "You can't sell hockey items in the middle of a heat wave. If they don't get this muddle straightened out in time, they'll have to wait until next fall. And this is the year the Huskies are news."

Unknowingly he had introduced a word which was anathema to Stanton Carruthers.

"Exactly what is this muddle?" Carruthers inquired.

"They had some informal system for splitting the promotion take among the players," said Elman.

The razor-blade titan knew about superstars. "And now, I suppose, Siragusa wants to change the split."

"Wrong! He's not talking about any split at all. He says he's not peddling the team's name. He's peddling his own name, and why should some rookie get any share at all?"

Stanton Carruthers had forgotten he was not in his own office. His fingers were steepled and his tone inquisitorial.

"You mean that there is no standard contract arrangement about promotions in use throughout the League? I find that extraordinary."

Elman was gratified by the variety of emotions his account was evoking. "Things are better than they were a couple of years ago. They were all playing it by ear, then."

"Of course, the law of professional sports is still in its infancy," Carruthers mused to himself. "You might say that the trading decision was the first cornerstone."

Everyone could see a lecture coming.

"You will recall, in that case, the player maintained that

his club had no right to sell his contract without his consent. He contended that, if he could be forced to move to another city and work for another team at the whim of his employer, he had been reduced to an unconstitutional state of peonage."

"Peonage?" It was an involuntary protest from the bond dealer, who had remembered the salaries involved in baseball. "At a hundred thousand dollars a year?"

"Precisely." A wintry smile illumined Carruthers' face. This was the only kind of peonage he liked to deal with. "The court held, in effect, that what the club had bought for one hundred thousand dollars was the right to make the most efficient use of the plaintiff—whether by playing him, benching him or trading him. But I can see how the problems raised by this young man from Holland's team would make an interesting companion case."

Thatcher tried to divert Carruthers from a discourse on companion cases through the ages. "You mean the court could decide that the club had also bought the right to make the most efficient use of the player's publicity?"

"I can see that I have not made myself clear," said Stanton Carruthers in the accents that convicted timorous clients of stupidity.

He was trying it on the wrong man.

"No, Stan, you haven't," said John Thatcher forthrightly. "What did you mean to say?"

Carruthers chose his words with offensive care. "The courts are beginning to be interested in the right of self-exploitation. Suppose that a singer becomes very popular and you wish to sell pictures of that singer. Many jurisdictions believe that the singer has the right to the benefits accruing from the exploitation of his personality, and that you must obtain a license from him. That is reducing it to its simplest terms. But a difference exists between the talents of this young man—is Siragusa his name?—and his personality. If he wished to sell the personality alone, without any reference to his team employment, without wearing a uniform, for instance, a very pretty problem would be raised. In the absence of a carefully worded contract clause the club might be held to have purchased only his talents."

"Wait a minute!" It was Elman, in anguished protest. "You're saying that not only his teammates wouldn't have any right to share. You're saying that management wouldn't either. And management always gets a cut."

Carruthers was triumphant. "Interesting, isn't it?"

Representatives of television, manufacturing and retailing stared at him in consternation. But before they could enlarge on the distinction between theory and reality, their host tapped a spoon against his glass and rose to his feet.

"I know that you are all waiting impatiently for our principal speaker. Many of you will remember Professor Arthur Gimble from your own student days and . . ."

On the whole, the evening might have been more educational for the Levoisiers than it was for John Thatcher.

12

DIGGING IT OUT

IN GREAT NECK, the roast beef was still in the oven.

"What's the matter?" Eileen Levoisier demanded, emerging from the ritual bear hug.

Pete had never been able to understand how she worked it. With her face buried somewhere around his armpits and without a word spoken, she always knew precisely how he was feeling. He was glad he had had a dry run with Paul Imrie.

Now she sniffed delicately.

"You've been drinking beer." This was not accusation; it was analysis. Eileen could follow Pete even better than Imrie. Already she knew there was bad news, it had broken at practice, he had talked it over with Paul. "Do you want another?"

"No, I'd like some coffee," he said, putting off the evil hour.

While she was in the kitchen, he slumped dejectedly onto the sofa. With his legs stretched out and his long, almost simian, arms extended along the top of the bolsters, he gazed around the room. He could see his son's hockey stick in the hall. Well, one thing was certain. Come hell or high water, Joey was starting college next year.

Eileen was back with a tray in record time. While he stirred in cream, she perched on the arm of the sofa, letting him set the pace. After two gulps, he grounded the cup.

"You know our skating clubs?" he began.

Silently she nodded. Pete was simply priming the pump. He always had to work himself into a difficult subject. The question itself was preposterous. For Eileen Levoisier actually ran the two clubs. She hired and fired the staff, kept the books, saw to it that rowdies and drunks went elsewhere. During the game season she arranged rare appearances by Pete, strategically timed for maximum effect.

"Well, I think they maybe in trouble. Billy's going into competition with us."

"Billy Siragusa?" Eileen frowned. So far it did not seem too bad. "I suppose if he wants to start a club somewhere, he's got a right to. Why do you think it will hurt us?"

"It's not exactly one club. He was talking to me this afternoon." Pete paused. "He pretended he wanted to thank me for giving him the idea. Said it was smart not to waste time on a hockey camp somewhere in northern Ontario. The money was here in the suburban belts and you could work it on a year-round basis. But he's got really big ideas, Eileen. He's planning a whole chain—the Siragusa Skating Clubs. And he's starting right in our backyard."

"You mean he's coming into Nassau County?"

"That's right. He says this is the right location for him. He's out here a couple of days a week anyway."

Eileen sat up. "Never mind what he says. What Billy means is that we've spent five years and a lot of money promoting skating interest in this area. Now he means to cash in on it."

Pete nodded. "That's what I thought, too. I figure he plans to start by siphoning off our customers."

"That slimy little creep! If I could only get my hands on him! He doesn't even know how serious this is. And to think we used to have him to dinner when he was new in town. I should have put rat poison in his plate."

There was a grunt of accord from the sofa. During Billy's first month with the Huskies, Pete himself had helped him with his slap shot. Maybe he should have aimed one at Billy's head.

"But we've got to face facts, honey. The clubs may have to go."

"Not on your life. So we're in for a fight. What makes you think Billy is going to win?"

"First off, there's his name." Pete sighed. He should have realized that Eileen would instinctively favor a struggle to the death. "You can't dodge it. Billy Siragusa is the name all the hockey nuts go for."

"It's so unfair. You've spent five years with this team and you've always been shortchanged. When they were losers, you had to shore them up. Now that they're winning, you play with the second-string wings because they want something called balance. Why, the only time you're on with Paul is for penalty killing. Billy Siragusa!" Her voice was filled with loathing. "What's so marvelous about him anyway?"

"He scores goals."

"So do you!"

Pete was doggedly factual. "Not as many."

"You don't get the ice time he does."

"Oh, be honest, honey. Billy's the big hero of the season. Remember that game on Christmas Day? Because if you don't, everybody else does."

Eileen had retreated to the opposite sofa. She was bristling at Pete as if he were the enemy. His ability to see another point of view angered her almost more than anything else.

"I remember everything about that game, even if you

don't. Sure, Billy scored the winning goal? Because you'd already scored twice, that's why!"

A lifetime in professional hockey shaped Pete's reply. "It's the winning goals that count."

"And what about assists? You've got more assists than Billy has."

Pete did not bother to say that this was a statistic only a wife could treasure. He moved to new ground.

"Besides, Billy is going to have more than his name going for him. You should hear the kind of things he's talking about. It's more like a country club than a skating rink—initiation fees and yearly memberships, saunas and whirlpool baths, cocktail bars and singles nights." With each refinement Pete sounded more dejected. "On top of all that, if it goes over in New York, he says he can work a franchise system. The dance studios have done it, so why not him? A membership would be good at any branch. A guy on the road wouldn't have to hang around the hotel bar. There would always be a party at Siragusa's. Do you see us competing against something like that?"

Eileen did not have her usual ready answer. As the catalogue unfolded, her fury turned to bewilderment.

"He must be shooting a line," she protested. "It would take a millionaire to start on that scale. Billy doesn't have any money. Oh, I know he's supposed to be a superstar. But he's still playing under his old contract."

"He'll hold out for something big this summer. I'll bet he gets one of those five-figure, three-year jobs," Pete said wistfully.

Eileen was more single-minded. "Even so. Grant him the big contract and throw in a big bonus while you're at it. That still wouldn't be enough."

"He says he'll get financing!"

"Financing!" she gasped. "Are you talking about banks? I trudged from one bank to another for five months before we could get backing for our first club. Half of them wouldn't even talk to me. They said there was no market for skating clubs. And you know the kind of loan we finally got."

"It was easier the second time."

"All right. But we were doing it on the cheap. We put up a rink with a locker room, a hot-dog stand and some canned music. We weren't trying to talk a bank into a whole series of Playboy Clubs."

There was a long silence. Eventually Eileen came to the same conclusion as several graduates of Harvard University.

"You know," she said thoughtfully, "we may be too old-fashioned. Hockey is turning into big business these days. I could take another run around the banks and see if they've changed. Billy may find we can give him a real fight."

Pete was still gloomy. "Don't count on it. Somehow I got the feeling that Billy wasn't going to banks."

"Then where was he going?"

"He didn't say." Pete hesitated. "But Billy's got a lot of important friends."

Eileen snorted. "Billy's friends! I know their kind. They're generous when it comes to pouring champagne into him. But they're not shelling out just to help Billy make himself a fortune."

"You'd be surprised what some of Billy's friends will do to help him." Pete told her about the Siragusa jerseys and the license royalties that were not going into the team kitty.

In many ways Eileen Levoisier and Paul Imrie resembled each other. She immediately began totaling the sums Pete had lost on the kitty during the last five years. Cries of indignation accompanied each addition.

"It's highway robbery!"

"Milt wanted to put his foot down on the whole idea. But Mrs. Post rolled right over him." Once again the grapevine had worked perfectly. "Of course, Billy's been her fair-haired boy for months now."

"Not to the point where she was willing to steal for him." Eileen studied her nail polish. "Billy may be even lower than I thought. He's twenty-three, and Mrs. Post is a widow. Do you think it's possible that—?"

"No, I don't!" Pete said brusquely. But his voice betrayed him.

Eileen pounced. "If you don't think that, you think something else," she declared with absolute conviction. "What is it?"

"I don't think anything," he said unconvincingly. But he was cornered and he knew it. "I was just wondering, that's all."

Eileen was an old hand at the extraction process. She curled herself into the corner of her sofa and dropped her voice.

"Then what is it you were wondering?" she coaxed.

Pete, too, had changed position. With elbows planted on knees, he cradled his jaw between massive hands. The pressure accentuated every line and scar on his face.

"Well, you don't have to look very far to find a friend of Billy's with money," he began obliquely.

Eileen's eyebrows flew up. "Mrs. Post isn't buying Billy a bunch of clubs as a present. And owners don't go into business with players. It isn't as if she's interested in skating clubs. It's people like us who try to make a buck by starting a business."

"You should hear her going on about Billy." Pete still clung to the indirect approach. "She really got to Paul today, telling him how Billy has to be kept sweet."

"I can imagine. We all have to be very, very nice to Billy so he'll play his best hockey for us. Silly old cow!" Eileen ended dispassionately.

Pete winced, but he came from a world where women are harder on women than men will allow themselves to be.

"I didn't mean that exactly. Mrs. Post is dead serious about keeping Billy sweet." He took a deep breath before crossing his Rubicon. "But I'm not sure it's got anything to do with the way he plays hockey."

He had riveted his wife's attention.

"What else could it be? You claim they don't have anything else to do with each other." The implications of Pete's speech began coming home to her. "You don't mean—but that's impossible. She couldn't be paying him off for something."

"I said I didn't know anything. I could be imagining

things," Pete qualified hastily. "Still, you've got to admit it's funny. The police have been around the Garden off and on ever since that guy Moore was murdered. But the last couple of days they've been all over the place. I know for a fact they've grilled every single one of the mainte- nance men. Then, suddenly, just at the same time, Billy Siragusa has money coming at him from all sides."

Eileen was transfixed. "You mean Mrs. Post murdered this man and now Billy is blackmailing her?"

The minute somebody else put his private suspicion into words, Pete could see how ridiculous it was.

"Go on, Eileen. Mrs. Post take a gun and shoot some- body in the middle of an airport?" he mocked. "It's plain crazy. So is the idea of Billy being a witness. When he's got a lot of autograph hounds on his tail and Neil Gruen waiting in a snazzy Cadillac, he's too pleased with himself to notice anything."

"Then what did you mean?" his wife prodded patiently.

"Mrs. Post took it hard when she found out about Moore's plans for the Huskies. We all knew about that. But she was trying to work other people up, too. She was hoping that if enough of us got mad, she could stop the thing cold. What if she's afraid now that she worked some- one up so much he lost his head? Billy could have over- heard her doing it."

Eileen reflected for a moment, then shook her head. "No. In that case, she might want to hush it up. She might let Billy get out of contributing to the kitty. But she's not coughing up the kind of money you're talking about."

"Billy acts as if he's on Easy Street for life," Pete said with gentle persistence.

"Billy is a poor boy from the wrong side of Toronto. Until now he's played hockey for nickels and dimes. He probably thinks that being in the Stanley Cup finals will take care of him for good."

"He couldn't think that."

Eileen had been diverted to a new track. "By the way, what is the play-off money for the finals?"

Pete was more relaxed now that he'd told Eileen the worst. "You must be the only wife in the League who has to ask that," he teased. "If we make it all the way, it means seven and a half thousand."

Eileen brightened. "Oh, that would be nice."

"It's not much to save two clubs from going under."

"No, but with a boy headed for college, it will be a help." She shook away this problem. "And the more I consider it, the more I think you must be wrong about Mrs. Post. She couldn't take that kind of chance with the whole team watching."

"All right," said Pete amicably. "But one thing's for sure. Billy expects a lot of money to be coming from somewhere."

13

DELAYED CALL

THE NEW YORK CITY police were talking with more people than Pete Levoisier realized. Inevitably they had decided to move on from the boiler room at the Garden to the sixth floor of the Sloan Guaranty Trust.

"Be careful," growled the Commissioner when he heard the intentions of his dauntless subordinates. "Be very careful."

Nothing could have been more correct than Captain Kallen's request for an interview with Charles F. Trinkam to discuss Mrs. Clementine Post.

Nothing could have been more cordial than Mr. Trinkam's immediate designation of a date and hour.

But Charlie knew all about being careful, too. Accordingly three men were assembled in his office to receive Kallen.

"This way I can tell him how Clemmie was foaming at

the mouth about that poor guy Moore with a clear con-
science," he said.

For the first time in his connection with the Huskies,
John Thatcher approved of the role he was expected to
play. "Because I can follow you with a description of the
situation at La Guardia. The Holland-Moore sale had
been abandoned, and Mrs. Post reconciled to Moore's
continued existence, while the victim was still very much
alive."

"But what am I supposed to do?" asked Dexter
Younghusband nervously.

Charlie was beginning to enjoy himself. "You can give
him the dirt you've picked up at rinkside," he said cheerfully. "Don't be bashful. Remember, the only one who's a
customer of the Sloan is Clemmie Post."

Within moments this program was being carried out.

"She was ripe for murder," Charlie said with gusto.
"She wanted him drawn and quartered. According to her,
Moore was the wolf coming down on her precious fold of
ewe lambs."

Kallen's face had been steadily falling. He did not have
to be a mind reader to guess that this narrative would be
more restrained if it really incriminated Mrs. Post.

"All right. Everyone seems to agree that she was mad as
hell," he said. "But exactly why? She'd never had any
trouble with Holland. Why did she expect so much with
Moore?"

Charlie was ready and waiting with his list. "One, he
was a boxing promoter, which meant he wasn't the type
she was used to associating with. Two, he expected to be
an active partner, not a sleeping partner. Three, he was
talking about moving the club to Nashville."

Kallen rubbed his chin consideringly. Trinkam sounded
as if he were opening the bag, but he was merely repeating
the contents of all those statements on file at headquarters.

"Let's take them one by one. This boxing-promoter
idea, for instance."

"I know what you're going to say. But you have to take
Clemmie with a grain of salt. You can't believe every word
she says."

"Thanks," said Kallen, not very grateful for the good advice. He had ceased believing anything a murder suspect said some twenty years ago.

"I don't mean it that way." Charlie grinned understandingly. "Half the time she's not trying to kid you, she's trying to kid herself. When Clemmie turned up at the Sloan, she knew all about Moore being on the up-and-up."

"How do you know?"

"I offered to check him out for her, and she told me her lawyer had already done it. You've got to remember that for years she's been eating her cake and having it too. Whenever she wanted to meddle with the players, she acted as if she were the general manager, not Forsburg. On the other hand, if there was some dirty work that had to be done, then she pulled her great lady act and was above the battle. She was burned up about Moore because she knew damn well he wouldn't go along with that."

Kallen was not convinced, but he wanted to tackle the last point on Charlie's list. "Now about transferring to Nashville. We've been in touch with the people in Tennessee who would have been Moore's partners. Three of them had agreed to come in on the deal. And they didn't know anything about relocating the Huskies. They said they were being asked to buy into a New York team."

"It may have been a long-term dream of Moore's. You don't move franchises overnight. And then, he could have wanted to see how the season came out. Teams usually leave if they're in difficulties where they are. Your guess is as good as mine, but Moore sounds like a hardheaded guy who wouldn't even have tried to move a successful team."

"Then, according to your story, Mrs. Post didn't have anything to worry about for a while?"

But the easy way out never had any appeal for Charlie Trinkam. "Good God, she was perfectly capable of working herself into a state—even if it didn't make sense," he rejoined heartily.

Captain Kallen was beginning to find that a little of Charlie Trinkam went a long way. Hopefully he proceeded to his next witness.

"And you agree with this, Mr. Thatcher?"

With care, Thatcher explained that he had not been at the original interview.

"A shame," Charlie murmured. "It would have been an eye-opener for you."

Thatcher hurried on. "But I was at La Guardia when Moore told Mrs. Post that he would not be buying Holland's share of the Huskies."

"Did he tell her outright, so that she couldn't misunderstand? Mr. Trinkam here seems to think she was pretty confused about a lot of things."

Charlie was only too willing to share the fruits of his indefatigable researches into Woman. Before he could get them all hauled off to the paddy wagon, Thatcher took matters into his own hands.

"I think that Trinkam merely meant Mrs. Post is not above sugarcoating her own motives. In any event, she was sensible enough to draw her own conclusions before arriving at the airport. She had already reasoned that the success of the Huskies' road trip would raise the price beyond what Moore was willing to pay. A buyer, after all, wants a low selling price, and, with the Huskies becoming popular favorites, the price was mounting. I might add that she was quite correct in her deductions."

"Are you sure of that? Did Moore say so in so many words? Could Mrs. Post have misinterpreted him at first, then learned she was wrong?"

"All I can tell you, Captain, is what I heard. Moore and Holland agreed in my presence that the deal was off. Moore very good-naturedly realized that he would have to content himself with collecting his debt and forgo acquiring the Huskies. Later on, Holland told both Trinkam and myself that his father would be annoyed at his not selling the team. I do not see any room for error."

"Then could Moore have been misrepresenting his decision?"

There were limits to how far Thatcher was willing to follow the police into the area of surmise. "I can think of no reason why Moore should indulge in such tortuous behavior. Admittedly I only met him for a few minutes. If you can think of a reason, go ahead."

Robert Bruce's spider had nothing on Captain Kallen. Now he took on Dexter Younghusband.

"Then let's forget about the owners. What about the rest of the people associated with the team, Mr. Younghusband? They weren't any too happy about Moore's plans either, were they?"

Younghusband squirmed. Already he had forgotten Charlie Trinkam's excellent counsel.

"They had been working together for years and they now were doing very well. Naturally feelings of loyalty had developed," he gabbled.

"You mean they didn't want Moore taking over?" Kallen translated relentlessly.

"Oh, I wouldn't express it that way."

"I'll bet you wouldn't!"

Younghusband, now thoroughly demoralized, looked for support. What he saw was not encouraging. Charlie Trinkam was smiling diabolically. John Thatcher seemed to be contemplating a drastic cutback in the PR department.

Unwisely Younghusband remembered that the best defense is offense. "You've forgotten that the Huskies had just returned from a road trip, haven't you?" he said with the engaging didacticism encouraged by his profession. "They were out of touch. They'd been busy winning games, not worrying about maneuvers between Mr. Holland and Mr. Moore."

"And how fast did they get back in touch?" growled Kallen threateningly.

Younghusband did not see the pitfall. "They were worn out. They were mobbed by their admirers. There was no time for long discussions."

"So that, as far as you know, most of them still thought Frank Moore was taking over, and they thought so right up to the murder?"

Younghusband moaned softly. "That's not what I meant at all," he said in despair.

Thatcher remembered that he had a duty to come to the aid of beleaguered Sloan troops, no matter how undeserving. "You will recall that Younghusband had not seen the team during the road trip. And at the airport he was in charge of the arrangements and the press, so he was fully occupied. I expect that, as far as he knows, there could have been any amount of communication."

Fervently Younghusband agreed.

But Kallen had found the hole in the dike and he was not giving up now. Charlie and Thatcher had both admitted the worst at once. Consequently their testimony had sounded innocuous. Younghusband, by repeated evasions and equivocations, managed to make the Huskies appear as a group of habitual assassins. From Kallen's point of view, this was equally unrewarding.

"The way you tell it," he concluded disapprovingly, "they could have drawn lots for the pleasure of shooting Moore."

Younghusband was reviving as the captain reached for his hat. He made a rather touching speech about the Huskies being a simple band of brothers.

Kallen smiled grimly, then delivered his valedictory. "Not any more they're not. A little thing called money has reared its head."

14

LEADING THE RUSH

Toys, as every progressive parent knows, can be educational. So can toy fairs. Not that Walter Bowman, for one, learned much from the trade show at the Coliseum. Like the rest of Wall Street, he already knew too much about the ghost of Christmas past.

"Spot Wheels bombed," Battel Industries admitted sadly and unnecessarily. So had Mister Wingo, Pollution

Pop-ups and other much-touted items. "But buying is picking up and inventories are way down. On top of that, our R & D is developing a hot new line—" With industrial espionage lurking behind every teddy bear, he stopped short.

Walter Bowman did not press for specifics. He knew all about the optimistic projections for next Christmas that hardened producers of space rockets and talking dolls invariably make before the rest of the nation has finished storing this year's decorations. Instead, he returned to the Sloan and dictated a report embodying his findings. At the moment, Walter Bowman was bearish on toys.

So, in short order, was Mrs. Clementine Post.

"No, I did not know the Toy Fair was in town," she said impatiently.

Billy Siragusa was ingenuous. "I didn't even know they had them. But we went down there on business—Phil and I. And while he was talking, I looked around. God, you should see the things they've got!"

Recent developments had taught Clemmie Post one lesson. Billy Siragusa's innocence no longer disarmed her—at least not during conferences in the Husky offices held at his request. So she smiled perfunctorily, then directed her inquiring look toward the man sitting at Billy's side.

"Yes," he responded pleasantly with a bob of the head. "Billy and I went over to the Fair to talk to the Battel people. They're starting production for next year. It's hard to believe, isn't it?"

Clemmie Post discounted this childlike wonder. Phil Ferguson, who affected ornate cuff links in a silk shirt, was a lawyer.

"The Battel people?" she asked cautiously.

"Yes indeed," said Ferguson, beaming. "Biggest toy-makers in the country. They're scheduling a brand new hockey game—Power Play. And Billy's signature will be on every box!"

This was news to Clemmie, despite a promotion department designed explicitly to coordinate endeavors like this.

All she said, however, was, "Fine. That will be good for Billy—and good for the Huskies."

But she had been precipitate. Phil Ferguson was still some distance from his point.

"In addition, Billy just received an offer from Jellcoe," he said, with a nod enjoying silence upon his client. "Four commercials—"

"For a shampoo," Billy burst forth. "I wash my hair and say—"

"No doubt Mrs. Post knows the kind of commercials Jellcoe has in mind," Ferguson cut in smoothly. "Now, Mrs. Post, you can see that these are very advantageous offers."

By now Clemmie was asking herself what the catch was.

"I'm sure," he continued persuasively, "you're as eager as we are to see that they work out in the most advantageous fashion for Billy here."

His proprietary tone took too much for granted.

"We don't have to worry about Billy," she said with an assumption of amusement. "He's already talked me into letting him out of his contributions to the players' kitty."

Past concessions did not interest Phil Ferguson. Like Battel, he was looking forward.

"What we wanted to raise with you," he said pensively, "is the other split in Billy's promotional earnings."

He was going too slowly for his client. "Why should I split with management?" Billy asked aggressively.

After a long look in his direction, Clemmie chose to address herself to the lawyer.

"Mr. Ferguson," she said, forcing herself to remain reasonable, "as you know, the owners always get a share of the Huskies' promotions. We've done it that way for years—"

Ruminatively Ferguson shook his head. "Well, now, I think Billy's got a pretty good question there, Mrs. Post. I've looked over his contract, and I'm not altogether sure it covers this." Despite his phraseology he did not sound uncertain.

Clemmie stared at him, then reached into a drawer for a

printed form. Brandishing it across the desk, she said, "Well, look again! It's Clause Sixteen—"

"I've read it," he said without moving.

Belatedly Clemmie Post realized what she was facing. "Billy, will you please explain—?"

But Siragusa had been carefully coached for today's performance. "I think I'd better leave the talking to Phil," he said with a humility that deceived no one, least of all Clementine Post.

Ferguson was too practiced to let his satisfaction show, but he did allow a moment for Siragusa's defection to sink in before he went on: "Now, Mrs. Post, there's no need for bad feelings. Once you hear me out, I'm sure you'll agree. Let me set your mind at rest about one thing. When anybody wants the Huskies to sponsor a product, management gets a cut—"

"That's what I just said!" she cried.

He might have been congratulating a student. "You say it, we say it, the contract says it."

Genuinely at sea now, she replied, "Then what are we arguing about? Billy isn't the first Husky to make commercials—or endorse products. Paul Imrie was on for some deodorant last year. And Pete Levoisier endorsed some hockey sticks a few years back. They didn't make any trouble."

But Ferguson was not interested in Billy's teammates. "Imre and Levoisier," he said, elaborately detached, "were salable because of their association with the Huskies."

"Well, what team is Billy supposed to be playing for?" she retorted. "Billy, for heaven's sake, what is this?"

Mrs. Post had always found it easy to bypass Coach Milt Forsburg when she wanted to talk to her star player. But Phil Ferguson was a different proposition altogether.

"We plan to market Billy Siragusa—the public personality," he said sturdily. "Quite apart from his employment by the Huskies."

Billy's enthusiastic nod told Clemmie that this rationale had already been explained to him—and adopted.

"Public personality?" she said scornfully. "What are

you talking about? There wouldn't be any Billy Siragusa if it weren't for the Huskies. I'm the one who made him!"

It was Siragusa who replied. "Look, Mrs. Post, you gave me a chance to show what I can do. And I'm grateful—"

"Grateful?" she mocked him.

"But that's as far as it goes," he finished determinedly.

Phil Ferguson observed this exchange benignly. But he set his client a good example by dropping the subject of gratitude.

"Mrs. Post," he said, "let me give you an example. Dwight Eisenhower was made by the U.S. Army, in your sense of the word. But when he sold his memoirs, they didn't ask for a cent. That's because he was selling something personal to himself—exactly what Billy will be doing."

"Do you think you're another Eisenhower?" Clemmie flung at Siragusa.

But Billy had picked up the signal. Pretending he was not listening, he sat back, withdrawn from the conversation of his elders. And even in repose, Clemmie realized as she glared at him, he was a sight to gladden a sports fan's heart. The alertness that made him first man after the puck was always there. One spring would have taken Billy across the room.

It was a salutary reminder, if she required one, that Mrs. Post needed Billy. With a real effort she controlled her growing distaste for his lawyer.

"Well, I don't know what you're talking about. No!" she said, raising her hand when Phil Ferguson leaned forward to resume his lecture. "As you know, Billy's contract comes up for renewal this summer. If you want a new clause inserted—well, I can't promise anything now. But, assuming Billy keeps up the good work, I know that we'll want to show our appreciation—" She stopped, because both visitors were shaking their heads.

"We came up here today," said Billy, who had forgotten that he was not listening, "because I wanted this settled—now. I've got plans. . . ."

Ferguson responded to another part of Mrs. Post's

statement. "I should warn you that Billy's contract will need substantial revision before I can advise him to sign, Mrs. Post. As it stands—"

Unceremoniously Clemmie interrupted. "There is no need to discuss it before the season is over."

"If you prefer it that way," Ferguson conceded. He then dissipated any triumph she might have felt by adding, "But in that case, we will insist on deciding the matter of the promotional moneys. These offers Billy has received from Jellcoe and Battel cannot wait."

"That's right," said Billy.

Clemmie, swinging between them, suddenly realized that one source of her discomfort lay in being outnumbered. Siragusa and Ferguson were feeding each other lines.

She, too, could use some help. Her thoughts turned first to Milt Forsburg, then to her lawyer. Then . . .

For once, she thought, Win Holland's total indifference to hockey might be a help.

"If you want a fast decision," she said icily, "we will have to get some other owners down here. I am certainly not making any major changes in our arrangements without their approval."

This disconcerted both men. "Win Holland?" Billy Siragusa said. "But he never handles anything like this. You're always the one—"

Ferguson suspected delaying tactics. "As Billy says, Mrs. Post, you have executive authority. Of course, we know that there are other owners. But you run the team."

"Not on something like this." Clemmie was already dialing. "I'll get Win Holland over here right away."

But things did not go that smoothly. Mr. Holland was unavailable, said the receptionist who answered the phone.

"You mean he isn't there?"

"He's in conference. Can I have him call you back?"

"No, that won't do. Please tell him that Mrs. Post is on the line."

The receptionist protested, to no avail. The Clementine Posts of this world are born knowing how to disrupt office routines. Their techniques, however, are less effective when relayed secondhand.

"I'm sorry, Mrs. Post," breathed the same voice moments later. "I did give your message to Mr. Holland, but he can't take any calls right now. He would be happy to come to your office tomorrow."

Phil Ferguson had followed half of this conversation. When Clemmie hung up, he said, "Too bad. But I guess we'll have to go ahead without him."

"No," said Mrs. Post firmly. "If he can't come down here, we'll have to go up there."

"But he's in conference."

Nevertheless he was not altogether surprised to find himself and his client swept out to the street and into a taxi.

Their arrival at Forty-seventh Street bore out Ferguson's misgivings. Once they were past the door with the nameplates—Holwin Enterprises, Inc., Holland Newspapers Corp., Holland International, Ltd.—the air became thick with indignation. The receptionist was aghast. Win Holland was furious. Holland's companions were puzzled and resentful. Clemmie Post, with regal unconcern, swept aside all opposition until she was firmly ensconced in the corner office. Ferguson and Billy Siragusa trailed in her wake like camp followers.

Tight-lipped, Holland performed introductions. "Clemmie, this is my colleague, Dr. Anton Dietrich, and this is Victor Jowdy from Fresno. We're in the middle of something rather important. Can't it wait?"

"Not according to Mr. Ferguson," replied Clemmie, smartly passing the buck.

Under the baleful gaze of three strangers, Phil Ferguson lost a good deal of his earlier cogency. Indeed, all of it as far as Win Holland was concerned. "It sounds to me as if you're trying to pull a raw deal. I don't see what the problem is, Clemmie. Can't you settle this? I've got a lot on my plate right now."

"That is very true, Mrs. Post," chimed in Dr. Dietrich.

"At this moment Winthrop should be speaking with our office in London."

But Clemmie was a quick learner. "I didn't think it would be right to make the decision myself. Not while you own twenty-five percent, Win," she said, underlining his obligations. "But Mr. Ferguson insists on an answer today."

"It's up to you, Clemmie. If you say yes, I won't gripe."

"I don't see how you can say that." The intervention came from an unexpected quarter. Victor Jowdy, a small neutral man with a low voice, was very serious. "It would just be throwing money away."

Cunningly Clemmie continued, "And we have to remember the team is going to be annoyed if they catch wind of anything like that."

"Why the hell should they catch wind of it?" Holland was unsympathetic.

"I expect Billy will take care of that."

"So they're upset." Again it was Jowdy speaking. "What difference does that make? Sounds as if somebody's going to be upset, no matter what."

"With the play-offs coming!" Clemmie gasped.

"I don't know anything about hockey, but I suppose there's something riding on these play-offs."

Billy Siragusa was galvanized by Jowdy's ignorance. "Our play-off money depends on those games," he said fervently.

"Then you've got nothing to worry about, Mrs. Post." Jowdy shrugged. "They're not going to let anything affect their play."

Clemmie Post relaxed. This was the right note to strike! Meanwhile Phil Ferguson struggled to shore up a rapidly eroding position. He addressed himself to Win Holland.

"It seems to me you're in danger of letting a very important decision for your team be made by a stranger. Mr. Jowdy himself admits he knows nothing about the game."

"No, but I can recognize a liability when I see one. You've got a real asset in this team, Holland. You don't want to go spoiling it."

Win Holland's teeth glinted briefly. "You mean, you don't want me to," he rejoined.

Ferguson had restrained himself, but now he was too hard-pressed to be overly considerate. "You can't expect your opinion to carry much weight, Mr. Jowdy," he said severely. "After all, this isn't really your business."

"Now that's where you're wrong," said Jowdy. He glanced toward Holland, who was intently studying the lettering on a pencil.

"Mr. Holland didn't explain that I'm representing clients too," he continued. "And unless I find something better for the purpose, I'm advising them to attach Mr. Holland's interest in the Huskies."

There was a considerable silence before this produced any response.

Then, in an even voice, Clementine Post said, "Win, what are you up to now?"

15

FACE-OFF

DESCRIPTIONS of the elephant, it will be remembered, depend on the number of blind men, as well as the portion of its anatomy their questing fingers encounter. Of the six persons present during Clemmie Post's descent on Holwin Enterprises, only one left satisfied.

Victor Jowdy had crossed a continent in search of his particular form of ivory. Within the hour, he was on the phone reporting his strike.

"Mark," he said. "I've just come back from Holland's office."

Back in Fresno, Mark needed reassurance.

"I'm convinced we're doing the right thing," Jowdy told him firmly. "Holland's other assets could take a long time to find. He's got everything wrapped up in holding companies from here to Timbuktu. But you can't hide a hockey team—"

Fresno broke in.

"No, Mark," said Jowdy after patiently listening to anxieties he had heard before. "We don't know anything about hockey, but we do know Holland's percentage of the Huskies is worth good money. Now that they're winning, other people are probably after it. So this is the ideal time for us to move. . . ."

Unresentfully he listened to a hodgepodge of suggestions.

"Sure," he said finally. "I'm going to look it over very carefully. But I'm sure Holland's share will suit our purposes. What? . . . No, Holland was none too happy to have me turn up right now. What difference does that make? I didn't come east to spread joy."

Even in Fresno, Jowdy, Jowdy & Rosenzweig were not renowned harbingers of sunshine and light.

California was not the only place to receive immediate tidings of Victor Jowdy's intentions.

Reports of a bruised instep sent Jerry Drake hotfooting down to the Husky locker room. Every disability, no matter how minor, represented a potential intermission guest to him.

Paul Imrie was not only disappointingly fit, he was planning to skate.

"Oh, fine," said Drake, trying to think of the greater good.

He was about to leave when Milt Forsburg stopped him. "Maybe you know what this guy Jowdy is up to."

"As a matter of fact," Drake said in accents befitting the Voice of the Sloan, "I have just been in conference on that very subject—at the bank."

He was yielding to temptation. Drake could barely balance his own checkbook. But over the years he had taken harmless pleasure in furnishing oboists and xylophonists

with the financial nuggets that came his way. And he had
encountered John Thatcher in the Sloan lobby a half hour
earlier.

The attention he received was flattering. "Mr. Jowdy,"
he said, reverting to his symphonic manner, "is not buying
the team. He is planning to attach Win Holland's share—
to help settle some debts. It is a standard business proce-
dure." Drake enunciated this with neither blush nor ac-
knowledgment.

"You mean, Jowdy just takes over from Holland?"
Forsburg asked.

By now, Drake was giving a creditable imitation of
John Thatcher. "On the contrary," he said magnificently.
"Jowdy and Holland will no doubt take the entire pro-
ceeding to court. There are likely to be disagreements, at
least about valuation."

"Court." Milt Forsburg seized on the word. "That
might mean some changes around here."

"Not immediately. The litigation may take several
months," Drake rejoined.

That, however, was not what Milt Forsburg was talking about, as he explained.

"If the owners get into enough of a legal mess, the NHL
steps in. The League manages the club!"

"You mean they assume responsibility for day-to-day
running of the team?" Drake said. "Is that good or bad?"

Forsburg shrugged. "They leave the team pretty much
the way they found it."

Paul Imrie could not resist. "It might be good for you,
Milt. At least you'll be sure of a job!"

"Knock it off, Paul," he growled.

"Cheer up, Milt," said Imrie unrepentantly. "This gets
Clemmie off your neck. She'll be frozen out for as long as
this hassle between Jowdy and Holland goes on."

Forsburg considered this, then came up with another
unexpected benefit. "And if Clemmie doesn't have a say in
what happens to us, guess where that leaves Billy."

Paul grinned. "Happy days are here again."

"Paul," Forsburg said, shaking his head, "the way things
are right now, the less said the better."

He was addressing the wrong man.

There were many versions of the conference at Forty-seventh Street besides Paul Imrie's, and most of them found their way to Great Neck that evening. By the following morning Eileen Levoisier had decided to ignore the discrepancies and concentrate on one common detail. Mrs. Post had taken Billy Siragusa to an owners' meeting.

She switched off the radio as Pete, yawning hugely, padded into the kitchen.

"Oof," he said. "Boy, I feel good. What time is it anyway?" He squinted at the wall clock. "Nine? Mmph . . ."

Silently Eileen handed him his orange juice, then watched as he blindly hooked a leg around his chair, pulled it out, and collapsed at the table in the breakfast nook.

With the usual platter of ham and eggs, she came over to join him.

"Pete," she said, pouring coffee for both of them. "I've been thinking."

But she had not waited long enough. Pete was a slow waker. Eileen herself had been up since six.

"Drink some coffee," she said, since she knew how Pete was in the morning. "And be careful—it's hot."

Gingerly he took a sip, shook his head and opened his eyes wide for the first time. "Hey," he said, making a discovery. "You're all dressed up."

Eileen was not wearing slacks.

"I've decided to go into town. Pete—"

"You look great," he mumbled, his mouth full. He leaned toward her and added, "You smell good, too."

These compliments heightened her uncertainty.

"But," he said lazily, "don't spend all the play-off money. We haven't got it—yet."

This was her opportunity. Despite carefully applied makeup, she bit her lip in indecision.

Levoisier misread her expression. "I was just kidding," he said earnestly. "Spend as much as you want!"

"As if I would," she retorted. This exchange had long

antecedents. Eileen could remember it as far back as the two furnished rooms in St. Catherine's when the Levoisier family had no bank balance at all.

"What the hell!" said Pete expansively. "That's what money's for!"

"Uh-huh," said Eileen. "You know, Pete, we've come a long way. . . ."

"Mmm," he replied, not hearing a syllable.

This made up her mind. "I'll pick you up in Mineola this afternoon," she said, draining her cup, then rising to collect her purse and gloves. "No, you don't have to catch a ride with one of the boys. I'll be back in plenty of time."

She took her coat from the closet, then whisked out the back door, pausing only long enough to blow him an airy kiss.

Pete grinned sleepily after her, then poured himself another cup of coffee. When Eileen started answering questions before he asked them, it usually meant something. But while he was still half unconscious, he was not going to do any heavy thinking.

Except about something he had noticed before. Eileen looked nice in pink.

In the driveway, meanwhile, his wife was deciding the debate she had been conducting with herself—in her own favor.

"You could call it shopping," she said defiantly.

Clemmie Post was dealing with her correspondence when the maid ushered Mrs. Levoisier into the spacious living room. She put down the paper knife and inspected her visitor over half glasses.

"Oh—Eileen," she said, pausing fractionally before the name.

Eileen smiled her player's wife smile.

"Sit down," Mrs. Post said. "I'm afraid I'm terribly rushed this morning—as you can see."

What Eileen saw could have been a photograph from *Vogue*. Mrs. Post, in a sweeping gown, sat at an elegant Directoire desk. An untidy heap of letters surrounded a silver vase containing yellow roses.

"Be good, Eileen," she admonished herself, accepting the cool invitation. Not only did she do her own housework; she took care of the Levoisier Skating Club taxes, mortgages and payrolls from a secondhand rolltop in the basement.

"I hope you haven't come to tell me something's the matter with Pete," Mrs. Post said. "I know there's a lot of flu going around."

Resolutely Eileen beat down a flicker of guilt. "Pete is why I came," she began. This was not the opening she had planned, but it would do. "He's worried—and I am too."

Clementine Post moved over to sit opposite Eileen.

"We've been hearing rumors," Eileen said grimly.

"I suppose that's inevitable," said Clemmie. "Let me just say this. Win's sale of the team won't involve any of the players. That much I think I can be sure of. Otherwise, I am as confused about the future as you are."

"Then, this Mr. Jowdy's not going to move the team the way Mr. Moore was," said Eileen with an innocence that would not have deceived her family for a second.

"No!" said Clemmie explosively.

"Naturally it worried us," Eileen lied fluently. "Pete and I have interests here in New York—"

But Mrs. Post was not attending. "If only," she said bitterly, "Win Holland would take care of *his* interests during the off season. Not now, when the Huskies are going into the play-offs."

Eileen made a rapid decision. "But what I really came to talk to you about," she said, "is Billy."

Clementine Post froze briefly. When she replied, she was very much the older woman enlightening a new bride.

"Now, Eileen, I've always made it a point never to discuss the treatment of one player with any other player. And if you just think for a minute, I'm sure you'll see that's the only way to keep harmony. Every member of the team is an individual case, and, after all, it really isn't anybody else's business what he's agreed to. Pete, for instance, has a right to have his privacy respected."

Two red spots were blazing in Eileen's cheeks. She sounded very determined as she said, "That depends on what's being agreed to. When it comes down to taking money out of our pockets to put it in someone else's, it certainly is our business."

Mrs. Post had perfected her justification of the kitty raid. "We all have to expect some adjustment now that the Huskies are so successful," she explained easily. "But you're mistaken if you think anybody is being favored. The new system applies to everyone, just as the old one did. All of that will be regularized next year."

"I'm talking about what you're doing this year!"

By now, fresh instructions for the maid were forming in Clemmie Post's mind. *She* descended on the Huskies; they did not descend on her.

"You must remember that Billy is very young and inclined to talk too much," she said, phrasing the thought unfortunately.

"He may talk too much for you," Eileen retorted, "but I don't know how we'd ever find out anything if Billy didn't babble. Nobody else is telling us. If it wasn't for him, the team probably wouldn't have found out about the kitty until the season was over."

They were bound to differ on this subject. Mrs. Post regularly celebrated the end of the season by flying off on a round of visits to her married children. From her point of view, it was the ideal time for embarrassing news to break.

"Certainly the players would have been informed of my decision," she proclaimed. "It was made in the best interests of the Huskies. After all, that's what I care about, and I expect everyone, from the rookies to the veterans, to be willing to make some sacrifices for the team."

Eileen would have loved to ask what sacrifices Mrs. Post was making. But she was not risking a serious quarrel with her husband simply to relieve her feelings.

"You said the new kitty system will apply to everyone. Is that going to hold for everything else you're doing?"

Clemmie Post's mouth clamped into a thin line. "I don't know what you're talking about."

"Billy seems to know," said Eileen, steel in her voice. "He has lots of arrangements in mind, and he seems to think they're just for him."

Clemmie was too incensed by this reminder of Billy Siragusa's treachery to guard her tongue.

"Oh, Billy has plenty of ideas. But he may find they're not going to come to anything—for him or for anyone else," she snapped. "Nothing has been settled."

For years Eileen had been filling in what Pete left unsaid. Clementine Post presented no difficulty at all.

"I see," Eileen said slowly. "If Billy's extra money is going to come from the other players, he gets it as a matter of team spirit. But if it has to come from the owners, then the team spirit stops right there."

Clemmie did not like what was said, but she was even more disturbed at how it was said. Eileen no longer sounded outraged. She sounded like a bridge player who has located the thirteenth trump.

Clemmie managed to produce a passable smile. "Eileen, you're jumping to conclusions. All I meant was that nothing can be resolved while the ownership is in doubt. The NHL may take all that out of my hands."

Even to her own ears it sounded weak. To Eileen, it was transparent. "The NHL doesn't have anything to do with skating clubs," she said roundly.

Clemmie Post's eyelids flickered. "Skating clubs?"

"Yes! And that's what I want to talk about."

Scarcely was the ultimatum out when the telephone rang.

Clemmie sprang to her feet as if, Eileen thought, there was no maid waiting for something to do.

"Yes . . . yes. But hold on—" her eyes strayed back to Eileen—"I'm going to put you on the other phone."

Without apology she swept out of the room. Her clear soprano, muted by distance, gave way to extended silence. As the seconds passed, Eileen realized that somebody was telling Mrs. Post something—at length.

"No!"

Then, more silence.

The phone was beginning to hypnotize Eileen. What would happen if she picked up the receiver . . . ?

She almost did not make it back to her chair before Mrs. Post reappeared.

"Now what were we talking about?" she said imperiously. "As I told you at the outset, Eileen, I'm busy today."

"Skating clubs," Eileen said, conscious that time, or something else, had cost her momentum.

"Skating clubs?" repeated Clemmie, unsure how to meet the attack. "Oh, that's right. You and Pete own two, don't you?" This, if she had realized it, was precisely the wrong tone to take. A significant portion of the Levoisier income came from the skating clubs.

"Yes," said Eileen. "And Billy is planning to invest in them, too."

"So?"

"Do you know how much it costs to open skating clubs, Mrs. Post?" Eileen said hotly. "Or how hard it is to get financing?"

Raising her hand, Clemmie signaled a halt. "Eileen," she said grandly, "I do hope you haven't come to ask me to lend you money."

Truly flabbergasted, Eileen gaped at her.

"Because," said Clemmie, smoothing her skirt with elaborate care, "I make it a point not to involve myself with team players."

"Do you?" Eileen struggled to get the words out.

"Always," said Mrs. Post.

Eileen was wondering how far she dared go, when Clemmie forged ahead.

"Sometimes I worry about these outside activities so many members of the team seem to have," she said. "I'm afraid it will take their minds off hockey. Really, to hear some of them talk, you'd think they weren't interested in anything but money."

"Some of the team have wives and children," said Eileen sarcastically.

But Mrs. Post was impregnable to the shaft. "Even Billy is beginning to act that way. And it would be so simple if he just left things to me."

Eileen Levoisier was not feeling kindly toward Billy Siragusa, but she knew that professional athletes had been poor men as long as they left their interests in the hands of management. With malice aforethought, she said, "Billy thinks he's found a gravy train. And his luck seems to have started with hiring that lawyer he keeps telling the others about."

Clemmie snorted.

"I sometimes think," Eileen continued artlessly, "that maybe Pete should get himself a lawyer, too. Say, in time to negotiate his new contract."

"You may find that more expensive than you think," said Clemmie, rising. "And now, Eileen, I'm afraid . . ."

It was at the front door that she provided the final straw for Eileen's morning. "Did I tell you when you came in," she said, "that I think your fun fur is absolutely delightful."

"That goddamned rich bitch!" Eileen was talking to herself as she set off toward Lexington Avenue. But her heart was not in it. She was too preoccupied with the question tormenting her for the last ten minutes.

Why had Mrs. Clementine Post hung up on Billy Siragusa?

16

A RUDE GESTURE

CHARLES EVANS HUGHES once went to bed assuming he had been elected President of the United States. According to the best modern scholarship he enjoyed a sound untroubled slumber. Thanks to the miracle of modern communications, and a very considerable expenditure by the Sloan, New York Husky fans were granted no such post-campaign respite. Until California was heard from, they were staying as wide awake as possible.

The Huskies won their ninth game in a row in Madison

Square Garden at 10:30 P.M. Straightaway their fans, although emotionally drained by two hours of high drama, fortified themselves for another vigil. Tonight's victory had moved the Huskies into first place of the Western Division—one full point ahead of the Chicago Black Hawks. More immediately important, however, the Black Hawks were playing their last game of the season that very evening, at eight o'clock, Pacific Standard Time, or eleven o'clock, Eastern Standard Time.

On the home screen, New Yorkers met Jack Stenhouse, sportscaster for the Oakland Seals. Stenhouse cultivated a low-keyed, friendly approach.

". . . wire services say that the Huskies have just picked up that all-important win," he announced. "And we understand that Channel Two in New York has just joined us, here in beautiful California, for tonight's game between the Seals and Chicago. Greetings to all you folks back East. As you know, a Black Hawk loss tonight would leave the Huskies in uncontested possession of first place."

New York, however, did not want friendship. It wanted facts.

"What's the score?" shouted Alvin Fischer (and many others) at the set.

"We're just three minutes into the first period," said Stenhouse cheerily.

"Oh, I don't like him as much as Jerry, do you?" commented Mrs. Fischer.

Her husband eschewed personality. "The score, dummy! What's the—?"

"The score," said Jack Stenhouse easily, "is one to nothing. The Black Hawks' goal . . ."

Alvin Fischer growled.

Mrs. Fischer rose. "And you talk about soap operas! I'm going to bed."

Alvin barely heard her.

"The usual Chicago razzle-dazzle on the power play!" said Stenhouse, giving credit where credit was due.

"Razzle-dazzle!" Fischer rasped. "Don't make me laugh!"

". . . but the fine young Oakland team is fighting back."

"Fine young jerks," said Alvin Fischer sourly.

From the bathroom came a final admonition. "Don't stay up too late, Al."

"You, too," said Alvin Fischer.

"What?"

"Nothing, nothing," he said irritably.

At midnight, E.S.T., the Black Hawks led the Seals two to one at the end of the first period. By now Alvin Fischer hated not only Jack Stenhouse but the whole state of California.

Intermission featured the wife of the Seals' goalie.

Fischer got up and circled the living room morosely in his stockinged feet.

". . . a schoolteacher before we were married," said Mrs. Gorham with a mad laugh. "Now I'm just a wife and mother . . ."

"That's wonderful," said Jack Stenhouse.

"Stupid broad," said Alvin Fischer awfully.

His wife spoke from the bedroom. Fischer listened. Then: "No, I didn't say anything. What? . . . How can I go to bed before I see what happens?"

At twelve forty-five, Chicago led three to one.

Alvin Fischer lay sprawled in his easy chair, staring hot-eyed at his television set.

". . . our friends back in New York are probably watching tonight's game with a lot of interest," said Jack Stenhouse with a chuckle.

"You're a crumb," said Alvin Fischer. "You're a born loser. And so's that lousy team of yours."

At one o'clock, California scored.

"Hey hey!" Alvin shouted.

Mrs. Fischer, in flannel nightgown and curlers, appeared in the doorway.

"You're still up," she said, stifling a yawn.

"What does it look like?"

"Can't you read about it in tomorrow's paper?"

Alvin gave her a look.

"All right, all right," she said, disappearing again.

Alvin resumed his communion with California. Three to two, Black Hawks.

"And you've got a lousy organist too," he added as an afterthought.

But at seven minutes after one o'clock, Oakland tied the game up.

"Of course, the Seals would be happy with a draw," said Stenhouse. "But the fans in New York will be disappointed. . . ."

"You're a pansy!" said Alvin Fischer.

At one-thirty, the team captain of the Black Hawks registered a protest against a linesman's call that quickly escalated into a time-consuming controversy. At one-forty, a portion of the goalie's net required attention. At one fifty-five, play was again halted until a scoreboard light could be repaired.

Alvin Fischer went into his kitchen.

This time his wife had her hands on her broad hips. "How many beers is that?" she demanded. "And what time is it? Honest to God, Al, it's only a game. . . ."

After a mighty struggle, Fischer controlled himself. "Go to bed."

"What's . . ."

He could trust himself only so far. "Go to bed!"

He stationed himself foursquare before his Spanish pecan console.

". . . a driving Black Hawk rush," Stenhouse said. "A fine save . . ."

"A save like that my mother could make!" said Alvin Fischer.

". . . a pass to LeBow. LeBow skates the puck to center ice . . ."

By now, Fischer was reaching into history for his invective.

"LeBow. Used to play for the Rangers. Don't give me LeBow . . ."

LeBow scored.

"Good old LeBow," said Fischer emotionally.

". . . the Seals lead," said Jack Stenhouse. "I'll bet they're biting their nails back in little old New York. . . ."

"Little old New York," snarled Fischer, fingers curling around his beer can. "Just hold Chicago, will you?"

". . . pass to LaFreniere . . . pass to Rivers . . . with four seconds . . . three seconds . . . And there's the buzzer! The game's over. The Seals win it, four to three. And in the Western Division, the Huskies are in sole possession of first place. . . ."

"What happened?" Mrs. Fischer demanded.

Fischer drew a deep breath. "What do you think happened?" he said. "The Seals creamed them. The Huskies made first!"

"Thank God, it's all over," said Mrs. Fischer.

"It's all over—but the play-offs," her husband corrected her.

But in point of fact, he too was wrong.

The Huskies still had one game of the regular season to play on Wednesday night. Therefore, at three o'clock on Tuesday afternoon, they were well into their practice session at the Mineola rink. It would have been understandable if their fighting spirit had slackened. But there was no danger of that with Billy Siragusa around.

Dispassionately Milt Forsburg decided that he should have taken Billy off the ice ten minutes ago. With the play-offs coming up, it would be a shame if Paul Imrie managed to do him serious injury. And no one could say that Paul wasn't trying. Unfortunately, even Imrie was not likely to drop all pretense and simply break his neck. And that was all that would do any good. Milt Forsburg had already been through an interview with Billy before the rest of the team arrived. It was enough to make him wish his superstar's burgeoning head cold were pneumonia.

"Towel!" yelled someone from the ice.

Forsburg expelled his breath. The decision had been taken out of his hands. Now Billy would have to come off the ice, he thought, as he watched a trainer stanch the blood flowing from Siragusa's nose. It had not been Imrie this time. It had been Pete Levoisier who had delivered the punishing body check, driving Billy's face into the boards. And everyone knew what was eating Pete. Billy had delivered the good news publicly, after his workout with Milt.

"Pete, I wanted you to be the first to know. My lawyer

has given me the go-ahead. We'll be opening the first Sira-
gusá Club in Great Neck."

Pete had been poker-faced.

"Where?"

Billy enjoyed telling him. "It's just off Northern Boule-
vard."

"That's where my club is."

"I guess we'll be neighbors. My club will be half a
block from yours." Billy sneezed. "We should be opening
next season."

"A lot can happen between now and then."

"Yeah. At first I thought maybe you wouldn't like it
much. But, hell, your place may not be there any more."

"Shut-up!" snapped Levoisier.

There had been silence in the dressing room after Pete
pushed his way outside.

Now Billy was leaving the ice, using the towel to mop
his mask of blood. Forsburg was mildly surprised at the
satisfaction he derived from the sight.

Billy had reached the bench. Yes, Pete had done a real
job on him.

"You'd better get that stitched up," Forsburg said duti-
fully.

Reddened teeth showed in a derisive grin. "Sure, coach.
We're all taking your orders. So far."

"Then you'd better call it a day. And remember to pick
up those cold pills the trainer put out for you."

Siragusa was already ducking into the doorway. But he
looked over his shoulder to say, "I'll be glad to get out of
here. I've still got a few people to talk to."

Forsburg's eyes returned to the ice. It was unbelievable.
Pete Levoisier was skating and stick-handling even better
than usual; Paul Imrie was working the puck out of the
corners with demonic skill.

Within minutes Forsburg was engrossed enough to be
bellowing at a rookie defenseman: "When you've got a
two-on-one, the place for you is in between. You're not
blocking a shot. You're blocking a pass and giving the
goalie a clear line of sight. Let him take care of the shot."

As if in eerie punctuation, a sharp crack resounded

through the resonant echo chamber of the rink. Every head swung toward the same corner.

Eileen Levoisier and Billy Siragusa were confronting each other. By some unfortunate mischance she had arrived to pick up her husband just as Siragusa, fully dressed, was heading for the exit. Forsburg had no trouble imagining what their exchange had been like. Everyone could see its consequences. Eileen was still in follow-through position, arm across body, palm flattened. Billy was a frozen statue, the marks of her fingers standing out clearly on his cheek.

Softly cursing, Milt Forsburg wheeled to the ice. Pete Levoisier's shoulders were hunched, his hands tight on his stick. With a lurch in his stomach, the coach realized that Pete's teammates were not moving to restrain him. They were moving to leave him an open path.

But Billy Siragusa had been as alert as Forsburg. He was not insane enough to exacerbate Levoisier now. With a mock salute to Eileen, he prudently retired along one side of the building. Eileen, after a moment of immobility, gave a half-strangled sob and fled up the other.

Milt Forsburg hurried over to Siragusa. "Have you gone crazy? Don't you know enough to leave the wives alone?"

"If the Levoisiers think I'm going to stand still and be their punching bag, they've got another think coming," Siragusa muttered in a furious undertone.

Regretfully Forsburg noted that Eileen had not managed to undo the trainer's recent suture work.

"You've got nobody to blame but yourself," he retorted. "Why don't you wise up? You're gunning for everybody in sight because the League may take over the team. Well, get it into your head that it's out of our hands. Nothing can be done."

Billy's body, almost whippetlike in street clothes, arched with intensity. "A lot can be done about Jowdy," he lashed back. "I haven't even started."

"What's that?" asked a new voice. "Does someone want me?"

Forsburg's heart sank as he turned toward the two men

who had emerged from the dressing room. God, why couldn't they have stayed there longer? For that matter, why had Holland brought Jowdy to the rink in the first place? Wouldn't he ever learn?

Win Holland seemed to read his thoughts. He smiled apologetically.

"I know you don't like visitors hanging around all afternoon, Milt. But Vic has to see what he's getting."

"I want to talk to you!" Billy Siragusa thrust forward to within a foot of Holland. "You can't unload the Huskies now. You've got to wait until after the play-offs."

Holland did not come from the same breed of scrappers as most of Billy's associates. He contented himself with raising his eyebrows and stepping back a pace. This response goaded Billy further.

"You act like you've got nothing riding on this." He was shouting now. "As if you and Jowdy are in some separate world. Well, you're not. We're right in there with you, and I'm not standing by while you shaft us."

He had said enough to catch everyone's attention. Out of the corner of his eye, Forsburg saw the players gliding silently closer.

Victor Jowdy could have been discussing the weather. "I think you may not have understood the other day. Mr. Holland isn't doing anything. I'm the one who's made the decision."

"You! What right do you have to step in like God, when we're the ones doing the work?"

"Don't try that on me! I don't have any obligations to you or anyone else here. The people I have a responsibility for are in Fresno, California. And you don't know a thing about their rights."

Billy was now probing at random, determined to find a weak spot. "Maybe not. But you'd be surprised how much I know about what's going on here. Some of us know a lot more than we've let on."

Jowdy blinked in confusion. For the first time he looked toward Holland for guidance.

Siragusa, delighted, continued his tirade. "Do you think you're the first one to have cute ideas about taking over the Huskies? Well, someone else was ahead of you, and he stopped being a problem damned fast. Haven't they told you about Frank Moore?" His glance raked the ice. "We got to meet him at a practice session just like this, and we remember all about it."

"Billy—" Milt Forsburg stretched out a hand.

Angrily Siragusa shook it off and turned to leave, hurling one last remark at Jowdy.

"Get Mr. Holland to tell you what happened to Moore after that practice. It might make you think twice."

17

SCREEN SHOT

BILLY SIRAGUSA went home to nurse his head cold and his grievances until face-off time, Wednesday night. It did not occur to him to speculate on what was happening in the interim. As far as he was concerned, the New York Husky Hockey Club disappeared the moment he absented himself. In spite of a crash course in the larger verities by Neil Gruen, he still believed that the only materialization of the team occurred when he stepped onto the ice. It was beyond his comprehension that Victor Jowdy saw the club as a series of bookkeeping entries, that a television network saw it as a block of time, and that the Sloan Guaranty Trust saw it as an advertising vehicle. An advertising vehicle, however, of astonishing success and duration.

This last aspect was responsible for the conference on Wednesday morning in the Sloan's PR Department.

"Yes, indeed," said Dexter Younghusband, rubbing his hands. "I assure you we regard it as a pleasure and a privilege to sponsor the play-off games."

John Thatcher examined the gathering with a critical
eye and decided that it presented a sorry spectacle. Mrs.
Post and Milt Forsburg, on one side of the table, were bal-
anced by Win Holland and Victor Jowdy on the other. He
himself was in the chair and had just put his signature to a
very handsome undertaking for a minimum of four games
and a maximum of twenty-one. By rights he should have
been assisting at a celebration. He had been prepared for a
monumental display of Husky self-satisfaction. Instead he
was in danger of being swamped by the prevailing
Weltschmerz.

Nor was it the outsiders who were to blame. Victor
Jowdy was projecting an aura of substantial contentment.
The new Sloan contract, as he had been quick to note, was
going to mean a very nice extra dollop in the Husky cof-
fers. Thatcher himself was modestly pleased with the results of the current season and even prepared to look forward to the next. Any deficiencies in enthusiasm from
where he sat were offset by Dexter Younghusband at the
foot of the table. The auxiliaries were more than doing
their part.

The ones who were not celebrating were the owners of
the Huskies. Win Holland's detachment was understandable. He after all, was preparing to sign off this ship
and hand over to Victor Jowdy within the week. It was
Mrs. Clementine Post who was the big surprise. Long ago
she had constituted herself poetess laureate of the Huskies, hymning their greatness in despair and defeat. And
what was she doing now, at this redemptive moment,
when she should have been bursting into a hallelujah
chorus? As nearly as Thatcher could tell, she was thinking
about something else.

Every appeal to her by Forsburg or Younghusband had
been met by an initial confusion, then a noncommittal
reply. Forsburg was again soliciting her agreement where
it should have been automatic.

"We'd like to start thinking about the television coverage for next season. The sooner the better, wouldn't you
say, Clemmie?"

Mrs. Post looked up from the polished mahogany she had been studying. "What's that?"

"Next year's contract. With the Sloan."

"It seems a little early to decide."

This had been her stock answer for over an hour. Now she drew fire from heavier guns than those of Milt Forsburg.

"What do you mean, too early?" demanded Jowdy. "Don't you want to sign while the going's good?"

She hesitated, then said dubiously, "Well, I suppose it couldn't do any harm."

Jowdy rolled his eyes to the ceiling in exasperation, a pantomime which normally would have set the fur flying. But Mrs. Post had already retired into her thoughts.

Dexter Younghusband's professional forte was kindling docile consumers with his own zeal. Instinctively he took over.

"First we have to consider the overall programming of the play-offs," he said like a baby-sitter promising a treat to good little children. "All sorts of groups would like exposure on these shows, and we want to do the right thing by everybody concerned." He paused, inviting them to share his vision of an importuning horde, a clamor of irreconcilable demands, and finally the stroke of legerdemain with which he resolved all difficulty.

Thatcher noticed that, as Younghusband waxed fervent, he reduced, rather than increased, the number of his listeners. Victor Jowdy had been alert as long as they were discussing dollars and cents. Other considerations obviously bored him. Milton Forsburg had abandoned any pretense of attention. He was frowning at Mrs. Post.

"It's the intermissions that are a challenge," Dexter Younghusband confided. "Jerry Drake will do his usual splendid work for us during ice time. But we have to get the proportions right with our guests. The NHL, the players' association, the American Olympic Committee, have all expressed a desire to appear. And, of course, we mustn't forget the Sloan."

Thatcher admired this way of putting it.

"But we have to face facts. What the listeners really like

to see is a hockey player. Now, the North Stars' Ed Grangier is out for the rest of the year with a separated shoulder and we're trying to get him. But in order to achieve a proper balance we should have a Husky, too. Unfortunately none of them have been injured." Younghusband laughed lightly at his own pleasantry.

Milt Forsburg was the only one who had heard, and he was not amused. "The Huskies are all fine," he declared.

Jowdy had been idly leafing through his papers. Provoked by some demon of boredom, he took issue with this statement. "The one who was yelling at me yesterday, he sounded sick."

"He's got a cold," Forsburg corrected.

Clementine Post swung around in her chair. "Who's got a cold?"

It was as if Win Holland were trying to spare Forsburg. "It's Billy Siragusa," he intervened from his side of the table. "He just came down with it."

Mrs. Post's accusing gaze never wavered from the coach's face. "Why didn't you tell me?" she demanded.

"Thought you knew." Forsburg was laconic. "Billy said he was getting in touch with you."

Clementine Post colored. "I suppose he missed me," she said defensively. "I've been out a good deal."

"That must have been it." Forsburg's agreement bordered on sarcasm.

John Thatcher was interested in the tone of the disputants. This had been his first meeting with Forsburg. By all reports, the coach should have been the harried, deferential employee of a great lady. Today, however, he was playing a different role.

Jowdy's reaction to this bickering was quite different. "I thought Siragusa was supposed to be your big star. Isn't it worth talking about when he comes down sick?"

"For God's sake! He's got a cold, not a broken leg," Forsburg protested. "The play-offs don't start till next week. He'll be all right by then."

Mrs. Post was endlessly twisting the rings on her wedding finger. "I hope you're taking care of him."

"What do you expect me to do, Clemmie? Invent a

cure? It's up to him. If he went to bed early last night instead of helling around at Gruen's place, and if he takes his pills, then he'll be okay for tonight."

They glared at each other.

Thatcher was beginning to feel the way Victor Jowdy looked. "What difference does it make?" he inquired impatiently.

He might have detonated a bomb. Even Win Holland emerged from his reverie to join Milt and Clementime Post in rebuking ignorance.

"He's our first-string center . . ."

". . . the Huskies' high score . . ."

"Billy is our superstar . . ."

They all spoke at once, defeating one another's efforts. Thatcher amplified his original contribution. "But tonight's game, you told me, doesn't make any difference."

Mrs. Post bridled. For a moment she was the old Clemmie, high priestess at the shrine of the Huskies. "The fans come to see Billy, they expect to see him. We'd be cheating them if he didn't play."

The lineup in the room had jelled. Clemmie, Forsburg and Holland spoke for the world of professional sports. Victor Jowdy and Thatcher represented the forces of sanity. Dexter Younghusband was sadly torn.

"It doesn't make sense," Victor Jowdy said in his low-pitched, emotionless voice. "You've got a lot riding on that kid. And he sounded to me as if he was running a fever or something. Stands to reason you ought to save him up for your big contest."

Clemmie Post was more than polite, she was amiable. "No, you don't understand. Billy has an obligation to the public. It's not just a question of winning games. The Huskies have to put on a show, even if there isn't anything at stake."

Thatcher raised an eyebrow. According to Charlie Trinkam, Clemmie had flailed herself into a fury at the mere mention of Franklin Moore. Yet here she was, taking the opposite approach with Victor Jowdy. She was trying to make friendly overtures. Either Clemmie had decided, for reasons of her own, to be devious, or she had revised her basic thinking. Possibly she had finally realized that it was Win Holland, not his unfortunate creditors, who posed these recurring threats to the Husky status quo. But if relations between Mrs. Clementine Post and Jowdy were less frigid than Thatcher had anticipated, this was not true of those between her and Forsburg.

The coach was deliberately introducing a new irritant.

"Billy was telling me he'd like to be rested," he said blandly. "If he doesn't feel better, that is."

Clemmie had a thin skin. "You just said he'd be all right tonight."

"Maybe you'd like to talk to him yourself?" Forsburg was obscurely amused.

"No, I wouldn't!"

It was said sharply enough to silence the table. Milt Forsburg nodded as if at suspicions confirmed, then glanced around the room. "Anything else?" he asked. "Otherwise I'll be getting on."

Younghusband sounded disappointed. "We haven't settled about the intermissions."

"Don't worry about it. You're getting Grangier as a start. After that, somebody on the Huskies is bound to have a bad knee."

He was anxious to be gone but not, it developed, quick enough.

"I'll come along with you, Milt," Mrs. Post announced.

He halted in shrugging on his coat. "I was planning on running some errands before I go down to the Garden."

"Where?"

"On the East Side."

"Exactly where I'm going," Clemmie said firmly. "We can share a taxi."

John Thatcher received the impression that her response would have been the same if Forsburg's errands had taken him to Yonkers.

Punctiliously Thatcher saw his visitors to the elevator. By the time he returned, Jowdy was in full flight.

"That's a great team you've got. The owner doesn't care about next year's television contract, and the coach doesn't care whether his players are falling apart."

Holland tapped the papers on the table meaningfully. "What are you complaining about, Vic? You saw the figures. They're making money."

"It must be the miracle of the century. On top of everything else, they're using hospital cases to play with."

Approaching severance from the Huskies had relaxed Win Holland. "That wasn't fever with Billy yesterday, that was temper," he joked. "You heard the trainer yourself, Vic. And believe me, those trainers know more than most doctors."

"If there was nothing wrong with him, then who the hell does that kid think he is?"

"At the moment, he thinks he's God."

Victor Jowdy was disapproving as he turned to Thatcher. "You should have heard Siragusa. He was trying to give me a hard time, claiming that I didn't have the right to get an attachment. It's none of his business, of course. What I can't figure out is where he ever got the idea it is."

"Well, Vic, you've met Clemmie Post and you know how it is when women start managing the show." Holland was elaborately reasonable. "She made a favorite out of Billy Siragusa, and he thinks if he wants anything at the Huskies, he just has to yell hard enough."

"Oh, yeah?" Jowdy's dark eyes were shrewd. "And how long has the yelling been going on?"

Win Holland became vague. "Things have been uptight around the Huskies for the last month or so. Billy's taking advantage of it."

Thatcher doubted if the lawyer from Fresno would be content with this generalization. But apparently Jowdy could supply his own details.

"You mean since Moore was murdered?"

Holland sighed with relief. "I'm glad that's out in the open. I was damned if I was going to be the one to tell you, Vic, but I thought you'd probably find out yourself. Particularly after Billy's little spiel."

"Oh, I knew about it already. There's not much about the Huskies I don't know." Jowdy's assessment was convincingly impartial.

"Then, according to Billy, you were taking a real chance when you came out to Mineola."

Jowdy did not hide his contempt. "You mean those mysterious threats of his? He's just a kid trying to make a big impression. But I am worried about Franklin Moore, all right. Not because he was murdered, you understand."

Thatcher could see Win Holland was lost. So he asked the question for him, although he could guess the answer. "Why?"

"If there's that much interest in the Huskies, then I'd better move fast. Or somebody else will."

For the first time, Victor Jowdy smiled.

18

AN OPEN NET

"GAME TIME is seven-thirty," said Miss Corsa, preparing to depart for the day.

Was there a hint of triumph in her voice? John Thatcher, by dint of adroit footwork, had avoided seventy-seven games of the hockey season to date. But all winning streaks come to an end.

"Thank you," he said, a good loser if ever there were one.

There was no danger of his forgetting that the Huskies were sandwiching his day. Too few hours had been granted him for other weighty considerations—primarily the future of fish farming as painted by some optimists in Miami.

But at tonight's game, one of his chickens—The Year of the Husky Contest—was coming home to roost.

"I don't suppose you know the approximate time the

winner will be announced, do you?" he asked, knowing full well that the great unveiling was scheduled for the second intermission. When Miss Corsa did not deign to reply, he hastened to add, "Not only am I attending the entire game, I am subsequently going downstairs to the party for the team."

A hockey game, even followed by champagne in the locker room, was small price to pay for calamity narrowly averted. It had not been easy to persuade Bradford Withers that Jerry Drake should do the honors on behalf of the Sloan. PR, and John Thatcher with them, had feared that Withers on ice might crown the season in more ways than one.

When Thatcher and Withers reached the lobby of Madison Square Garden that evening, the faithful were already filling the escalators, eagerly pressing toward the upper tiers. Excitement and anticipation crackled in the air, as if the play-offs were beginning tonight.

"John," said Withers, disentangling himself from a fan club carrying a banner that read: WHEN YOU'VE SAID SIRAGUSA, YOU'VE SAID IT ALL, "there's still plenty of time before face-off."

Four small boys wearing Husky caps cut between them while Thatcher asked what Withers had in mind.

"Seeing that this is the last game of the season, we might go down and wish them well," Brad said.

Thatcher suggested that hockey players might be like opera stars, preferring to receive after the performance.

Withers agreed in principle. "But Clemmie's party will be jammed," he said. "Right now, there will be no one down there. Normally, I wouldn't think of it. But with tonight's game, there's no pressure. I think we can risk dropping by."

As was so often the case, he was proven wrong almost immediately. The corridor outside the Husky quarters, when they at last reached it, was overflowing.

"Other people had the same idea about seizing this last quiet moment," said Thatcher, raising his voice above the din.

Withers plowed on, an oceangoing vessel cleaving through a flotilla of tugs, to the only open door.

"Forsburg's office," he said informatively, disappearing inside.

Thatcher stepped back to let a large group of well-wishers exit before he followed. In the interval, Withers vanished.

"Listen, everybody," someone bellowed from the solid mass of humanity. "Clear out! We've got a game to play. The parties come later. Now, I want everybody out of here!"

John Thatcher, who could take a hint as well as the next man, found that the crowd had closed in behind him.

"That means you, too," the voice continued irascibly. "Talk to Billy after the game. All of you—will you get out of here?"

Slowly the logjam began to break. Through the remnants, Thatcher caught sight of two uniformed players ducking into the adjoining room.

"Come on!" came the plea. "Let's clear the room, huh?"

Thatcher posted himself to scrutinize the outgoing tide for Bradford Withers. Instead, Coach Milt Forsburg appeared, escorting—or ejecting—Mrs. Clementine Post.

"Milt," she expostulated, barely nodding to Thatcher, "Billy's cold sounds terrible. Maybe you shouldn't play him at all—"

Forsburg's face was etched with fatigue. Gruffly he said, "That's what that guy Jowdy said. Look, why don't all of you let me run the team—for tonight at least?"

Before Clemmie could reply, Win Holland loomed behind her.

"Have you seen Vic?" he asked, craning around.

Forsburg was not cordial. "He was down here a few minutes ago. Hell, everybody has been down here."

"I guess he's gone back upstairs," said Holland, setting off after Clemmie. "Well, good luck, Milt. I'll see you after the game. Clemmie! Oh, Clemmie!"

"Boy! It should be some party!" Forsburg muttered to

himself advancing on diehards still congregated around his desk. "Look, will you people please scram?"

When he finally tore himself away, Bradford Withers' dignity was unimpaired.

"Clemmie's sent down champagne," he said approvingly as Thatcher trailed him up the ramp. "It's a great night for the Huskies—and it must be a great night for her."

By the time they reached the auditorium, Bradford Withers' untroubled view of things received ample support. The organ was booming a spiritied medley of tunes; fans cheered the empty ice, the officials and even the maintenance men. The loudspeaker came to life as Withers and Thatcher reached their seats. "Ladies and gentlemen—the Vancouver Canucks!"

Across the rink, the visiting team skated onto the ice to a healthy greeting of applause, punctuated by ritual booing.

". . . and the New York Huskies!"

A dazzling arpeggio underlined the flourish. The vast audience was on its feet, yelling lustily. It took two national anthems to restore a semblance of order. Finally the referee conferred with the team captains—and play was under way.

The taut stillness of the face-off erupted into a ferocious scramble that resolved into a symmetrical ebb and flow up and down the ice.

"The game's starting off slow," said Withers knowledgeably. A full-throated roar almost drowned his words. The Huskies had disrupted the minuet. In four fast spurts, they advanced the puck into Vancouver territory. There was a tangled mass of players before the Canuck's net, a forest of sticks wickedly jabbing. The goalie flung himself face down on the ice, blocking a savage drive by Paul Imrie.

The galleries groaned sympathetically, the linesman swooped down on the puck. From both benches, players clambered over the rail to speed onto the ice and replace the starting strings.

One minute and forty-five seconds had passed.

From almost directly behind the Sloan box, a fan shouted a question: "Why aren't you using Billy?" His neighbors took up the cry and turned it into a chant. "We want Billy! We want Billy!"

The Huskies had taken command and were bearing down on the Vancouver net. This time, the goalie was not quick enough. A slap shot—and the Huskies scored their first goal. Players tousled the hair of Pete Levoisier, the fans responded generously. But the chant soon resumed.

"We want Billy! We want Billy!"

Billy Siragusa, however, remained on the Husky bench until three minutes later. Then, like a hero coming into his own, he responded to Milt Forsburg's wave.

John Thatcher's first impression was that Siragusa was less columnar than his teammates. Despite bulky padding, he skated with supple grace, his bare head held high. At last Thatcher understood some of the rhapsodies he had been hearing for weeks. Siragusa was a knight without his helmet—or youth as it has been idealized over the ages.

But it was when he started a one-man rush that Thatcher fully appreciated the magic that enraptured his admirers. With small, sure strokes, Siragusa stitched the puck along the ice, as neatly as a seamstress plying a needle—a stick's width beyond one opponent, inches past another. Surefooted as a cat, he seemed inviolable. Suddenly, shockingly, he was smashed to the ice by a bruising check from a Vancouver defenseman.

Madison Square Garden did not boo—it gasped.

But Siragusa was back on his skates. For the first time, his head was down. At breakneck speed he was racing the puck. A sudden curve, and he caught it, taking it to center ice, where he stood for a moment surveying the field, his stick poised.

He was not a hockey player to the men and women watching him with breathless attention. He was a young prince.

Slowly Siragusa skated out of Husky territory, deliberately toying with the Canucks. First a lazy circle, tantalizingly open, then a flick to the right, teasing the puck past an outthrust stick. Then, almost negligently, Siragusa passed to Imrie.

"Magnificent," said Bradford Withers, echoed by applause that was tribute, pure and simple.

"A remarkable performance," Thatcher conceded.

During the second period, the Huskies scored four more goals against the hapless Canucks, each of which was hailed with delirious joy. By now Coach Forsburg was letting his second and third lines carry the game. Every newcomer was tumultuously greeted, but at intervals the cry would come: "We want Billy! We want Billy!"

You could scarcely blame the young man, Thatcher thought, for seeking to exploit his immense popularity. Because Billy Siragusa was not a young prince, but a poor boy from Toronto. Hockey had given him the key to a golden future.

Second-period play was barely over when microphones appeared at center ice. Jerry Drake followed, clutching a sheaf of papers.

". . . tremendous response!" Drake's familiar modulations were amplified and distorted by the sound system. "It gives me great pleasure to announce the name of the winner of the Sloan Guaranty Trust's Year of the Husky Contest."

Unperturbed by isolated jeers, he paused dramatically, then reached into an inner pocket for an envelope.

With an assistant hovering nearby, he opened the flap with painstaking care.

"Mrs. Margaret Billars!" he yelped happily as a buzz rose from the stands. "Yes, one of the Huskies' lady fans . . ."

Thatcher closed his eyes briefly at this witless invitation to a Women's Lib raiding party. When he opened them, he discovered another matter he would have to take up with Dexter Younghusband.

Despite the envelope and the pretense of secrecy, Mrs. Billars was present.

". . . eighty-three years young," said Jerry, as two of his aides solicitously ushered a vigorous elderly woman to his side, despite her attempts to shake them off. "Congratulations, Mrs. Billars!"

Mrs. Billars responded with a curt nod.

"And you attend every game, do you?" said Jerry.

Thatcher was not convinced that this was enough to acquit the Sloan of charges of collusion. However, his attention was reclaimed.

Mrs. Billars signified that she did indeed attend every Husky game—by a tight nod.

"Well, now," said Jerry Drake, straining slightly. "And I suppose you're looking forward to attending the play-off games. . . ."

The galleries caught on to Mrs. Billars faster than he did. This nod sparked a healthy round of applause. Only then did Jerry Drake fully assimilate his predicament: he was standing in the middle of Madison Square Garden, before television cameras and microphones, with a woman who did not propose to say one word.

". . . proud of our Huskies, aren't we?" said Jerry Drake with his much-loved laugh.

Mrs. Billars compressed her lips and folded her arms.

Whatever frenzy this was producing in the television booth, where Dexter Younghusband was in charge, it did not distress the Sloan contingent nearer at hand.

Thatcher was mildly amused—and curious to see how Drake would extricate himself.

Bradford Withers, predictably enough, saw nothing amiss.

"This contest," he said, "was a fine idea, John."

Jerry Drake was now babbling nervously as he cast hysterical appeals in the direction of the television booth.

"Oh, it was nothing," said John Thatcher modestly. "I wonder which one of them is going to win?"

"But the Huskies are ahead four to one," Brad protested.

The game was never in doubt, and neither was intermission. Mrs. Billars, a popular winner, stalked off the ice without having uttered a single syllable.

This refreshing interlude came to an end too soon for Thatcher and most of the other fans. The anticlimactic third period of the Huskies' anticlimactic game began.

"We want Billy! We want Billy!" By now, there was an intimidating flavor to this demand. But the home-town fans had to wait until late in the period before they got what they wanted. There were only three minutes left in the game when Billy Siragusa skated back onto the ice to hysterical acclamation.

Before the cries could die away, Siragusa and a Vancouver wing were jammed together in the corner, battling for the puck. There was a confused flurry of sticks, a signal from the referee, then a storm of catcalls from the crowd.

"A two-minute penalty," said Brad Withers in disgust. "And with not much longer left in the game, I'm afraid that's the last we've seen of Billy tonight."

He had forgotten one technicality. The Vancouver power play swept over the blue line, wheeled with precision, passed the puck back and forth, then scored their second goal of the evening. Derisive cheers floated down, together with the chant: "We want Billy! We want Billy!"

"That's right," Withers reminded himself. "That goal releases Billy from the penalty box."

The timekeeper was already swinging open the door. Siragusa headed swiftly to the face-off circle. He was halfway there when, with his first departure from grace, he stumbled. His stick slipping from his grasp, he sprawled on the ice.

An affectionate roar showed that the fans loved him for his mistakes as well as his excellences. But Siragusa did not scramble sheepishly upright. Instead, he heaved over onto one side.

"What's the matter?"

"My God, he's hurt!"

Siragusa's arm jerked convulsively, then his whole body contorted into a fetal curl.

"He's in pain!" someone shouted as Siragusa was blocked from sight. Teammates and linesmen had skated up to form a ring around him. There was a moment of indecision before a Husky trainer stepped onto the ice. He was just approaching the huddle when one of the linesmen broke away to skate to the officials' table, shouting something as he advanced.

Thirty seconds, forty seconds passed.

"He's not getting up."

"How bad can it be?"

As if in reply, Paul Imrie turned toward the sidelines.

"Dammit, hurry that thing up!" His bellow was audible to the first row of seats. Those who could not hear him could see the desperate, imperative gesture he made with his stick.

For Billy Siragusa was leaving the ice of Madison Square Garden on a stretcher.

19

PENALTY KILLER

TEN MINUTES later the team physician was in Milt Forsburg's office.

"Billy's dead."

"Before you could even get him to the hospital?" Forsburg said incredulously. "God, that's terrible. I knew it was bad when he didn't get up, but I didn't think it was that bad. How in hell did he get hit? I didn't see anything, did you?"

Dr. Baines ignored the questions. Instead he said, "I've called the police."

"Have you gone out of your mind?" the coach exploded. "What do the police have to do with this? Christ, you've really balled things up now."

"It wasn't a natural death."

"How the hell can you tell? He could have had internal injuries. You know that as well as I do."

"This was no hockey accident."

Milt Forsburg glowered. "You're taking a lot on yourself, aren't you?"

The doctor looked at him pityingly. "One murder you

can soft-pedal, Milt. But after two murders, then every-thing comes out in the open."

The news was slower penetrating to other parts of Madison Square Garden. Bradford Withers, with that strange authority he reserved for social niceties, had said immediately at the end of the game, "We had better wait for fifteen minutes, John, and then go down to the dressing room. We want to assure them of our concern."

By the time he and Thatcher reached the entrance to the Husky quarters, the police were already there and a routine had been established. Everyone seeking admission was asked a single question.

"Did you come downstairs at any time during the evening?"

"Why, yes," answered a puzzled Withers. "We were down here just before the game to wish the team well. Actually we never got any further . . ."

Smoothly the policeman cut him off with an emotionless announcement of Billy Siragusa's death. Captain Kallen would be very grateful if the gentlemen would wait so that he could speak with them later. Perhaps they would follow this officer?

Thatcher stiffened at the mention of Captain Kallen, but Brad Withers was above such considerations.

"A fine young man," he said with appropriate gravity. "And such a promising career ahead of him. Tragic things, these accidents."

He was still producing a flow of banalities when they arrived at Room 306 to join a select group. As usual, the trainers were better informed than anyone else.

"It was cyanide," said a portly middle-aged man. "I helped with the stretcher and Doc Baines wasn't in any doubt. Sure, they'll do a post-mortem, but they already know."

"For Chrissake, that stuff kills in a minute or two. How could you give it to someone in the middle of a game?"

"You've forgotten the cold tablet." Another trainer shook his head sadly. "It was the only thing Billy took. You know how rotten he was feeling. I warned him not to take the pills before or during the game. But when he went to the penalty box, I passed him over the bottle."

His companions gaped.

"You mean they think you planted a cyanide tablet?"

With unshaken composure, he replied, "No. Didn't you see the way they latched onto the bottle? And the way they sliced open a couple of pills? They think somebody switched bottles. If that's right, a lot of people are going to remember those pills were sitting on Forsburg's desk for almost two hours."

Thatcher had heard enough so that his subsequent interrogation held no surprises. Only one part of his account really interested Captain Kallen.

"Did you notice anything on the desk?"

Thatcher explained he had been too far away to observe details.

"I assume Siragusa's cold tablets should have been there," he ventured, half expecting to be snubbed.

But Captain Kallen was forthcoming.

"I suppose the trainers are talking," he said without rancor. "But it will all come out in the morning papers anyway. The bottle that Siragusa had in the penalty box was filled with cyanide pills. We're not sure yet when the switch was made. But he slammed his bottle down on Forsburg's desk when he came in at five-thirty. And he promised not to take any until after the game because they're loaded with some kind of depressant."

Thatcher was thoughtful. "Theoretically, then, the substitution could have been made any time after Siragusa's last use of the medication?"

"Sure," Kallen agreed. "If he was following the trainer's instructions, he hadn't taken any tablets since noon. But one thing we've got to go on. Siragusa's bottle had lost the label on the back. The trainer remembers that distinctly. The murderer supplied a fresh bottle, with both labels intact. That's why I'd like to get hold of someone who took a good look at the bottle on Forsburg's desk."

"You think people's memories are that good?"

"You'd be surprised at what people remember. In the

meantime, I'm working on motive. And I'm learning a hell of a lot."

Kallen brought the interview to an end by asking Thatcher to wait across the hall in case anything further developed.

The room there was occupied by those who had already been questioned. As if by right, the owners and the coach had taken the most comfortable corner where a few armchairs were pulled around a low table that now boasted an overflowing ashtray. The players were sitting with their wives or with each other.

Win Holland beckoned to Thatcher almost eagerly. "I'm trying to talk some sense to Clemmie," he said. "Maybe you can help."

"You may call it sense," she retorted. "I don't know what's gotten into everybody tonight."

Thatcher did his best. "It's not surprising that people are on edge after what's happened."

She ignored him. "First there was Dr. Baines. Calling the police that way, without even bothering to consult us."

"What was there to consult about?" Holland asked wearily. The relaxed assurance that had marked him at this morning's conference was gone. There was stubble around his dark jaw and his hair was rumpled.

But Mrs. Post was not really concerned about the team doctor. She was simply listing minor irritants before zeroing in on her major complaint.

"And then someone has been talking nonsense to the police—about my giving Billy a lot of money. Captain Kallen kept harping on the arrangements for Billy's promotions. He even implied I might know about Billy's investments."

Holland did not sound very sympathetic. "Why can't you face facts, Clemmie? Somebody murdered Billy Siragusa tonight. And the way you've been giving him special treatment lately, the boys in the dressing room must have had it in for him."

"Don't be absurd, Win. That wasn't what Captain Kallen had in mind at all." She hesitated, the anger in her voice subsiding. "He seemed to be looking for some connection with Franklin Moore. But what hurts more than anything else is that someone should be violating our privacy. We've always made it a practice at the Huskies not to talk too freely to outsiders."

"For God's sake!" Holland blew up. "This isn't a question of a new defense. Of course Kallen is asking about Moore. He asked me about Frank, too. When you've got two murders . . . Oh, hello, Vic. Pull up a chair."

Thatcher regarded the potential new owner of the Huskies with curiosity. Victor Jowdy was still now identifying with the team.

"I don't know why the police want me to hang around," he grumbled. "This isn't any of my business. And what's all this about cold tablets anyway?"

Jowdy either had not asked Captain Kallen that question or he was pretending he had not.

"Poison," Holland replied briefly. "In Siragusa's pills. Somebody switched the bottle."

"What bottle?"

Win Holland had had enough. "Cut it out, Vic. You were with me yesterday when the trainer gave them to Billy. You made some crack."

"Did I?" Jowdy was uninterested. "Well, it's today they're asking about. I told them there was a mob traipsing in and out of the coach's office."

"That's thanks to Clemmie," Holland said sourly. "And her cute ideas about parties."

That reminded Clemmie of another wrong. "Billy said he wasn't staying after the game. You heard him. He was going on to a party at Neil Gruen's club. Do you realize that if the trainer hadn't passed the bottle to the penalty box, Billy would probably have died at the Golden Dove? And then the Huskies wouldn't have been involved?"

Both Holland and Jowdy began to reason with her. Soon all three were wrangling in savage undertones. Any excuse to get away would do, thought John Thatcher, catching sight of a familiar face. Without compunction he rose and made his way to the far corner.

Pete Levoisier, who recongized him at once, seemed pleased at the encounter.

"Honey, this is John Thatcher from the Sloan. You know, they're sponsoring the television," he said to the woman at his side. "My wife, Eileen."

Mrs. Levoisier explained the warmth of the greeting. "It's nice to see someone who isn't part of this mess," she admitted. "If I have to talk to Milt Forsburg or Betty Duval again, I'll scream."

Thatcher agreed that hours of intimacy on the night of a murder could be a strain. "Would you rather not talk about what's happened?" he asked. "I imagine the police have questioned the team very persistently."

Mrs. Levoisier did not look well. Although it was quite warm in the room, she was wrapped in her coat with her hands pushed into the sleeves. Her face was colorless with exhaustion.

"In a way, it's a relief to talk," she said. "I don't mind the facts, it's the hinting I can't stand."

Thatcher understood. "It is unpleasant, but murder inevitably spawns exaggeration and vague rumors."

With a wan smile she corrected him. "There was nothing vague about whoever ran to tell the police that I was in Milt's office tonight."

Pete squeezed her arm through the coat sleeve. "We explained that to Captain Kallen, honey. He believed you."

"Contact lenses," she told Thatcher. "Pete forgot them in the car, so I had to drop them off. I wasn't going to hide the fact, but someone was in an awful hurry to tell the police before me."

"They just wanted to know who came by before the game," Pete said.

"Well, I hope they're checking on Neil Gruen," she replied tartly. "I see he isn't penned up here with the rest of us. Why don't they concentrate on him instead of the Huskies?"

Pete had no trouble with that one. "Someone's been shooting his mouth off. The police know damn well how the team felt about Billy."

"Well, I'm glad." Eileen reversed her position. "I think you all ought to shoot your mouths off."

Her husband looked at her reproachfully.

"Don't you see, Pete? That bottle was there for hours. Anybody could have taken one of those poison pills."

"Nobody but Billy had a cold."

"I know that. But did the murderer? My God, Pete, you have all those play-off games. Every time you go into that dressing room I'm going to wonder if somebody has sprinkled poison around."

Pete Levoisier tried convincing Eileen that her fears were groundless. But Thatcher was developing misgivings of his own. Bradford Withers should long since have emerged. Yet the door had opened time and again on figures far more intimately connected with the Huskies. Players, management and wives had all been released. What could Brad be saying to keep Captain Kallen glued to his side with a full-scale murder investigation in progress?

It was another five minutes before this question was answered. When Withers finally appeared he was solemn, as befitted a responsible citizen discharging his civic duty. Nonetheless, to the experienced eye, he radiated lively satisfaction.

Good God, thought Thatcher involuntarily, what has he been up to now?

"I hope you haven't been kept waiting, John," he said, as courteous as ever. "But Captain Kallen needed me longer than I expected."

With sinking heart, Thatcher said, "What did he want to know?"

"First he asked me about who else was in the dressing room and what they said. Then he asked me what was on the desk."

He came to a full stop.

"Yes?"

"Well, there was a great deal on that desk." Withers turned innocent eyes on his vice president. "At first I thought it was one of those observation tests, and he was going to ask me something else. But he came back to it again and again. I thought it only right to satisfy him."

"I'm glad of that."

Withers became judicious. "Now I've decided he had trouble taking it in."

"That must have been it. By the way, Brad, what was on the desk?"

Brad was astonished. "Why, champagne, John. And while Clemmie is a fine woman, I couldn't help being worried. The Sloan, in a way, is responsible for the Huskies, and I wanted to be sure that everything at the party was first-rate."

"Yes," Thatcher said. "The Sloan certainly wouldn't want anything shoddy."

"I knew you'd agree with me. That's why I read the labels. I explained to Kallen that I wouldn't dream of doing such a thing if I were a guest in a private home."

"You read the labels?"

"I did," Withers admitted. "And then, because that medicine bottle was there, I happened to glance at the labels on it, too. Both of them."

"Both of them?" Thatcher echoed in a voice he did not recognize as his own.

Bradford Withers liked to make everything crystal clear. "Yes. The one on the front and the one on the back."

He had drawn a cordon around the people who could have murdered Billy Siragusa.

20

ON THE FLY

POLICEMEN all over the world are experts in the aftermath of murder. Inevitably they become sensitive instruments, calibrated to record deviations from the norm. By the time Captain Kallen had spent ten hours at the Garden, had conferred with experts at headquarters, and had reviewed the reports of his staff, he knew he was in for trouble. Certainly there were expressions of bereavement—from the lead editorial in *The Times* to his own son, whose bantam team would not skate that afternoon in deference to Billy Siragusa's death. But another sentiment, still muted and uncertain, lurked behind these formal observances.

The news vendor on the corner was an omen of things to come. "We've been robbed," he croaked, making change. "We've been robbed of the Stanley Cup."

Once the initial shock faded, several million Husky fans were going to see the tragedy in exactly that light. When that time came, Captain Kallen did not want to hear what city officials from the mayor on down would say to the police captain in charge—not unless said captain had already executed a warrant for the arrest of the murderer.

Unfortunately Brad Withers' artless disclosure simply made things worse.

"The hell of it is," Kallen said, dreamily surveying the wall of his office, "that Withers doesn't seen to be the observant type."

His subordinate's role in these self-communings was

that of devil's advocate. "Withers told the same story again and again," he countered.

"That could be because he was rehearsed, Joe."

Until now their exchange had been a formality. But at this point, Joe came back to earth.

"Can you imagine anyone rehearsing that bozo? Besides, that story about reading the champagne labels rang true to me. Particularly when he got red in the face talking about it."

Kallen sighed. "Okay, but look where that leaves us. Siragusa arrives at the Garden with a bottle of pills that has just one label on it. We've got a lot of witnesses to that. By the time Withers is nosing around, we've got a bottle with two labels. And who's had access to that office in the meantime? The team, some of the players' wives, the owners, and a president and vice president of the Sloan. That's who! Arrest any one of them, and we've got half of New York on our necks. People see the Huskies as the victims. They won't go for Clemmie Post or Paul Imrie in the cell block."

Joe coughed. "Victor Jowdy," he said with a wealth of meaning. "He's on the short list, too."

"Oh, so he's the one you like," Kallen grunted.

"I don't know if I do," was the frank reply. "But nobody in New York cares one hoot in hell about him."

"You realize that the guy you've picked is the only one without a motive. And he's got an alibi on the Coast for Moore's murder."

"Siragusa was sore at him."

"It would be more helpful the other way around." Kallen paused. "I'll tell you what bugs me about Withers' story. When you first look at it, it seems to let everybody in—everybody who had anything riding on Siragusa, that is. But suppose Withers hadn't noticed a thing. What would we be left with? One bottle when Siragusa arrived, another bottle when he died. So Withers isn't giving us anything extra when it comes to pointing the finger at the people who were in Forsburg's office. On the contrary, all he does is eliminate one man."

Joe consulted a chart, then leaned back and whistled.

"So that's where you're looking? I'll say one thing for you, Captain. You sure can pick them. If we have to arrest him, it'll make as big a stink as if we charged Clemmie Post."

"I can't arrest a man because a witness clears him completely. But I sure as hell can talk to the one guy who came into Forsburg's office after Mr. Bradford Withers."

When Captain Kallen was shown into Neil Gruen's room at the Golden Dove, he noted that Gruen was clear-eyed, fresh and alert. Kallen himself now had the drawn pallor of a man who has been without sleep or fresh air for too long. Everybody he had seen during the long night at Madison Square Garden had been similarly haggard. Even Phil Ferguson, roused from his office at nine o'clock, had been up too late listening to bulletins on his newest and deadest client.

But if appearances were any indication, Gruen had not only enjoyed a good night's sleep, he had begun the day with an invigorating sauna.

It was envy as much as suspicion that made Captain Kallen brusque. "You've heard that cyanide has been definitely established as the cause of Siragusa's death?"

Gruen agreed that the news had been on the radio for hours.

"I understand that you went down to the Husky dressing room last night."

"That's right. Just before the game."

"You say you've been listening to the bulletins, so you know that the poison switch was made then. Didn't it occur to you to get in touch with us?"

If Gruen recognized the accusatory trend of the captain's questions, he was not allowing it to ruffle him.

"I'll be glad to do what I can, Captain, but I don't see that I can help much. I wasn't down there very long. Forsburg didn't want a lot of visitors hanging around, and you couldn't blame him. Extra people are only in the way."

"In that case, why did you go down?"

"Just to deliver a message. I'd heard Mrs. Post was

throwing some kind of celebration after the game. Billy had already promised to come to a party of mine. I was simply reminding him not to spend too much time there. Give it half an hour and come to my place, I told him."

Kallen had been feeling his way. Now his voice sharpened.

"This was a party for Siragusa you were giving?"

"Sure—because the Huskies were going into the play-offs in first place. A lot of my customers are hockey fans."

"So Siragusa's a friend of yours. You throw parties for him. But . . ." Kallen deliberately built suspense. "But you don't bother to ask what's wrong when he collapses and is carried off on a stretcher. Everyone who had anything to do with Siragusa hung around the Garden last night— everyone except you."

Gruen had no doubt he could explain. "You've got it all wrong, Captain." He leaned forward earnestly. "This was a big party I was throwing. Some very important people were coming. I left the Garden during the second period to see to things at this end. When I got here, I went straight to the kitchen to talk to the chef and the wine steward. I didn't get the news until I came out front. Then my bar-man told me he'd seen it on television. He thought Billy looked real bad."

"And you let it go at that?"

"Of course not. You can't tell anything from television. It could have been a sprained ankle, or it could have been a fractured skull. I called the Garden."

"What did they tell you?" Kallen knew the staff of the Golden Dove would confirm this story, but would Gruen realize that there was a log of incoming calls to Madison Square Garden last night?

"A couple of thousand other people did the same thing." Gruen shrugged. "I got about three busy signals. Then the crowd started pouring in here. They told me that Billy was dead. TV had it an hour later."

"You gave up calling without getting through?"

"When they're dead, they're dead, Captain. Billy Siragusa wasn't going to do anything for me ever again."

"And just what had he done for you?"

"It was good for business, having Billy here at the Golden Dove," Gruen said coolly.

Kallen got the message. Neil Gruen was prepared to defend himself against suspicion of murder. He would not justify his general conduct.

"So Siragusa wasn't a friend. He was just useful. Is that it?"

Had the question sounded too much like a trap? The owner of the Golden Dove changed tactics instantly.

"What the hell?" He was grimacing wryly. "If you want the truth, in some ways Billy was a pain in the rear. But in other ways you couldn't help feeling sorry for him."

"You seem to be the only one who managed."

"I suppose you've been hearing how cocky he was," Gruen said. "He could be hard to take, but only the last couple of months. And anyway, you're getting the wrong slant if you've been talking to people like Clemmie Post and Milt Forsburg."

"Then give me the right one," Kallen asked comfortably.

A flicker of wariness crossed Gruen's face, but he did not hesitate. "Billy grew up poor. He took to hockey the way kids used to take to the Golden Gloves. It was the way he was going to pull himself up."

"You mean he had too much too soon?"

Gruen disagreed. "It's not that simple. I didn't start making it myself until I was thirty-five. But things were different for me. I never had all my eggs in one basket. When some deal went sour, I could go on to the next. And by and large, I haven't done badly."

There was a touch of complacence in this last, an invitation to behold a finished work of art. Kallen obliged and was tempted to agree. Neil Gruen was encased in beige suede slacks and an orange velours pullover. His black hair was carved into an elaborate frame, accented by silver sideburns and a wide streak over one temple. It all looked very expensive. Gruen had a question of his own. "Look, Captain, do you know anything about hockey?"

"Well, I watch the games."

"No, no, I don't mean that." Gruen waved a scornful

hand at a small television set. "I mean the way hockey looks to a player. Billy was a full-time professional by the time he was fourteen. Then, after junior hockey, he went to a farm team. In the old days all the players went that route. But now hockey's signing up college kids. They can always get another job. Billy never even graduated from high school. He was a very scared boy last fall. Then Clemmie Post picked him up. Suddenly he's a superstar! They're writing magazine articles about him, they're interviewing him on talk shows, they want him to endorse products. It was coming at him from all directions, and he lost his head. Given a year or two, he would have straightened out. It's a shame he didn't get them."

"Very touching," Kallen commented appreciatively. "But none of it explains what I really want to know."

Neil Gruen did not move a muscle.

"Why did you send Siragusa to Phil Ferguson? Why did you set things up so that everyone at the Garden had it in for Siragusa? What were you getting out of it?" Kallen rapped the words out.

Gruen deliberated for a moment. "Sure, I recommended a lawyer to Billy, I'm not denying it. Why should I? But you didn't get the rest of that from Phil Ferguson."

"Ferguson told us about Siragusa's claims on the Huskies—which we already knew about. Everything else, according to him, is a privileged communication," Kallen said ironically.

Gruen was saddened. "Now, Captain, I was just giving Billy some good advice. He didn't know how to handle his success. He was thrilled at having a swank apartment and meeting people he'd read about. He was spending like a wild man. He could have wasted it all and ended up fifteen years from now with a lot of debts. The Husky owners were planning to make a mint out of Billy. I put him onto a lawyer so he'd get his fair share—and sock it away."

"So you were just doing a good deed. You didn't have any other interest in Billy's affairs?"

Neil Gruen was examining a manicured hand. "You're going to have to be more specific than that," he remarked.

"Siragusa was talking about a cháin of fancy skating clubs. He was planning to start in a big way. And don't tell me he was so ignorant he didn't know he'd need backers. Did you hear these plans of his?"

"Yes, I heard them. Sometimes Billy couldn't talk about anything else."

"And were you going to be a backer?"

"I probably would have been. As far as I know, there was nothing on paper yet."

"Nothing on paper?" Kallen was openly challenging. "Siragusa told people he was ready to start, that he'd decided on locations."

"Billy was probably shooting his mouth off."

"But there was a market survey? Do you know that?"

Gruen was becoming uneasy. He had dropped his former loquacity. "Yes, there was a survey."

"Who paid for it?"

"I did."

Captain Kallen sat back, triumphant. "So," he growled, "you footed the bill for the survey, you were going to be a backer. Why were you so ready to finance Billy Siragusa?"

But Neil Gruen had caught his second wind. "A good investment, Captain," he said blandly, "is always a good investment."

Kallen was beginning to think he had tangled with an eel. He hastened to attack from an unexpected angle.

"And Mrs. Post? Was she putting up money for the same reason?"

Gruen took his time. "'Mrs. Post is the only one who can tell you her reasons," he said at last.

"All right, forget about her reasons. Was she shelling out for these clubs, too?"

"Billy never mentioned her."

It was said naturally enough, but the police captain pricked up his ears. Was it too restrictive?

"Did anybody else tell you she was going to finance him? Did she talk about it herself?"

"No." Gruen was firm. "Absolutely no one mentioned Mrs. Post to me in connection with Billy's clubs."

Kallen subsided, baffled. The answer was unequivocal. But he had dealt with literal truth-tellers before and he recognized the symptoms. Every particular was accurate but the total impression was misleading. Forcing the pace, he realized belatedly, impaired the efficiency of the inquisitor as well as the inquisited.

But he traversed the same ground several times before admitting defeat. It was Gruen's growing geniality, more than anything else, that finally convinced him his shafts were falling wide.

"And now what happens—to the clubs, I mean?" he asked in conclusion.

Gruen was at ease. "With Billy gone, I suppose the whole thing folds without ever getting off the ground." He reached for a cigarette. "It's a pity, a real pity."

Captain Kallen could not decide whether he was referring to the collapse of his financial plans or to the death of Billy Siragusa.

21

GOALS AGAINST

DEATH MAY BE the great leveler, but only in the better world beyond—as the obituary pages attest. In life, Billy Siragusa had occupied a modest niche in the pantheon that America reserves for its public notables. Death translated him. Throughout the United States and Canada he was mourned, even by those who had never known his name. Very few people can remain untouched by the poignancy of youth cut down, especially when it is unfolded before their eyes—again and again—by the magic of videotape.

For those few who can, television was ready with an extra throb. Cameras, accompanied by an unctuous interviewer, invaded a modest stucco bungalow on the east side of Toronto. Billy Siragusa's mother remained stony-faced; his father, midway through a description of the backyard rink he had once built, broke down and wept helplessly into his hands.

"The Siragusas," CBC quavered, "are not alone in their grief."

But Billy Siragusa was not only a fallen gladiator, he was also a murder victim. The front pages erupted: photographs of the blanketed body leaving Madison Square Garden vied with police releases about potassium cyanide; Husky players, their collars turned up against the cameras, were shown entering Centre Street; doctors, druggists, executives of Coldine, Inc., and the entire Vancouver squad were quoted.

Press agents for the Huskies came up with a dignified statement of shock and grief.

It did not suffice.

"Sure, sure," called one of the reporters crowded into Bob Riley's office. "But why can't we talk to Pete? For that matter, where's Milt? And Clemmie? How about Clemmie?"

Riley forgot that he was currently team spokesman. He put down his typewritten script and tried explaining.

"Come on, you guys. Be reasonable. We've got cops in and out of the dressing room. We've got photographers sneaking into the rink at Mineola. That's all we need—a bunch of reporters bearing down. Have a heart. The team has to get ready for their first play-off game. Things are bad enough—" He broke off, picked up his notes and began again. "That's off the record. Now, I've got a few things for you—"

"Clemmie isn't skating against Minnesota next Tuesday," said somebody from the back of the room. "Why doesn't she give us a break? We've given her plenty."

Riley shrugged. "Me, I just talk for the team. You'll have to ask Mrs. Post."

"She's not available," a chorus replied. "And what about Win Holland?"

"Look, I don't know anything about the owners!" Riley insisted.

"Are the police allowing the team to leave town?" asked a legalist from *The New York Times*.

"Yes," said Riley shortly. "The Huskies are cooperating wholeheartedly with the investigation." He glanced down and found a sentence at hand. "We all hope that it will be completed before the team has to travel to meet the North Stars. Now, I have a few words—"

"That's in three days, and the police haven't made a helluva lot of progress—not unless they're keeping something quiet."

"Have they talked to Levoisier again?"

"What about this rumor that Paul Imrie swung on Billy just before the game?"

This was too much for Riley.

"Listen! You got questions for the police? Ask the police. Now, do you want to hear about the play-offs, or don't you?"

"Sure," said one of his tormentors. "Tell us about the play-offs, if you haven't got anything better."

Riley took a deep breath, counted to ten, then began reading. "Despite the tragic loss of a valued teammate, the Huskies are holding practice sessions to prepare for their upcoming games against the Minnesota North Stars. They're proving they're real champions, that they don't knuckle under when the going gets tough. They're doing it because that's the kind they are—but they're doing it for Billy, too. He would have wanted it that way."

"Stop," said somebody. "You're breaking my heart."

Associated Press, however, hurt Riley even more.

"Now, where have I heard that before?"

Nevertheless the stories fabricated from this skimpy material gladdened many hearts—including Riley's.

As one headline put it: THE HUSKIES WANT A WIN FOR BILLY.

Clemmie Post arrived at the Husky offices with another

headline. She flung the paper toward Milt Forsburg as she entered, then swung around the desk with a flounce.

This headline was not aimed at sentimentalists.

POLICE PROBE LOCKER ROOM TENSIONS

"I thought we were absolutely clear," she said ringingly. "Bob Riley is acting spokesman for the Huskies, and no one else says anything at all. I want to know who's responsible for this."

Someone besides Riley had been talking to a reporter for the *News*. He had provided enough straw for an experienced brickmaker.

Forsburg shifted. "Somebody blabbed," he agreed. "But you've got to expect that."

"Anybody who feels like that," she cut in crisply, "shouldn't be playing on my team!"

She glared at Milt for a moment, during which he kept his eyes firmly fixed upon his shoes.

"Well?" she said finally. "Do you know who's responsible for this tissue of lies?"

"No," he replied without adding that he had a pretty shrewd notion of who had been talking. Most of his players were keeping their thoughts about Billy Siragusa to themselves these days. But Paul Imrie did not play it safe, on or off the ice.

". . . saying that Billy could get anything he asked for! That he was the only member of the team I treated fairly. Good God! When I think of what I've done for all of them—"

Unceremoniously, Forsburg broke in. "Win Holland was out at practice today," he said. "He didn't seem so upset about the story. And it's his team too, isn't it?"

She looked as if one of her dogs had bitten her.

"Besides," Forsburg continued ruthlessly, "the cops have already got the full story—they know how everybody felt about Billy. And they're a lot more dangerous than the newspapers. Now, if that's all you wanted, Mrs. Post, I'd better get going. I've got a lot of things to do!"

With an effort, she maintained her composure. "No, I

want to hear about the team. How are the Huskies doing, Milt?"

"What do you want me to tell you?" he asked. "That they're going to win it for Billy?"

This rebuff caught Mrs. Post where she was most vulnerable. Since the night of Billy Siragusa's murder she had remained in virtual seclusion. Wealth and privilege shielded her, while Forsburg and the Huskies ran the gauntlet. It was natural—but it was resented.

"We're doing the best we can," Forsburg finally relented enough to say. "That's about all I can tell you."

Clemmie tried to recapture her old authority.

"Perhaps I should move the boys into a hotel while they're preparing for the play-offs," she said. "I'd be willing to foot the bill—and it might be wise."

Puzzled, Forsburg studied her. "No, it wouldn't," he said. "Taking guys like Levoisier away from their homes would just make it twice as hard on them."

"There would be fewer distractions," she argued.

"Mrs. Post," Forsburg said, without a trace of humor, "some distractions the guys like. And then—"

She waited until he found words for what he wanted to say.

"Right now, it's hard enough practicing together. Nobody wants to be locked up with a poisoner. You ought to understand that."

Distressed, she put both hands palms down on the desk. For one terrible moment, he thought she might be near tears.

"Pete's okay where he is," he said gruffly.

She seized at the change of subject. "Are you starting him?"

"I have to," said Forsburg. "Not that he's going to take Billy's place."

But this time Clemmie Post did not follow his lead. "He's going to have to try. The Huskies are a solid team. They should be able to put up a fight. After all, they did finish in first place."

Forsburg was not encouraging her even by silence.

"First place—with thirty-one goals from Billy," he reminded her.

Petulantly she said, "Billy's dead. Can't we forget him?"

"Maybe you can," he said deliberately. "But we can't. We've got reporters crawling all over us. We've got cops waiting every time we come off the ice! We've got to go play in front of thousands of people—while everybody is wondering who killed Billy. Sure, we'd like to forget him. But it isn't possible!"

"All right, all right!" she snapped resentfully.

From under heavy-lidded eyes he watched her cautiously.

"There's another thing," she began evenly. "Your contract for next year—"

Forsburg stood up with the air of a man at the end of his patience. "Never mind," he said.

"I thought it might help," she said, trying to placate him, "to know that we want you back."

"Sure you do," he said. "Mrs. Post, would you want to talk about my contract if Billy was still alive?"

"Milt!"

"Look," he said truculently, "Billy was after you to get rid of me. You know it, I know it, and the police know it. So if you don't mind, I'll wait before I talk contract with you, Mrs. Post."

She too had risen by now.

"But, Milt—"

"Thanks anyway," he said, picking up his hat. "Oh, by the way, are you coming out to Minnesota with us?"

"No," said Clemmie Post. "I don't feel—"

"I didn't think so," said Forsburg. "I'll tell the guys that you wished them a lot of luck."

22

RAGGING THE PUCK

ON TUESDAY, the Western Division play-offs began at the Metropolitan Sports Center in Bloomington, Minnesota. The game was preceded by a two-minute silence in memory of Billy Siragusa. In a larger sense, the whole evening was testimony to his loss. The Huskies went down to a humiliating defeat, 8-2. For over two hours Jerry Drake was poignantly reminded of the *Death of Siegried*.

Wednesday night he moved on to *Twilight of the Gods*. This time the score was 8-0, in favor of the North Stars.

By Friday the leitmotif in Great Neck might have been *Sometimes I Feel Like a Motherless Child*.

"Aren't you going to do anything?" Eileen Levoisier asked in rising exasperation.

The focal point of the Levoisier living room was a broad, low fireplace, flanked by two sofas. At the moment Eileen herself was the only vertical line marring this predominantly horizontal composition. She was gazing at the sofas, each of which contained a man stretched full length. Except for one arm trailing limply to the floor, Pete Levoisier might have been laid out for his funeral. His eyes were closed and he did not answer his wife. Paul Imrie was constitutionally incapable of complete repose. His hands were locked behind his neck, his head was raised an awkward two inches.

"Have a heart, Eileen," he pleaded. "We're not the kind of heroes who get up and do things. We're the boys who lose games. And not just one. But—"

"I know you've lost two in a row," Eileen interrupted.

Imrie was now hitting his stride. "And when we're not having the pants beaten off us, we're down at headquarters explaining to a bunch of nits that we didn't kill Billy. Anybody who reads the sports page knows we'd have waited until after the play-offs."

"Oh, God, can't the police do something more useful than that? Anyone can tell that Pete wouldn't hurt a fly. You just have to look at him."

"Maybe *you* just have to look at him. The police seem to be looking at that picture of him belting Jacques Devereux," Imrie murmured.

Eileen knew all about that picture. So did most of the Western world by now. Her mother in Edmonton, Alberta, had called up about it. Pete had chosen the night of Billy's death for one of his rare shows of force. Rising from a collision, he had thrown off his glove and landed a haymaker. This was bad enough. But, as the film showed, he had also knitted his heavy brows and bared his teeth in a carnivorous snarl.

"It's so unfair," Eileen brooded. "If it had been you, Paul, it would have made a lot more sense."

Imrie grinned proudly. "Eileen, do I hear you right? Is that coming from the woman who landed one on Billy herself?"

"That's totally different. Billy was asking for it."

Imrie could not have agreed more. "That's what I always say when they start picking up their teeth."

Pete still had his eyes closed, but he was listening.

"I wish you two could find something else to talk about besides Billy. I'm sick and tired of the whole damn subject," he said grumpily.

This was so unlike him that Eileen was taken aback. "Oh, Pete, you're just edgy because you've spent hours being grilled by the police."

Paul Imrie intervened. "Eileen, light of my life," he said liltingly, "Pete isn't in the dumps because the cops have been asking him about his motive. They've been asking him about yours!"

She gaped at him. "You've got to be joking. Why me?"

With open enjoyment, he explained. "You've been too free telling people you wished you'd fed Billy rat poison when you had the chance."

"I never heard anything so foolish."

Like many people with a quick tongue and a long-suffering family, Eileen Levoisier had often been saddened and dumfounded by the unforgiving nature of neighbors and acquaintances. But she had exercised her license too long to start counting costs now. Pete might be thrown into black gloom by police suspicion of his wife. Eileen was merely irritated.

"If they're wasting time that way, it's no wonder there's still a poisoner running around the dressing room."

The results of this remark were not encouraging. Pete was still giving a fine rendition of a candidate for last rites. Paul Imrie had lost interest in the conversation and was about to fall asleep. Eileen realized that they were both tired, but she did not belong to the tribe that lies down under the blows of fate.

"You need beer," she discovered. "I'll go and get it."

If that doesn't work, she told herself, I'll have to start cooking. The smell of food had never been known to fail with those two.

Such drastic measures were not necessary. The clank of the tray revived them. Eileen stepped back, leaving the cans unopened. Pete swung his feet to the floor. He opened three cans, handed one to Eileen and stretched another across the coffee table. It was still a good six inches clear of his guest. Like a man fighting his way through heavy seas, Paul Imrie struggled erect.

Eileen felt as if she had moved mountains.

The rules of the game required that Pete and Paul be free from badgering during the first round. But the minute Pete discarded his empty, she attacked.

"You can't tell me you've been spending hours around that police station without some idea of what's going on. They must suspect somebody."

"Sure. You and me for starters," Pete muttered.

But Paul Imrie on his feet was a different man from Paul Imrie supine. He was quartering the room, a beer can poised for punctuation.

"Come off it, Pete. They're not wild about any of us as possibilities."

"They keep asking me about my skating clubs and how Billy was going to put me out of business," Pete said stubbornly.

"Yeah, and they've asked me how much my endorsement business slipped since Billy became a big name, but none of that makes any difference."

"Why not?" Eileen asked. "To someone who didn't know us, it might sound like a motive."

Paul was now on the balls of his feet as he prepared to one-two her argument. "Don't you believe it. The cops have got some sense. They know we're not worth anything if we're connected with a losing team. I got endorsements last fall because the Huskies were winning. We go back to the cellar and I won't be able to give my name away. And it won't do your skating clubs a helluva lot of good, either."

"We'll see about that." Eileen was bristling automatically. "But then why are they asking all these questions?"

"First, Kallen was really interested in us at the beginning. Hell, you can't blame him for that. I was going to kick Billy's teeth in, you were telling everybody about rat poison, and Pete was trying to mash him in practice. But Kallen realizes that what I said before is true. If we were going to kill Billy, we'd have waited until he won a Stanley Cup for us. Because say what you will—" Imrie was grudgingly appreciative—"Billy was a beautiful hockey player."

There was a constrained pause. Imrie had evoked the perfection that was Billy Siragusa on ice. Then Eileen cleared her throat and said firmly, "That was the first reason. What's the second?"

Instead of answering, Imrie cocked his head at Pete. Eileen had seen this kind of silent byplay before.

"Oh, for heaven's sake!" she chided. "We're not talking

about boys being boys. The whole world is going to know the inside dirt about the Huskies."

Pete was running a meaty hand through his thick hair. "Anyway," he said mildly, "I already told Eileen about the way Mrs. Post was behaving."

"Then you know the second reason," Imrie shrugged. "The cops want to know all about the special favors Billy was getting. They want to know how much it added up to. And they want to know why he was getting them."

"I can't believe it," Eileen protested, "if you mean that Mrs. Post was being blackmailed by Billy."

"She was acting plain crazy," Pete said.

"Yes, but you've got to remember that she *is* crazy—about the Huskies." Paul Imrie had come to rest, backed up against the fireplace with his elbows on the mantel. He was totally serious. "Look, Pete, you're never going to figure out Clemmie Post until you realize that she doesn't understand hockey."

"She's owned the Huskies for over five years," Eileen objected.

"She honestly thought that if she didn't give in to Billy, he might not play as well as he could. If Clemmie Post has done only what we know about, if she hasn't shelled out any money for his schemes, then maybe it wasn't blackmail. But you've got to admit, Eileen, somebody sure as hell poisoned Billy."

"He could have been killed for some reason other than blackmail."

Paul Imrie admitted that many people had been annoyed by Siragusa and some had been threatened by him, but he clung to one point. "Billy was making money for all of us."

Pete Levoisier had been staring at the beer tray, studying the circles of condensation as if they had a meaning. He liked to order his own thoughts before condemning those of others.

"You're both going off half-cocked," he said slowly. "The cops know we don't have two loonies in the team running around killing people. The reason they like the

idea of blackmail is that it ties Billy in with the murder of
that guy Moore. If you forget blackmail, what's left?"

Imrie produced a lopsided smile. Pete rarely called
down his quicker-witted companions. When he did, he was
almost always in the right.

"I'll give you that, Pete. We keep forgetting about
Moore because we didn't know him. None of us even
talked to him. We heard about his plans secondhand, from
Mrs. Post or from Holland."

"Even Milt Forsburg was on the sidelines," Levoisier
agreed.

"Of course, from the cops' point of view, Billy was the
wrong person to be murdered," Imrie continued. "You
can tell that from the way they keep harping on Jowdy.
And I don't know that I blame them. If Jowdy had gotten
that dose of cyanide, you could see some reason to it.
Maybe Clemmie Post was knocking off anyone who mus-
cled in on the Huskies. Maybe Win Holland was knocking
off everybody he owed. Maybe Milt wasn't chancing his
job on any changes. But that doesn't do you any good with
Jowdy alive and kicking."

Pete was very sour. "Mostly kicking," he said, remem-
bering some of Jowdy's comments yesterday. "He says the
Huskies don't look like a team any more."

Whatever somber thoughts this remark might have oc-
casioned were stifled by Eileen Levoisier. She had listened
intently to Imrie, and she had an idea. Afraid of making a
fool of herself, she said tentatively, "I suppose that Mr.
Jowdy didn't have a cold before the murder?"

Predictably her listeners reacted differently. Her husband turned to stare. Paul Imrie gave way to strangled
shouts of laughter.

"Eileen, you ought to be on the force," he said, upon
recovery. "Kallen thought of that one, too. He got all excited when he found out Jowdy was in the dressing room
when Billy's pills were first handed out."

Eileen's eyes were sparkling. "Then that could be it. He
could have said something about needing one himself that
confused the murderer. Maybe he was taking them and it
was an accident that Billy was poisoned."

Imrie shook his head decidedly. "No way, Eileen. Look, this was out in Mineola. You know what that dressing room is like—"

"No I don't," she interrupted.

"Well, there's barely enough standing room for us, let alone the equipment. The trainer gave Billy a bottle of pills before practice and told him to take one. Sure, we all heard. You couldn't help it, being that close. But the point is, Jowdy was with Holland right in the middle of us. If he'd said anything about having a cold himself, we'd have heard. Besides the man says he didn't have a cold. If he was a murderer, he might lie. But not if he was supposed to be the victim."

Eileen was discouraged. "All you do is say that my explanations are no good. Well, what other ones are there?"

"There's the one about Milt Forsburg," Imrie said instantly. "Personally I think it's a lot of baloney, but the police seem to like it. First Moore was going to change coaches, so Milt shot him. Then Billy was going to make Mrs. Post fire Milt, so he came up with cyanide. How crazy can you get?"

Eileen was ready to favor any theory that shifted suspicion from the players, but even she was doubtful.

"A winning coach?"

Imrie spread his hands. "I suppose it could have come to a showdown, but that was a long way in the future."

"There's another thing," Pete supported him. "You remember when the cops came out to Long Island just after Moore was shot? We were talking about Milt then, and Billy said he knew Milt hadn't killed Moore."

All three of them recognized the implications of this statement at the same time.

"Say, if Billy knew Milt didn't do it . . ." Pete began.

". . . then maybe he knew who did," Imrie finished.

"Didn't you even ask him?" demanded Eileen, who could not comprehend such a lack of curiosity.

Imrie explained to her. "That's what Billy wanted, for us to ask him a lot of questions. So nobody did."

Eileen ground her teeth.

"Anyway, we thought he was just sounding off," Pete apologized. "Probably that's all there was to it."

"And if not," Paul Imrie rounded off the discussion, "then we're back to where we started—blackmail."

23

STICK HANDLING

BETWEEN MAN and secretary there exists a relationship that can take many forms, as the Huskies' third loss in a row served to illustrate. At the Sloan, John Thatcher was given the opportunity to match Miss Corsa's high standards.

"The score," she reported when he arrived, "was six to one."

"A great disappointment, Miss Corsa," said Thatcher, repressing a temptation to cite the murder tally to date.

Without emotion, Miss Corsa indicated that Mr. Thatcher would find his mail sorted and waiting.

Elsewhere things were different. In the tower suite, Miss Prettyman fairly itched for her letter opener. Instead, she was treated to a detailed play-by-play account of last night's ill-fated action. Miss Prettyman (whose hobby was African violets) spent most of the morning supplying exclamations of insincere sympathy. Down in Public Relations, Gloria was fairly run off her feet, purveying endless cups of coffee to fuel a litany that began with muted lament, then escalated into stream-of-conscious melancholia. Even Mrs. Norris, in Everett Gabler's office, was not untouched. Everett believed in striking while the iron was hot. He dictated a lengthy memorandum to the chairman of the board advocating reappraisal, however agonizing, of the Sloan's decision to drop *Thursday Night at the Symphony*.

All over the city secretaries with better things to do were dealing, one way or the other, with the New York Huskies.

Oddly enough, one of the few places rivaling John Thatcher's sixth-floor suite in decent reticence was Holwin Enterprises.

"I'm sorry the Huskies lost again," said Judy, giving her eyelashes a last-minute touch as her employer appeared at the door to his office.

Win Holland shrugged this off unconcernedly. "Judy, we're going to be busy in here for the next hour. Hold any calls, will you?"

Putting away her paraphernalia, she promised to do so as Holland turned to rejoin Anton Dietrich and Victor Jowdy.

"Okay, Vic," he said, shutting the door behind him, "we'll be free for a while. You're lucky you caught us in. Anton and I were just leaving for the Plaza. One of our English suppliers is in town, and we're due to have a talk with him."

Dietrich, who had been pensive since Jowdy's unexpected arrival, nodded agreement.

"This won't take long," said Jowdy.

Holland sat down, tilting back his chair. His complete relaxation suggested that he had all the time in the world.

Anton Dietrich, however, could not contain himself. "You're planning a trip. Mr. Jowdy?" he said, glancing toward the two-suiter at Jowdy's feet.

"That's right," said Jowdy. "I'm going back to Fresno."

His observant, obsidian eyes registered the flick of Dietrich's head, as he went on: "You'll be getting my registered letter—but I thought I'd better stop by and tell you myself. I've been in touch with my clients. We've decided to drop our plans to attach the Huskies."

"Ah!" Dietrich breathed, spanning his temples with thumb and finger in a posture eloquent of intensive thought.

Holland had a slower reaction time.

First, he came upright. Then, with a glance at Dietrich, he pulled at his lower lip. Finally he said, "Well, you've really sprung something, Vic. I suppose I should have seen it coming. But . . ." He let his voice trail away.

Jowdy, a firm believer in not advancing unnecessary explanations, remained silent. Otherwise he might have agreed that Win Holland should have seen this coming.

But any surprise Holland felt took second place to other considerations.

"Dammit," he said robustly, rising to stare out the window. "I'm beginning to think that damned team is a jinx!"

This roused Anton Dietrich. "Events have been most unfortunate," he began. "It has not been a happy progression. However, perhaps now—"

This formulation made Holland laugh aloud. "Happy?" he said, cutting in unceremoniously. "That's one way to put it, Anton. We've got a couple of murders. And the whole team is going down the drain."

"As I said—"

But Holland ignored his associate. "Just when I thought they could be of some use to me—if for nothing else than to help take care of your people, Vic. Now they're not even good for that!" Exasperatedly he reached for a pack of cigarettes.

Training and inclination kept Victor Jowdy from responding to this unguarded comment. Beside him, Dietrich also showed a marked disinclination to pursue the subject.

Nevertheless Holland continued. "It's been a bad-luck team from the beginning," he said. "You've been right all along, Anton."

"I have simply deplored the amount of your attention that they have demanded," said Dietrich formally. "Sports may be admissible as a hobby. But, when there are other more important affairs at hand—"

"They've been losers right down the line," said Holland. "In more ways than one."

The Huskies' bad luck was the last thing his companions wanted to discuss. A quick look between them produced a silent meeting of minds.

"Maybe so," agreed Jowdy. "But let's just say that the Husky balance sheet doesn't attract us any more."

"It doesn't attract me a helluva lot either," said Holland over his shoulder.

Anton Dietrich picked up Jowdy's cue.

"That, of course, is your decision to make, Mr. Jowdy. No doubt you have given it due thought. But, if you have decided not to attach the Huskies, that leaves us with another problem, does it not?"

Victor Jowdy could speak swiftly when he wanted to.

"Exactly," he said. "We still expect settlement of our claims."

In effect, Dietrich deplored this bluntness. "That is well understood," he said with a hint of reproach. "We are all serious businessmen."

Win Holland would have done better to remain silent.

"You'll get your money, Vic," he said, his mind obviously elsewhere.

This nettled Jowdy, who turned from Dietrich to the younger man. "When?"

"Please," said Dietrich pacifically. "There is no need for unpleasantness. Now, Mr. Jowdy, we have been quite frank with you. Holwin Enterprises has had certain liquidity problems, primarily in connection with our British venture. But, as Win said, we have a meeting this morning—and I can tell you that the problems have now solved themselves. If you will wait—for, say, three weeks—we can fully satisfy you."

Jowdy looked speculatively across the desk.

"As Mr. Holland will agree," Dietrich added suavely.

"Hmm?" said Holland. "Oh, sure, Vic. We got caught in a cash bind—but, hell, that happens to everybody. It's all coming out straight now. There's nothing to worry about."

Guarantees, no matter who made them, no longer interested Jowdy. "I'll take that back to Fresno with me," he said, without enthusiasm. "But one thing I should make clear. We know you're good for the money, Holland. That was why my clients lent it to you in the first place. But it was a short-term loan, not a long-term loan. Your liquidity—well, that's your problem."

"As I said," Dietrich began, before Jowdy waved him to silence.

"The Huskies no longer interest my clients. But you have other assets. If you don't meet your obligations to us, I can find them."

"But we will!" said Holland easily. "Didn't you hear what Anton was telling you?"

"I heard," said Jowdy. "I just want our position understood."

"Believe me, it is," Anton Dietrich assured him. "Consult with your clients, as you must. But I am certain they will agree that three weeks is very little time to wait."

Victor Jowdy decided to leave it at that. "We'll see," he said. "But right now I've got a plane to catch."

Holland escorted him to the elevator, where he made a final observation. "Well, it's a real shame. You put in a lot of time and energy on the Huskies, Vic. Too bad it didn't work out for you."

There were many replies Jowdy could have made to this, but he confined himself to the most neutral.

"Yes," he said.

Holland watched the elevator doors close, then returned to his office.

"This team causes nothing but trouble," Dietrich burst forth. "Always I have looked on it as a waste! And, Jowdy—whom I confess I do not like—"

"He's not bad," said Win Holland.

With an effort, Anton Dietrich abandoned Victor Jowdy for a happier subject. "Well, one thing is fortunate," he said. "This decision of Jowdy's comes at a reasonable time for us. London will be showing a profit. Then, once the Whipple merger is completed . . ."

His shift to optimism about Holwin Enterprises went unnoticed.

"I wonder exactly what made Vic change his mind," Holland mused aloud.

Dietrich was one of those ageless men who could be thirty or sixty years old. Suddenly he sounded venerable. "No doubt there are sufficient reasons. Jowdy is a shrewd man—and a hard man."

"There are plenty of reasons," said Win Holland ruefully.

"But one thing I can say," Dietrich continued. "Prudent businessmen do not involve themselves in situations such as this. Murder, Win, raises—many many questions. You would be wise to remember that yourself. I still wish profoundly that you were disembarrassed of this team. But now I think there will be more difficulties than I anticipated."

Holland translated this. "You mean, nobody will want to touch them with a ten-foot pole?"

Dietrich assented with a resigned gesture.

"I know somebody who'd disagree with you on that," said Holland, reaching for the phone.

"Win just called and told me," said Clemmie Post, drawing her fur coat over her shoulders with a shiver. "Jowdy has flown back to California."

The heating system in the Husky offices was capricious. Outside, soggy rain fell. Inside, dingy light yellowed the room without camouflaging its seediness. Yet, despite her surroundings, Clemmie Post sounded exuberant.

Her companions did not.

"He was probably afraid that someone would shoot him," said Paul Imrie, ignoring a headshake from Milt Forsburg. "Or slip some poison in his cocoa."

Clemmie Post refused to be deflated. "I thought it might help the boys to know," she said eagerly. "Before the game tonight. Don't you see what it means? It means that the Huskies won't get managed by the NHL. Win Holland —and I—will go on running the team the way we always have."

Forsburg knew what Paul Imrie was thinking about how Clemmie and Win Holland had run the Huskies.

"Sure, we'll spread the news," Milt said. "Maybe it will

cheer everybody up. God knows if anything can, the way things are going. But I don't see how Jowdy's beating it does us any good—unless the cops were on his tail."

As if this were not bad enough, Imrie added glumly, "Besides, how do you know what Holland is going to do now?"

Bewildered, she stared at him.

"Well," said Imrie, "he's always up to something. First he's selling to Moore—" He broke off angrily. "Christ! Everywhere you turn, somebody's been murdered."

"That's enough about murder," said Clemmie, her color heightening.

This time, Paul Imrie did notice Forsburg's warning frown.

Clemmie waited until he had subsided. Then: "You don't have to worry about Win Holland. I'm going to be in charge of the Huskies from now on—the way I always have been."

24

AGAINST THE BOARDS

EVERY WINNING streak comes to an end. The Huskies had learned that bitter lesson in Minnesota. Now it was the turn of the New York Stock Exchange.

On the sixth floor of the Sloan Guaranty Trust, purposeful activity was the order of the day. Like generals preparing for battle, trust officers reviewed their strategy and deployed their reserves. Dividends went winging back into capital without touching ground, cash accounts were raided, clients yearning to sell were cozened into holding fast.

John Thatcher stepped from the elevator and paused to savor the atmosphere. He could have reconstructed the week's averages even if he had just emerged from an extended bout of amnesia. Every man was at his desk, voices rose and fell in sonorous dictation, typewriters thumped rhythmically. Human passion was conspicuous by its absence.

It was a double surprise, therefore, to find Charlie Trinkam waiting for him, prowling the floor like a bear at stake.

"That woman is a complete lunatic," he announced as soon as Thatcher crossed the threshold.

It did not require extrasensory perception to identify the culprit.

"Mrs. Post?" asked Thatcher, enjoying the thought of a clash between these two redoubtable personalities.

"Who else?" Charlie tried to relieve his pent-up feelings by another half-turn on the rug. "She wants me to sell out over half her holdings."

Thatcher's amusement came to an abrupt end. "Now? With the market falling?"

"Naturally. I don't call them lunatics if they unload during the highs."

"What does she want the money for?"

"Three guesses!" snorted Charlie. "For that miserable two-bit team of hers."

Thatcher became thoughtful. "What good is money going to do her? She can't buy the Stanley Cup."

"Who cares what's going on in that midget brain of hers? Clemmie wants to throw her capital out the window. Then she'll come bleating to me about her income."

She would not be the first Sloan client who failed to appreciate this interrelationship.

"How much can she afford to lose?"

"Nothing," said Charlie stoutly. He was too instinctive a conservator for any other answer. "That's why I said I'd drop everything to talk it over with her. God, I knew we'd be in trouble once Ed Post wasn't around to sit on her."

Thatcher murmured something tranquilizing. But he

was more interested in Clemmie Post's present actions than in her past restraints.

"You're going uptown to reason with her?" he asked, an idea forming.

"Reason with her? I'm going to read her the riot act!"

"Splendid. I think I'll go with you."

Charlie, intent on maintaining his steam pressure, accorded this offer only an acquiescent grunt.

Mrs. Clementine Post, however, hailed Thatcher's presence as a bonus.

"Oh, you were both able to come. Good. It looks so much more impressive that way," she purred. "Now, you sit right there. You're going to back me up."

"If you think I agree to any of this—" began Charlie.

Clemmie's eyes widened. "You haven't even let me tell you what I want. All you have to do is guarantee that I have the money."

"Not for long, at this rate," Charlie ground out.

"Now, Charlie, you just listen to what's happened and you'll see that I'm doing the right thing."

"I wouldn't rely on it."

"That's because you haven't heard the news," Clemmie said triumphantly. "Victor Jowdy has left town."

Bankers had their own way of looking at this.

John Thatcher nodded approvingly. "Very sound," he commented.

Charlie was even worse. "What did you expect, now that the Huskies have turned into a lemon?"

"Don't you see?" Clemmie was sitting bolt upright behind the desk. "He's not going to attach Win Holland's share. He doesn't think it's worth a damn."

Charlie Trinkam was willing to try anything. If Mrs. Post could be diverted into the intricacies of hockey, she might forget her financial schemes. "Then it's your job to prove he's wrong. Get in there and go to work," he advised stirringly. "Don't you have the big player drafts coming up in a couple of months? That's what you ought to be thinking about. You've taken a big knock losing Siragusa. You have to reorganize whatever you have left and decide how you're going to supplement it."

Although Thatcher applauded the attempt, by the second sentence, he could see it was doomed to the fate of most heroic flourishes.

"And do you know what will happen while I'm doing all that?" Mrs. Post demanded threateningly. "Somebody else will show up to take Jowdy's place."

"Not the way the Huskies are playing."

"You don't know the first thing about it." Clemmie was growing excited and her voice was rising. "I've been through this twice, and I'm not going through it again. I'm buying Win out."

Charlie now proved why he was so valued by the Sloan. Instead of foaming at the mouth, he began to speak, slowly and distinctly. "It is true that all sorts of people have been interested in picking up a piece of the Huskies this season. That is because they have been a winning team. But now that they're losing, everyone will feel exactly the same as Jowdy. He dropped the idea like a hot potato, didn't he? So you don't have to worry about anyone taking his place."

"It's not that simple." Clemmie's mouth had set in a mulish line. "I won't be safe until I make sure it can't happen again. That man that Win keeps so quiet about—that Dr. Dietrich—he's always after Win to sell. And Win listens to him. He pays much more attention to him than he does to me."

Charlie was still in there fighting. "But that was earlier this year, when it made sense."

"Well, I'm not taking any chances. I've made up my mind. All you have to do is find the money."

It was time for the kid gloves to come off. "And what are you going to live on then?"

"For heaven's sake, Charlie! Money isn't any use unless you buy what you want with it. And all I want is the Huskies."

"Oh, yeah?" Not for one minute did Charlie believe that Mrs. Clementine Post contemplated any retrenchment in her style of living. "You don't want your apartment, your maid, your place in the Bahamas?"

Mrs. Post was stung. "You know perfectly well that I live very modestly."

Charlie started to tell her how much more modestly she was going to live, but his strictures were interrupted by the arrival of Win Holland.

"Well, Clemmie," he said after a round of greetings, "what's the big hurry? I was coming to the game tonight anyway."

"Never mind about the game," said Clemmie, breaking new ground with each word. "I want to make you an offer. Yes, Win, I've decided that I'm now able to buy your share of the Huskies." She leaned forward earnestly. "And, so that there won't be any misunderstanding, I've asked the Sloan to be here. That way, you can be certain of getting cash on the line."

But Win Holland had not reached the refinements. He blinked and repeated, "You want to buy me out? Now?"

"That's right." Clemmie smiled broadly. "I know we haven't always seen eye to eye. But there's no reason why we can't sit down and do the best thing for everybody."

"Let me get this right." Holland shook his head as if to focus anew. "There's a game tonight. By the time it's over, the Huskies will be out of the play-offs."

"What does that have to do with anything? If I don't mind, why should you?"

"You're going too fast for me, Clemmie."

"Why should I go slow? There's nothing complicated about this. It's a perfectly standard offer."

She had not convinced him. "It may be standard to you," Holland said grimly. "But there's a lot I'd like to have explained."

"Such as?" she challenged.

Holland seemed to regret his impetuosity. He hesitated, then said, "Look, why don't we just forget the whole idea? Everything's upside down right now. In a week the pressure will be off and we'll both feel different."

"Forget the whole thing?" Clemmie gasped. "I want to get this settled here and now. And I don't see why you're trying to weasel."

"All right then, if you insist. Back in November the Huskies were winning and we were making more money out of them than ever before. You weren't interested in buying then. And at no point since have you made me an offer. But when we get two murders and a losing streak, and everybody else is backing off from the team as if we had the plague, you're hot on the idea. And you're in such a hurry, you can't wait a couple of hours until we know the outcome of tonight's game. There's something going on that I don't know about, and I don't like it."

This was plain speaking with a vengeance. John Thatcher wondered how Clementine Post would answer the indictment.

She did not answer it. She filed a counterclaim.

"If we're talking about people's behavior, what about yours? For months you've been ready to sell out to any Tom, Dick or Harry who came along. You didn't care whether they knew about hockey, or even if they intended to keep the team in New York. It's only for me that you have so many questions. Back in November *you* were saying that a reputable buyer was all that counted."

"And you were begging me to stay with the Huskies," Holland rejoined promptly. "Now suddenly you want me out—and pronto!"

"Why should I make any explanations to you? You've never made any to me."

"You don't have to tell me a thing. And frankly, I'm beginning to think I'd just as soon you didn't."

"What do you mean by that?"

"For Christ's sake, how did we get into this? Like I said before, let's simply drop it."

But this was the one thing that Mrs. Post could not do. "No!"

The squabble continued for another hour with no sign of weakening on either side. A charitable man might have ascribed the increasing acrimony to superficial causes. Mrs. Clementine Post had not expected to encounter opposition, and thudding against a brick wall has never improved anyone's temper. Possibly it galled Winthrop Hol-

land to discover that his simple nay would not do. But
John Thatcher was rapidly coming to the conclusion that
charity might be a mistake. He could think of different,
and more sinister, interpretations of this rancor.

It was safe to say that Charlie Trinkam was the only
person deriving satisfaction from the scene. Early on, he
had tensed apprehensively at Clemmie Post's lavish invitation to Holland: *Stop asking these silly questions and
name your price. I won't haggle.* But as each offer was re-
buffed, he relaxed. The Post portfolio was looking more
and more secure.

Thatcher was calculating how long the same demands
and replies could be exchanged when Clemmie Post remembered her obligations. Glancing at the clock, she rose
and picked up her coat.

"I can't waste any more time on this now. I have to get
over to the Garden. Somebody has to show up tonight."

"Game time isn't for an hour," Holland reminded her.

"Some owners stop by and wish the team luck. Of
course, that's always been too much work for you," she
said nastily.

Holland bit back his first retort. "I'll be there later," he
said with a snap.

Clemmie insisted on the last word. "Naturally. Now
that you've developed such an affection for the team," she
replied, slamming the door.

It was Charlie who broke the ensuing silence. "Well,
well," he said cheerfully. "Too bad you couldn't come to
an agreement, but that's the way the cookie crumbles."

Holland was still staring at the door. "I don't know
what the hell has gotten into Clemmie," he muttered.
"She's not usually such a harpy."

"She was surprised," said Charlie out of his newfound
kindness to the world. "She didn't expect you to give her a
hard time."

It was clearly insufficient explanation for Win Holland
but he, too, was conscious of the timetable. "I suppose I'd
better grab a sandwich and get over there," he said, reluctance in every word. "Look, there's plenty of room in the
box. You two wouldn't like to come along, would you?"

"No, no," said Thatcher and Trinkam as one man.

This elicited a weak grin. "I don't blame you. I'm not looking forward to being cooped up with Clemmie."

"She'll get over it," Charlie encouraged him. "She thought if you were willing to sell to Franklin Moore, you'd sell to her."

The grin disappeared. "There's been a change since then," Holland said tightly. "Like two murders."

Only one part of Winthrop Holland's program had held attraction for Charlie and Thatcher. They too went in search of food.

"We should have realized what it would be like a block from the Garden," Trinkam said an hour later.

They were the only two patrons of the Iron Horse interested in their steaks. Men were lined three deep along the bar, eyes glued to a giant television screen. The air reverberated with Jerry Drake's hoarse voice.

". . . To Imrie . . . pass to Levoisier . . . Breton cuts in . . . steals the puck . . . two on one . . . save by Duval. Oh, what a save!"

The tumult transmitted from the Garden was echoed by ragged cheers within the restaurant.

"Good evening," said a voice above them. "Not taking in the game?"

Thatcher did not at first place the square-faced solidly built man. Charlie was quicker off the mark.

"Captain Kallen, isn't it?" he said joyfully. "Have you been watching it?"

Kallen shook his head. "Just taking a look around the Garden."

"If you've come in for something to eat, join us." Charlie was already pulling out a chair.

"Glad to."

Something in his voice told Thatcher that Kallen was not going off duty. But routine was suspended until the appearance of a corned-beef sandwich and a stein of beer. Then:

"You know, it's quite a coincidence my running into you tonight."

Charlie and Thatcher kept straight faces. They had both deduced that the Husky office was under surveillance.

"How so?" asked Thatcher amiably.

"I'd like to hear how bankers look at the Huskies," said Kallen, carefully removing traces of foam from his lips. "You know, there's a lot of big money connected with that team. Everybody's a millionaire. Or else they're making damned good money—and planning to make more. We're spending more time digging into business than anything else."

"We'll be glad to tell you what we can," said Thatcher. "Business can cover fairly broad ground, though."

From Franklin Moore to Clemmie Post, he thought to himself. With several other items—such as Billy Siragusa's machinations and Pete Levoisier's investments—in between.

But the police knew more about this, or most of this, than he did.

Kallen then jolted him. "That's true," he said. "But something came up, just this afternoon. I'd like to hear what you think about it."

Charlie froze and Thatcher almost complimented Kallen on his sources of information before the police captain continued: "Victor Jowdy. He flew back to Fresno today."

"So I understand," said Thatcher, still watchful.

Kallen shot him a look from under lowered brows. "Now, I don't want to say we've got anything against Jowdy. Sure, he was here. He had the opportunity—just like everybody else. We didn't have any reason to hold him. Or even to ask him to stay. It looks as if he told us everything he knew." He paused. "But then, all of a sudden, he takes off. And now, he's a continent away."

"His business here was finished," Charlie said. "It was natural for him to want to go home."

Captain Kallen took issue with this. "I thought his business was to buy out Holland's share of the Huskies."

Thatcher put down his fork. "Just a minute, Captain," he said with a glance at Charlie. "Jowdy was not going to buy Holland's share of the Huskies. He was going to attach it."

Even as he spoke, he wondered if Kallen were being disingenuous. Victor Jowdy's flight to California was not the only thing that had occurred recently.

"That's right," said Kallen. "But it boils down to the same thing, doesn't it?"

Thatcher chose his words with care. "Not quite," he said. "The end result might be the same—a change in the effective ownership of the Huskies. But the process—well, that's quite different."

He saw that Kallen was listening attentively and added, with a small smile, "You might say that very different forces are at work."

Charlie put it into vernacular. "Like red ink and black ink," he said.

"How do you mean?" Kallen asked.

"Buyers," said Thatcher, "are interested in an advantageous price—almost always in relation to time. You buy when the price is low and sell when it's high."

"Sure," said Kallen. "But attaching a property is the same, isn't it?"

"In many ways it's the reverse," said Thatcher. "Anybody attaching a property is not comparing values over time but comparing two values at one specific time—in this case, the asset to be attached and the debt to be satisfied. So, anybody thinking about an attachment is likely to act when the price is high—" He broke off for a moment.

"So," said Kallen, "it would make sense to buy the Huskies now, but not to attach them."

"Yes," said Thatcher, barely listening to him.

Charlie had been alerted by Thatcher's hesitation.

"John!" he exclaimed. Then he, too, fell silent.

Kallen was openly disappointed. "It's a shame," he said. "It looked good. Jowdy makes a sudden decision and flies home—"

Thatcher found himself providing a testimonial for a man he barely knew.

"Of course, I don't know Jowdy's reasoning," he said,

"but his actions make excellent sense to me. Sports fans may talk about waiting until next year. But any lawyer knows that time is valuable."

"Then, what I should look for," said Kallen, "is somebody who wants to buy the Huskies now. Right?"

With Clemmie Post's offer and Win Holland's refusal still ringing in their ears, neither Charlie Trinkam nor John Thatcher was going to rush into speech. Fortunately, a third Sloan voice rescued them.

"Score! Score! Score!"

Jerry Drake was screaming from a Madison Square Garden throbbing with pandemonium. The bar at the Iron Horse erupted.

"Levoisier scores again! The Huskies lead—three to two! With seven seconds left to play . . . five . . . four . . . three . . . two . . . it's *all over!* The Huskies win!"
Kallen had to lean forward to hear.

"There is something I think we could discuss," said Thatcher, sorting out his thoughts.

Charlie was on the verge of protest.

"About somebody wanting to buy the Huskies?" Kallen asked implacably.

Thatcher looked up at the television set.

". . . they're mobbing Levoisier. And Duval! The Huskies win it. Three to two. They're still in the play-offs. The never-say-die Huskies . . ."

"Not quite," said John Putnam Thatcher.

25

OFF SIDE

FROM THE Iron Horse to the Sloan Guaranty Trust was
no significant distance in time or space.

"Pete Levoisier—what a clutch performance," said
Billings the following morning. "The greatest game he's
ever played."

John Thatcher repeated an observation he had made to
Captain Kallen in a different context. "He could scarcely
have timed it better."

"An old pro," said Billings, who could give Levoisier at
least twenty years. "He's always been a money player, and
experience tells."

Stepping out of the elevator, Thatcher encountered one
of his own gnarled veterans.

"Surely last night was the final game of this intermina-
ble season," Everett Gabler was saying. "Good morning,
John."

Dexter Younghusband was cut to the quick. "But Levoisier saved the game! He scored the hat trick! Good
God—the Huskies are still alive!"

Dismissing hat tricks as jargon—whether of hockey or
PR it was difficult to tell—Everett said, "Presumably that
means another game tonight. John, I want a word with
you."

It had always taken more than a lengthened stride to
shake Gabler. But, trotting behind them, Younghusband
demonstrated his own brand of tenacity. "No, no," he
squeaked. "There are two days off. Thank God, the Huskies get a breathing space—"

190

Everett was in a tetchy mood this morning. "Breathing space, ha! Possibly that means the Sloan will be allowed to forget hockey, for a few hours if no more."

He was uttering this heresy as they entered Miss Corsa's office, and Younghusband swiftly tried capitalizing on this opposition error.

"Miss Corsa," he said breezily. "Wasn't last night tremendous? To think, there were people who wrote the Huskies off!"

He had misjudged his woman. Rabid fan or not, Miss Corsa's first loyalty from nine to five lay elsewhere. No frailty of hers was going to expose Mr. Thatcher to the tender mercies of his subordinates.

With utmost confidence, Thatcher said, "Good morning, Miss Corsa. Now, I have a full docket, don't I?"

Without batting an eyelash she agreed.

"The Pleydell estimates," Everett protested.

"Possibly later this afternoon," said Thatcher.

Younghusband was still lost in the stars. "John, listen to the brain wave we've had," he said, including Miss Corsa in a proud smile. "A documentary short, to be distributed by the Sloan. We'll call it *Husky Highlights*."

Sheer willpower kept Thatcher heading for his desk, despite this tempting target.

Miss Corsa herself, however, was not above seizing opportunities. Minutes later she appeared in his office, dictation pad in hand.

Thatcher swiveled to face her. "Possibly later this afternoon," he said brazenly. He had not cleared the decks to deal with his backlog of correspondence.

Miss Corsa suspected as much. Nevertheless, sauce for the gander did not sit well with her. She withdrew, trailing waves of silent rebuke.

Unrepentantly, Thatcher returned to the window. Contrary to appearances, he was not wasting moments that could be better spent on the Pleydell estimates. In fact, he was anticipating the PR department by mentally running off a few reels of his own. But his shooting script for *Husky Highlights* was not confined to ice time. And the commentary was not supplied by Jerry Drake. There were too many other color men . . .

A hockey player interested in business.

A businessman interested in hockey.

A woman who knew about both.

And, of course, Captain Kallen. At the Iron Horse, he had digested Thatcher's short review of commercial practice, then supplied the conclusion.

"That could explain both murders, couldn't it?"

Even though the Sloan was treading warily, Charlie Trinkam went one step further.

"My God, John," he said. "That's why the murders happened when they did, isn't it?"

Thatcher was not ready to answer questions, except indirectly. "Hockey," he said slowly, recalling a conversation in Central Park, "is a game of timing. People keep telling me that—as if timing weren't decisive in other spheres as well."

Captain Kallen quickly took this up.

"Like police work," he said, frowning at the packet of sugar he was fingering. "The hell of it is, we've got to go through channels. And by then it may be too late."

Thatcher did not pretend to misunderstand. Nor did he reply that the Sloan Guaranty Trust had to use channels as well. And in this instance, one of them was definitely closed.

For a moment, only Jerry Drake's voice burbling in the background had broken the silence. Then Kallen smiled blandly. "Unless, of course, someone brings things to a head."

"I suppose that's possible," Thatcher mused. "Although exactly how remains to be seen."

Captain Kallen then proved he was a realist. With a hopeful gleam in his eye, he said, "Well, thanks for your cooperation, Mr. Thatcher. *And* Mr. Trinkam. I guess we'll have to wait to see what happens."

Once Captain Kallen had left, Charlie Trinkam boiled over. "Now he wants the Sloan to gift-wrap his murderer for him."

A good night's sleep had settled the problem of which ribbon to use. Thatcher was still wondering how to tie the bow when Miss Corsa reappeared. "Mr. Withers is on the line," she announced, offering him another chance to shirk his duty.

But, in leaving her desk, she herself had opened the way for a blockade runner. Insouciantly Charlie Trinkam sailed in.

"Good," said Thatcher, carefully pausing before he picked up the receiver. "Charlie, I want to talk to you."

Not about Northern Illinois Gas, Charlie correctly inferred. Without regret, he laid a report in Thatcher's inbasket and leaned back to eavesdrop.

"Yes, Brad?"

"John, I've had an idea," came the dread words. "The Huskies are flying out to Minnesota tomorrow night at about five o'clock. It just occurred to me . . ."

Déjà vu assumed new terrors with Withers on the premises, thought Thatcher as he replied, "You mean that instead of a welcome home, the Sloan could organize a hail and farewell?"

That was not the way Brad cared to put it.

"I'm sure it isn't," said Thatcher bracingly. "Why don't you discuss it with Younghusband, Brad? I'm going to be a little too busy today for the Huskies. . . ."

With this prevarication, he escaped.

Charlie applauded. "Now that I come to think of it," he said, "they're made for each other. You've heard about 'The Face on the Cutting Room Floor'?"

"It will keep both of them innocently occupied and out of harm's way," said Thatcher, reaching for the buzzer. "At least until the Huskies fly out of town. I'd like a clear field."

"For what?" asked Charlie.

"To clear up a piece of unfinished business. Ah, Miss Corsa. I have some calls I'd like you to place, if you will. One of them will have to wait until lunchtime."

The rest of his instructions were enough to alert Charlie even before Thatcher finished by saying, ". . . then this afternoon, I'll want to talk to Captain Kallen."

Miss Corsa did not linger to hear Charlie's comment.

"He's already thanked us for our cooperation, John," he said.

"Yes indeed," said Thatcher. "I merely propose to see that we deserve it."

"Sure," said Charlie. With a lift of his chin, he indicated the phone. "So we cooperate with the police. How much cooperation do you think the Sloan is going to get from there?"

Thatcher had already considered this. "About as much as the trout gives the fisherman. I'm not relying on cooperation, Charlie, but on self-interest. Fortunately we have the right bait."

Charlie was openly admiring. "Well, John, that's one helluvan applecart you're kicking over."

"Nonsense," said Thatcher. "All we are doing is throwing off some close timing."

"As in hockey?" Charlie suggested.

"As in hockey," Thatcher agreed. "If nothing else, I think we may show a lot of people that Pete Levoisier is not the only . . . er, money player around."

It was two hours before the Huskies were scheduled to depart for Minnesota, and Charlie Trinkam's office was not where Mrs. Clementine Post wanted to be.

"It's getting late," she said, her crossed leg marking each passing second with the regularity of a pendulum. "I have to pick up my bag, then get out to La Guardia . . ."

Snapping his fingers, Charlie said, "That's right. You're traveling with the team, aren't you?"

"As I have told you several times," she replied tartly. "I decided I simply had to. All this can wait until I get back!"

"All this" was the massive analysis of the Post portfolio on Charlie's desk.

With as much delay as he could muster, he opened a folder. "I wanted to look into your tax situation. Now, if you sell these Southern Railway bonds, you might . . ."

"Charlie!" she said, sounding dangerous.

"Well, Clemmie," he defended himself, "you seem quite

determined to buy Win Holland out. You're not willing to accept his refusal—"

"I am not," she declared. "Sooner or later he'll sell."

Charlie abandoned the Southern Railway. "So, you're going to be making him another offer, aren't you?"

"Whenever and wherever I get the chance," she said forthrightly. "I would have gone over to talk to him today if you hadn't called!"

"There you are," he said triumphantly. "If you insist on going ahead, then you've got to know where you stand. Hell, the two of you might settle things out in Minnesota, for all I know. There's nothing much else to do there."

He was congratulating himself that he knew the way to a woman's heart when she surprised him.

"I'm going out to Minnesota to watch the Huskies win two games."

"Sure, sure."

"And we can talk about business when I come back."

She rose and began collecting her belongings. Charlie, with a smile calculated to charm birds out of trees, introduced another ploy.

"Hold it just a little longer, Clemmie. I need your signature on—now, where is it?"

Halfway into her coat, she watched him rooting around. Then, to his dismay, she said acutely, "Charlie, what is all this?"

"It's here somewhere," he murmured, leaning down to search the bottom drawer.

"You got me down here—and you've been trying to keep me. Why?"

"I need your signature—"

It did not wash.

"Is something happening?" she demanded, her voice rising. "Charlie . . . ?"

With an uninfectious laugh, he replied, "Happening? What could be happening? Clemmie you've got a case of pre-game nerves!"

"Too many things could be happening," she replied in a cold voice. "I'm going. Unless—you're not trying to keep me here long enough to miss my plane, are you?"

Putting on the best face he could, he said, "Of course I'm not. We'll talk about your portfolio once you get back. And Clemmie—I want to wish you all the luck in the world."

This sincerity backfired immediately.

"Nothing on earth is going to prevent me from going out to Bloomington," said Clemmie with narrowed eyes.

"Of course not," said Charlie Trinkam.

Only after she left did he mop his brow.

An hour before takeoff Milt Forsburg and Paul Imrie hurried up to the terminal where Pete Levoisier was standing, garment bag slung over his shoulder. Beside him was Eileen.

"What's this?" Imrie asked, as if the navy-and-red suitcase at her feet did not tell its own story.

"I've just decided," she said defiantly. "I'm going out to Minnesota too. I'm sick and tired of watching games on television. Does anybody besides my husband have any objections?"

Sheepishly Levoisier stooped to pick up her bag. "All I said was, who was going to keep an eye on the kids?"

"The kids can take care of themselves," she replied, following him inside. "They're not the ones who are in trouble."

Forsburg and Imrie, trailing close behind, exchanged glances.

"Of course," Eileen continued, "I'm not flying out in your charter, the way Mrs. Post is. I've got to take a commercial flight. But I'm sure I'll have a chance to talk to her out there!"

Her husband, plodding on ahead, did not reply.

"Cut it out, Eileen," Forsburg grunted. "Look, I can't stop you if you insist on coming—"

"I'd like to see you try!" she snapped.

"But I want Pete's mind on hockey—not on anything else."

She flushed angrily. "Pete's mind is on hockey," she said. "He proved it the other night. Where would you be now, if it weren't for Pete?"

"Take it easy," Forsburg said, lowering his voice. "You don't want to make Pete sound like Billy, do you?"

"He couldn't if he tried," she said. "And you know it!"

They were glaring at each other when Pete came to a halt by a bank of seats.

"Oh no, you don't," said Forsburg, seeing the garment bag deposited. "You're coming to the lounge with the team."

"I just thought I'd wait a while with Eileen," Levoisier began.

Forsburg was at the end of his patience. "I can't stop Eileen. But right now, I want you—and all the Huskies—in one place where I can keep an eye on you. That's the lounge. Now come on, Pete."

Paul Imrie was ready to second Levoisier when Eileen looked up from her chair.

"Go on, Pete," she said steadily. "I'll be all right."

"I don't like to leave you," he mumbled, embarrassed.

Her voice sharpened. "Go on. I'll be fine. And I'll see you tonight!"

"God willing," Paul Imrie added jocularly.

Eileen Levoisier was serious. "That's right," she said. "God willing."

"Hey, mister," said the cabbie. "You forgot your paper."

Pocketing his change, Victor Jowdy reached inside to retrieve the San Francisco *Chronicle,* although he already had assimilated the one fact that concerned him. The New York Huskies were leaving town in half an hour.

The receptionist at Holwin Enterprises still sounded helpless. "Mr. Holland hasn't come back yet."

"You're sure he's not going to Minnesota?" Jowdy demanded, just as he had earlier by phone from the airport.

Before she could reply, Dr. Anton Dietrich emerged from his office, topcoat over one arm. Hurrying forward, he caught sight of the visitor.

"Mr. Jowdy," he said. Meticulously he set down his old-fashioned briefcase and extended a hand. "You are back. I only wish you had given us some notice."

With the ghost of a smile, Jowdy said, "It was a sudden decision on my part."

Dietrich nodded. "Unfortunately, I am required to leave immediately. I am flying to London this very evening. Win, no doubt, will be back in minutes. Now I am afraid that you must excuse me . . ." Bending over for the briefcase, he glanced at the receptionist.

"Now, Judy. I shall be in touch. You have my address, and my telephone number . . ."

He was gone before she could get a word in. Shrugging, she returned to the problem of Jowdy. "Maybe," she said, "you'd like to wait in Mr. Holland's office."

It was a long twenty minutes for Victor Jowdy. He had made three trips to the door before he was rewarded by the sight of Win Holland striding into the office.

"Listen, Judy," Holland began apologetically, "I know it's time for you to leave, but I'd like you to stay for just a few minutes. I've got a letter—"

"Hello, Win," said Victor Jowdy.

In unfeigned astonishment, Win Holland turned to him. "Why, Vic," he said, forcing a smile, "what brings you back?"

"The same as before" said Jowdy.

"The same—" Holland rubbed his jaw. "Oh, my God, you don't mean you've changed your mind. You're going to attach, after all?"

Jowdy's brief concurrence made him roll his eyes slightly. "Sweet Jesus," he said. "Well, I suppose we'll have to chew it out. Judy, you can go. Oh, ask Dr. Dietrich—"

She had been waiting for this. Holland was already on his way into his own office when she spoke.

"Dr. Dietrich's left," she reported. "He said he had to go to London."

Holland's mouth fell open. "London?" he repeated, turning slowly like a man reeling from one blow too many.

"That's what Dr. Dietrich said, didn't he?" she appealed to Jowdy.

Jowdy supported her. "Yes, he told me the same thing."

But Holland was not listening. He moved to Dietrich's office with the others on his heels. Abruptly he sagged against the door frame, giving them a clear view. For a moment they all stared at the half-opened drawers, the papers strewn on the floor and the gutted file cabinet.

Victor Jowdy was the first to speak. "That makes two sudden decisions," he said. "I guess you could call it tit for tat."

"What the hell . . .?" Holland was murmuring under his breath, when he was interrupted by a clatter of activity in the reception room.

They all swung around, to see Dr. Anton Dietrich returning. He no longer clutched the thick briefcase. This was safely clasped by one of the uniformed men escorting him.

"Anton?" said Holland, stunned. "What's going on?"

With a venomous glance at Jowdy, Dietrich said, "My advice, Win, is that you say nothing—nothing at all."

It was not such bad advice at that, as Captain Kallen proved when he thrust himself forward.

"A. Winthrop Holland? I have here a warrant for your arrest . . ."

The charge was murder.

26

CUTTING DOWN THE ANGLE

FOUR WEEKS LATER, Charlie Trinkam was fulfilling his duties as a host. "I hear that it wasn't a bad game," he said in the interval between courses.

He would have been justly served, John Thatcher reflected, if three of his guests had immediately risen and left the restaurant. The game to which Charlie referred so slightly had been the last of the play-offs. Each team had already won three; each needed that fourth. The Huskies and the Montreal Canadiens had joined in a battle of titans. Twenty seconds before the end of the third period Paul Imrie had scored the tying goal. Ten minutes later Pete Levoisier had fired the screen shot that made the New York Huskies the first expansion team in the history of hockey to win the Stanley Cup.

Eileen Levoisier was aghast.

"Not bad! When it went into sudden death overtime?" But Charlie's social talents were having their usual impact. "Oh, well," she relented, "a lot has happened in this last month."

She was absolutely right. Winthrop Holland and his legal advisers were monopolizing the courts of New York State, Dr. Anton Dietrich was running him a close second, and the NHL was threatening an investigation of its own. But Eileen did not have any of these pyrotechnics in mind. She was referring to the happy combination of events that would shortly see the ground-breaking for the third Levoisier skating club.

As Pete had steered his team successfully through the first two rounds of the play-offs, Neil Gruen's ambitions to exploit a hockey personality recrudesced. Misled by his experience with Billy Siragusa, Gruen had presented himself in Great Neck with an engaging smile and a business proposition. There he came under the cool scrutiny of Eileen Levoisier. She had read his market survey with interest, then shown him the door. Within twenty-four hours the Levoisiers were in John Thatcher's office. Reluctant to hand them over to one of the hockey enthusiasts now burgeoning throughout the Sloan, he remembered Charlie. Anybody who had counseled Clemmie Post for over five years without once seeing the inside of Madison Square Garden was clearly the man they needed. In a remarkably short time Charlie had improved the original financial scheme and become a connoisseur of Eileen's cooking. Today he was celebrating the formal birth of Levrie, Incorporated, and returning hospitality.

"Speaking of sudden death," he said, regrettably single-minded, "now that you don't have Win Holland stirring things up, you can concentrate on Levrie, Inc. Let's hope you have a nice quiet season next year."

Paul Imrie and Pete Levoisier were only human. They both opened their mouths to explain that a quiet season was not a desideratum in the NHL, then reconsidered. Charlie's shameless ignorance of hockey was fast becoming a byword in the Husky dressing room.

"We don't have to worry about Holland, that's a fact," Imrie agreed weakly. "As if he didn't already have enough on his plate, they say he's in bankruptcy court, too."

This was news to Levoisier. "You mean he's broke?"

"That's one word for it." Charlie was in high good spirits at the thought. "It's why he killed two people."

Pete wagged his head. "I didn't know you could lose that much," he said humbly.

"That's a common viewpoint," Thatcher sympathized, "And it was the cause of the entire tragedy. Everybody assumed that a Holland has unlimited resources—including young Holland himself."

"The motive is plain enough," said Charlie. "I saw it that night we were with Kallen. It's the details I'd like to have explained."

Eileen objected to this summary dismissal of her major problem. "The motive may be clear to you. It isn't to us."

"As a matter of fact, we talked about Holland once," Paul Imrie chimed in. "We figured if Moore and Jowdy had been the victims, you could say he was knocking off everyone he owed. But Billy sure as hell wasn't lending Holland money."

Thatcher nodded approvingly. This sterling common sense boded well for the future of five skating clubs in Manhattan.

"Of course, Siragusa's murder was the key to motive. At first, it seemed as if he must have been killed because he was blackmailing Moore's murderer."

At these words, the Levoisiers and Imrie self-consciously looked elsewhere.

Charlie Trinkam chortled. "So you thought Siragusa was putting the bite on Clemmie, eh?" he asked tolerantly.

Pete blushed, Eileen stiffened and Imrie guffawed.

"But the only reason that blackmail came to mind," said Thatcher, riding the whirlwind, "was that Siragusa was worth more alive than dead to all of the suspects. Or so it seemed. Anybody murdering him had to assume that his death would plunge the Huskies into a losing streak. And who, among the players and owners, would benefit from that? We did not see the answer until we were explaining the difference between a sale and an attachment to Captain Kallen."

Pete Levoisier had recovered from his confusion. "Suppose you explain it to us," he suggested.

"A creditor wants to cover a debt for a certain amount —say, one hundred thousand dollars. He will go to the trouble of attaching assets only if he thinks they can be sold for about one hundred thousand dollars. When the value of an asset starts to plummet, he no longer wants it. You yourself saw how Victor Jowdy abandoned his plans as soon as the Huskies began to lose. That was exactly what Win Holland expected when he killed Billy Siragusa."

"Wait a minute!" It was Paul Imrie, holding up a detaining hand. "That's pretty fancy, isn't it? If Win Holland shot Franklin Moore just because he owed him money, then why not the same treatment for Jowdy? If something works once, you give it another try."

Thatcher shook his head. "No, it's a mistake to equate Moore and Jowdy. Moore was a creditor in his own right and ran his own business. When he died, his estate went into probate. Months would pass before his claims were pressed. But Jowdy was a lawyer representing clients. If he had been killed, his firm would simply have sent another man in his place."

"And even the New York police would have cottoned on," said Charlie merrily, "if Holland had started gunning down lawyers as fast as they could ship them in from California."

"But what good did it do him in the long run?" Levoisier persisted. "These debts weren't simply going to go away. Sooner or later, somebody would inherit from Moore. And Jowdy didn't look to me like the kind who was going to sit still just because the Huskies weren't any use to him. Holland wasn't getting anything from his murders."

"Oh, yes he was. He was buying time. He was willing to go to these extremes for time because of his overall financial situation." Thatcher paused, searching for shorthand. "He was in a very peculiar position, largely because of his investment in the Huskies."

Charlie grinned broadly. "As I understand it, John, the bankruptcy court has hired a squad of accountants who expect to spend a year trying to untangle Holland's affairs. I'm going to enjoy hearing you do it in a couple of sentences."

Thatcher had perfected a technique for ignoring Trinkam in these moods. Instead he collected the eyes of the other three and uttered the perfect curtain raiser. "Winthrop Holland began his career with fourteen million dollars."

There was a reverent silence.

Assured of his audience's attention, Thatcher continued "That was seven years ago, and he has been losing money steadily ever since. Holland viewed himself as a tycoon spinning a vast web, and he utilized all the tools of the trade—mergers, offshore havens, tax-loss possibilities and holding companies. Further obscuring the facts was the ease with which his name enabled him to obtain credit. The result, predictably enough, has been total confusion, not only for others, but also for himself. He did not know how badly off he was until last fall, when things came to a crisis."

Charlie was skeptical. "How can you be sure? He may have been keeping quiet about what he knew."

"I doubt it. A number of things happened then. Two of them are significant. His father cut off the supply of credit from the family bank. That, of course, could simply mean his father was more perceptive than he was. More revealing, however, young Holland changed the habits of years. Mrs. Post told us how he was never in New York for the hockey season. He was always busy elsewhere, with his chain of newspapers or his toy factories or his international trading company."

"Say, that's right," said Imrie. "You know, we'd barely seen him until last October. Then, suddenly, he was around a lot."

"Exactly. For some reason, he was settling down for the winter in New York—even though his major concern at the moment seemed to be in London. And any banker has suspicions when a man who is losing money disappears from his normal locations."

Charlie Trinkam vindicated this confidence in his profession. "Hiding from his creditors," he explained briefly.

Eileen Levoisier registered an objection immediately. "How could he hide from anybody? The sports pages had long articles about the Huskies last fall."

Thatcher's admiration for the Levoisiers was increasing by leaps and bounds. "That is precisely what ultimately led Winthrop Holland to commit two murders. Like almost all bankrupts on a heroic scale, he was confident that his current maneuver would put him in the black. To bring it to a successful conclusion required only six months. But during that six months he needed every asset he still owned. It had finally come home to him that one intransigent creditor could bring down the whole house of cards. So he decided that he and his assets were going to become hard to find. He came to New York, relying on the fact that the Huskies had never attracted wide publicity and that his ownership was virtually unknown. Clementine Post had sufficed for the casual coverage accorded a losing team."

"Now there's the kind of owner a team needs," commented Paul Imrie. "One who counts on losing."

"It must have been a shock to him when you started winning," Thatcher replied. "And long articles were being written about every aspect of the Huskies, including ownership. Naturally, the first creditor to surface was Moore, the hockey fan. He demanded one of two things—payment for notes outstanding or sale of Holland's interest in the Huskies. Holland could not afford either. He had no cash, and any sale of the team would have unleashed enough publicity to bring his other creditors down on him. Nothing would have disturbed them more than the suggestion that assets were being unloaded."

Paul Imrie did not pretend to understand the world of high finance. "Why weren't they disturbed already? He wasn't paying them."

"It was an annoyance that he was not present to discuss a schedule of payments. But they were not seriously worried—because he was a Holland. That thread runs through all his ventures. His arrangement with Moore shows that he was making the classic mistake of the rich man."

"And what's that?" Eileen Levoisier was making notes for the future.

Thatcher spelled it out. "The debt to Moore was incurred by Holwin Enterprises. But it could be satisfied by Win Holland's private share of the Huskies. That means he was personally guaranteeing the notes of his company instead of using the protection afforded by the corporate form."

Everybody at the table was now an expert on limited liability. "You mean the way we've set up Levrie, Inc.," said Pete Levoisier fondly. "If the skating clubs get into trouble, no one can attach our house."

"Yes, but Holland's enterprises were so dubious that Moore insisted on the protection of the Holland name. He was the kind of man who couldn't be put off. That was why he was shot."

"Just like that," Imrie marveled. "That's a tough game you boys play. Moore says he won't wait, and Holland kills him on the spur of the moment."

"Not just like that." Charlie's voice had hardened. "He set it up beautifully. Haven't you realized yet that he was trying to shaft you all?"

Three startled faces turned to Trinkam, who said, "I should have seen it earlier than I did. Clemmie herself told me that she wasn't talking to Moore."

"That's because she was so mad," Pete tried to explain.

"Forget about why she was acting that way and think of the results," Charlie advised. "Holland was passing himself off as a man considering a deal that had been suggested to him. Normally the two parties would have been the only ones to know anything about it. But Holland insists on telling Clemmie and is clever enough to tell her in such a way that she is hostile to Moore from the start. Then he goes further and sees to it that the whole team finds out. Before he's done, lots of people have a motive for stopping Moore."

Pete and Imrie were nodding like mandarins. Eileen had her own contribution. "You know, the big gripe on teams is usually that the owners never tell us anything. They move franchises and trade players without a word of warning. The first you know is that they tell you to be in Oakland on Thursday—even though it means selling houses and taking kids out of school."

"Holland didn't have to do all the work himself," said Imrie, recalling the details. "He told Milt Forsburg and Billy. They carried the ball from there."

"Yes, but he did more than broadcast Moore's offer," Thatcher said. "By antagonizing Mrs. Post, Holland became the only conduit of information. And I think we can assume that almost everything he said was inaccurate. Moore's prospective partners had never heard him mention moving the team from New York. Nor did he ever say anything to them about actively managing the team. Holland was fabricating items that would serve his purpose. For the same reason, he murdered Moore at the welcome home—the one place where all the suspects would be gathered together under circumstances of considerable confusion."

"He was making patsies of us!" Pete was indignant.

"I'm afraid so. He had to cover the weakness of his position, you see. Because if you ignored motive and looked at opportunity, what did you find?"

It was Charlie who bustled in with an answer. "You found all of us, including Brad, right on the spot, that's what. I don't think much of that argument."

"You would if you didn't overlook the obvious," Thatcher rejoined severely. Now was no time for Charlie to lose the confidence of his clients. "The only person who knew Franklin Moore was going to be at the airport was

Win Holland. The Huskies, including Forsburg, had just disembarked from a plane after a week's absence. Is it likely that they were carrying guns on the off chance of meeting Moore? Clementine Post's motive was blown sky-high as soon as she spoke with Moore, and she button-holed Forsburg the moment he was on the ground. Added to that is the fact that Holland's story about leaving Moore to find his own way to the city never rang true. Franklin Moore was a hockey zealot, the Huskies had returned from a triumphant road trip, the natural thing would have been for Moore to ride in the bus. Indeed, the only person likely to take him to the parking lot was always Holland."

Charlie Trinkam had never been the type to brood over defeat. He came rattling back with another challenge.

"At which time Billy Siragusa could have seen some-thing. So blackmail wasn't ruled out for the second murder."

"Most unlikely," said Thatcher unyieldingly. "Siragusa, and all the players, were mobbed by their admirers until the very end of the welcome home. The murderer would not have waited until the flow to the parking lot began. He would have acted earlier, when he still had some privacy."

Paul Imrie advanced his theory that Billy had been too self-centered to notice anything, anyway. "Unless some-body started shooting at him, of course," he added. "But say what you want about Holland lining us up, the police didn't really put the pressure on the team until Billy was killed. Then it seemed like a choice between us or Clem-mie."

"Captain Kallen was in difficulties as long as the motive eluded him. He realized very early that Holland had a magnificent opportunity, but that was offset by Mrs. Post's behavior."

"What was so special about Holland's opportunity?" demanded Imrie. "That damned bottle was sitting on Milt's desk for hours. And Clemmie was right in there with the rest of us. Milt practically had to throw her out."

"But it was the day before that was important," That-cher reminded him. "The murderer had to know that Sira-gusa was taking cold tablets, and had to see the original bottle in order to duplicate it. Mrs. Post was not at Mineola the day before the murder, would not have been in the dressing room in any event, and was avoiding Siragusa so effectively that she didn't even know he had a cold until the next morning."

"Strike one for Holland," said Charlie irrepressibly. "On the basis of past performance he should have waited until Clemmie was as good a suspect as he was."

"Time was running out on him and he was correspondingly desperate. He thought he only needed six or seven weeks more of grace, and Jowdy wouldn't give it to him. If we were readers of the society page, we might have guessed that Holwin Enterprises was in deep trouble by the fact that Holland's father chose to leave the country just when every other financier was rushing back to his desk."

"John!" exclaimed Charlie incredulously. "You're not saying you think old Archibald Holland knew what his son was up to?"

"I don't think he suspected murder. I do think he was afraid of bankruptcy. He probably thought life would be easier if he could not be cross-examined by Winthrop's creditors or court-appointed auditors."

"You may have a point." Charlie rubbed his chin reflectively. "I see he's still in Antigua."

"Not for long," said Thatcher. "I expect he's been hoping it would all blow over."

"Blow over?" Pete Levoisier thought he was dealing with maniacs. "Two murders and a bankruptcy? Not to mention all this stuff about Dietrich?"

"Hollands don't get much experience with that sort of thing," Charlie explained kindly. "It's taking Archie a while to adjust."

Eileen was impatient with these diversions. "Never mind that. You said Mrs. Post was avoiding Billy. Why?"

Thatcher gestured toward Charlie. "This is our expert on Mrs. Post."

"Nobody ever claimed logic was Clemmie's strong point. As nearly as I can tell, she encouraged Siragusa to think he could get anything he wanted by coming to her. It didn't do much harm at the beginning. He didn't want much, and it wasn't coming out of her pocket."

"You can say that again," growled three voices.

Masterfully Charlie swept on. "But Clemmie is no dope. She knew something was wrong with the Huskies, and she was rattled. Then Billy started raising the ante, and throwing his weight around. She began to be terribly afraid of what he might already have done. She had gotten to the point where she didn't want to find out anything. But Jowdy appeared and she was in a vise. Siragusa insisted she make all sorts of commitments before the NHL took over. His demands were pretty hysterical. To Clemmie it sounded as if he wanted the rewards he'd risked his neck for. Forsburg, of course, was urging her to delay making commitments. And when the chips were down, Clemmie wanted to be sure of Forsburg at least. So she was ducking her superstar."

"And she never was going to back his clubs?" asked Imrie.

Eileen laughed sarcastically.

It was Thatcher who explained. "No. Mrs. Levoisier here took a very long look at Niel Gruen's proposals. Obviously Billy Siragusa never clearly understood them. The clubs would have been owned by Gruen and his friends. Siragusa's share amounted to a royalty for the use of his name. But Gruen had certainly helped the boy to an inflated view of his participation. After Siragusa was murdered, Gruen did not want the facts to come out. He deliberately left Captain Kallen with an erroneous picture of the undertaking."

"As soon as I saw what he was up to, I realized that Mrs. Post hadn't done us dirt." Eileen sounded defensive. "And I told everybody right away."

"Sure you did, honey," Pete said amiably. "The trouble was, too many people were hiding something."

"Including Dr. Anton Dietrich. He may take the cake." Charlie turned to Thatcher. "Still, John, you had more luck than you deserved with your little trap. It wouldn't have been half so successful without our Anton."

Imrie and Pete had been far too busy with the Minnesota North Stars to follow the details of Win Holland's arrest.

"Trap?" asked Paul Imrie. "How did you work it?"

Charlie took up the tale with gusto. "John had an inspiration. Kallen was a very worried policeman when he understood Win Holland's motive. He figured he could get evidence on other aspects of the crime once he knew who the murderer was. And he was right. I see that he's found the drugstore where Holland bought the second bottle of pills and he's proved access to a gun that's gone, missing. But the motive was hypothetical. And if Holland's ship really did come in, there never would be evidence of how hard up he had been. Juries, according to Kallen, want a solid motive before they convict. So John decided to precipitate things."

At this signal, Thatcher smoothly took over. "I simply called Victor Jowdy and suggested that he return to New York with a renewed threat of attachment. The winning game at the Garden gave him a perfect excuse. Holland had just killed a man to prevent this. The odds were that he would crack under pressure and do something foolish."

Eileen was staring at him, horrified. "Like poison Pete and Paul, this time?"

"No, no, it was too late for that. He was more likely to forge assets in some way. He would have done anything to quiet Jowdy, even if it meant leaving a record. But, as Charlie has pointed out, the trap flushed Dietrich instead. And for very good reasons. Holland had not been losing all that money unassisted. Several million had found its way into an account belonging to Dietrich. He had been pacifying Holland with an illusory London venture while he made his final raid on the Holwin treasury. He knew far better than Holland that the assets would never cover the debts. When Jowdy called from the airport, he knew the game was up. He packed everything he wanted into a briefcase and was preparing to flee the country. The contents of that briefcase gave Captain Kallen everything he needed to prove motive."

Charlie wagged an admonitory finger. "It pays to listen

to Clemmie. She said Dietrich was Holland's evil genius and she was right."

"I believe she put it differently," Thatcher said dryly.

"A mere detail. Anyway, she's happy enough these days."

"Is she ever!" Imrie gave a hoot of laughter. "You should have seen her yesterday. She was carrying around the Stanley Cup like it was a baby."

"And what about you?" Pete Levoisier was too polite not to amplify for the benefit of the non-hockey element. "Paul was awarded the Lady Byng Trophy for the season."

"And what's that for?" Charlie asked.

Imrie was infatuated with his achievement. "It goes to the most gentlemanly player in the League," he said, virtue leaking from every seam.

He presented his profile for admiration. It had a black eye, a stitched gash along the cheek and a hideous swollen contusion on the jawbone. The other side was worse.

"They must be out of their minds," muttered Eileen.

"Every little bit helps," Paul chided her. "Play-off money, trophies, you name it."

"And that's another thing," Eileen went on. "Of course I'm glad you're coming into the skating clubs with us—"

"It will be a smash," Imrie interrupted. "Peter and Paul, the two stars of the Huskies, giving personal instruction. I can see it now."

"Yes, yes, I know it's a good idea. But since when have you been interested in investments? The only thing you've ever put money on is a horse."

"Now, now. I'm thirty-four, you know. It's time I started thinking about the future."

Eileen's brows knitted in thought. It did not take her long to draw the obvious conclusion.

"What's she like?" she asked.

Paul waxed enthusiastic.

"Wonderful! She's tall and quiet and beautiful." Then he grinned provocatively. "She's everything a woman should be—sweet and gentle and sympathetic."

But his barb missed its mark. Eileen was nodding in matronly approval. The girl sounded just right for Paul.

One tiger, Eileen Levoisier had always said, was enough for any house.

COMING SOON!
THE COAST-TO-COAST BESTSELLER!
DICK FRANCIS
WHIP HAND

A
GRIPPING NOVEL OF
THE POWER OF FEAR
AND THE PRICE OF COURAGE
"MORE THAN A HIGH-LEVEL
THRILLER" —THE NEW YORKER
"MEMORABLE...AMONG
DICK FRANCIS' BEST!"
—CINCINNATI POST
WATCH FOR IT!

FROM POCKET BOOKS

66